HONEY
the HILL RUNNER

by Stephen Breckell

First published in Great Britain as a softback original in 2017

Copyright © Stephen Breckell

The moral right of this author has been asserted.

All rights reserved.

All characters and events in this book, other than those clearly in the public domain, are fictitious and any resemblance to real persons, living or dead, is purely coincidental.

No part of this publication may be reproduced, stored in a retrieval system, or transmitted, in any form or by any means, without the prior permission in writing of the publisher, nor be otherwise circulated in any form of binding or cover other than that in which it is published and without a similar condition including this condition being imposed on the subsequent purchaser.

Typeset in Sabon LT Std

Editing, design, typesetting and publishing by UK Book Publishing
www.ukbookpublishing.com

ISBN: 978-1-910223-91-8

HONEY the HILL RUNNER

Chapter 1

Martha Hunney sprinted through the field, summer wet grass whipping her long lean legs, and rushed into the back entry leading to her home as though her life depended on it. She dragged off her drenched plimsolls and swilled her peat-stained legs in the trough outside the backyard gate near the water well. Barging in through the back door she tripped over the cat sprawled out on the floor and bumped into the kitchen table. Sarah looked at her and laughed. Martha rubbed her left knee, pulled her tongue out at her sister, and then bounded upstairs.

Sarah stood at the bottom of the stairs and shouted, "Hurry up, Martha and shape yourself, we've got to be in the village by eleven and it's half ten now. Mother will be mad with us if we're not on time. You should get up earlier if you want to go running on Saturday mornings – or run faster."

Martha, now standing at the top of the stairs, replied, "Stop fretting, Sur, we've plenty of time to get to the café. Mother said eleven and then we would have time to have a cup of tea and one of those delectable cakes that Mort bakes. The bus into town isn't until twelve, so you can go down before me if you want – I've still to wash my pumps off. I've got them filthy treading in a peat bog on the moor. And by the way, I did get up early enough and run fast enough, so there."

"You and your running. One day you'll get lost going up that hill to the moors. You shouldn't go running on your own up there. I don't understand what you see in running anyway, it's hard work."

CHAPTER 1

"Well, you wouldn't, Sur, because you're not a runner and don't have a runner's mentality. Anyway, I'm not just a runner; I'm a hill runner. I'm a specialist."

"Oh yes, I forgot: 'Honey the Hill Runner', as Teddy Moore calls you. Only you can't race on the hills because the authorities don't let girls race on hills or fells, do they, Honey?"

"One day they will, Sarah, just you wait and see. Anyway, you get on your way now, and I'll meet you in the village. Don't forget we're meeting Mother in Mort's café – not the post office."

"Oh, you're so funny, as if I won't remember that, Honey."

Martha laughed at the funny face Sarah pulled at her from the bottom of the stairs and said politely, "I'll clean my pumps and be with you and Mother shortly. And by the way, I didn't go running on my own, Shep came with me."

After putting on her raincoat and felt hat, Sarah set off on her pushbike. It had been raining most of the morning, after two weeks of warm, sunny weather. The early spring had been unusually warm in the countryside. This seemed to have raised the spirits of the local rural community, after a winter of frost, ice and snow and the near hurricane winds of late October and November of the previous year.

Martha cleaned her plimsolls in the dolly tub in the backyard of the cottage and carefully placed them under the overhang of the coal shed against the door. The rain was falling steadily and blowing away from the plimsolls. Martha was confident that they wouldn't get any wetter and in the position she had placed them the excess water in them would drain off.

She had decided to ask her dad if she could put them in front of the fire on the hearth if it was lit that evening. Her dad hadn't been lighting the fire over the past two weeks; there was no need because the evenings, as well as the days, had been warm enough. She hoped he would light the fire, or it would mean pushing newspaper inside the pumps to soak up the rest of the water, and then they would not be properly dry in time for her next run, which was to be on Monday evening after work – part of her training schedule she had devised. Not that Martha was a stranger to running in wet or damp footwear, especially after the long harsh winter. But she would rather have them dry for comfort at the start of a training run. She had spent all winter running in her damp, muddy plimsolls and her brother Oliver had said to her, "You must be used to running in those wet muddy pumps," when she moaned about their condition.

She had grumbled to him, "No, not used to it, Oliver. I just put up with it."

Martha slipped her short waterproof jacket over her cotton dress, wrestled her lace-up shoes on without untying them, and ran off swiftly down the bridle path parallel to the road that led into the village. She soon arrived at the café and sat down next to her mother. Sarah arrived at the café a little later after parking her bike at the side of Pringle's garage for the afternoon. She usually did this when she was catching the bus into town with someone or on weekdays when she caught the works' bus.

Sarah wasn't surprised to see Martha sitting next to their mother. She ignored her and said, "Hello, Mother, are you looking forward to spending all your money on me in town?"

"I don't think so, Sarah; just enough to get you and Martha a new frock each for you to wear at Matilda's wedding. You two can buy your own shoes, and whatever else you need, with your own hard earned money."

Martha interrupted, "I'll have a cup of tea and an almond slice, Sarah, they're delicious. What do you want Sarah to get you, Mother? Tea and a slice of that fruitcake you love?"

"If I get this, Honey, you can pay for our tea in town, alright?"

Martha ignored her sister's remark.

Their mother, Ruth, intervened before the sisters started arguing, "I'll have an almond slice, Sarah and a cup of tea. You'll pay for our tea in town, Martha for your cheek! It will probably cost a fair bit more than what Sarah is spending now."

Martha thought quickly and said, "I'm sorry, Sarah, for being so clever; I'll halve you with this and you can halve me with the tea. Okay?"

"That won't work, Honey, you heard what mum said, accept

CHAPTER 1

the consequences of your actions and take your medicine."

Martha pulled a face at Sarah, which she was inclined to do when she was in the wrong and had to accept it.

"Are we going to have something to eat and drink? Or debate who will pay for what, and then get straight on the bus without having anything at all." Before either had time to answer Ruth said, "Look, Mort's standing there whistling and rapping his fingers on the counter. You had better go and order, Sarah, before he asks us to leave because we're taking valuable seats up."

Martha sprang to her feet before her sister had moved, glided over to the counter and quickly blurted the order out. And then said, "Sarah will pay, Mr Johnson, the money's in her purse, she's loaded you know." She looked back at Sarah who was approaching the counter and carried on to say, "That's because she never spends anything."

"No, it's not, Mr Johnson, take no notice of her. It's because I'm careful with my hard-earned money," retorted Sarah.

"That's very wise, Sarah. That will be three shillings and sixpence please and no buttons like you tried on me the last time you were in."

"Oh, that was very grown up, Sarah."

"He's joking, Honey, aren't you, Mr Johnson?"

"If you say so, but the cost is still three shillings and sixpence please and still no buttons, Sarah. Now let me get your order." The two girls sat down next to their mother and started to discuss what style of dress each would like for their cousin's impending wedding. "I want a summery frock, one that I can keep for special occasions as well as church on Sundays during warm weather," commented Sarah.

"I do too," echoed Martha. "But I want some new training pumps, or more to the point, racing pumps as well. I intend to do a race, I need a pair with a bit more grip on that will stay together in a hard race, and not fall apart when I'm flying downhill to the finish."

Their mother interjected, ignoring Martha's comments, "Yes, young ladies, but there will be nothing too fancy. You know what your father's like. He won't want the young men of the village ogling at you, and you most certainly wouldn't be going to church in a frock like that either."

"Well, Mother," replied Martha, "it's a bit late for that. The boys are always ogling at Sarah. Well, more to the point, at her big bosoms."

"Stop that talk, Martha; this is not the place to say such a thing. You're supposed to be a young lady. Look at the people staring, and poor Sarah blushing. I won't have that sort of talk in a public place."

"Sorry, Sur, sorry, Mother," Martha said meekly, with her head bowed. "I shouldn't say such things," and then said in a whisper, "but it is true."

"That's enough, Martha, don't mention it again," Ruth reinforced.

Mort brought the food and drinks to the table. "There you are, ladies; enjoy it." He looked at Martha. "That almond slice will do you good for your running. There's lots of goodness in it."

"I might have two the next time, Mr Johnson," remarked Martha.

"Thank you, Mort," said Ruth.

"My pleasure, Ruth."

Martha poured three cups of tea, pushed one over to her mother and one to her sister then picked her almond slice up and ate all of it without saying another word, apart from muttering under breath, "I will do a race; a proper hill race as well."

Ruth and Sarah carried on talking whilst Martha sulked. "I've seen some material which I think will be just right for me, and it's actually made at our mill, Mother."

"Oh, and what material is that, Sarah?" her mother asked looking at Sarah with an 'are you sure?' glance.

Sarah read the glance and said; "Don't worry, I'm sure, Mother. I won't be changing my mind like you think I will. It's definitely the right material; it's a lovely small primrose print and I want a small frill on each of the plain half sleeves." She then reiterated, "I like it a lot. I just need to decide on the rest of the style. You will

CHAPTER 1

help me with that, Mother, won't you? And you'll definitely have to help Honey because she's no idea about fashion and style. She's more interested in her running pumps, aren't you, Honey?" Sarah questioned, glancing at Martha.

Martha gave Sarah a sideways glare and giggling, observed, "Of course you're right, Sur. Much more interested. In fact, I'm going to wear them with my fancy summer primrose frock," she said mockingly to her sister.

"All right that's enough you two, now finish your drinks. The bus is due in five minutes; look at the clock on the wall?"

Mort overheard Ruth and walking over said, "It's five minutes, Ruth," pointing at the clock.

"What do you mean, Mr Johnson, five minutes?" questioned Martha.

"Mort means the clock's five minutes fast," stated her mother.

"Oh," said Martha, slightly puzzled.

Mort then, quite unexpectedly, turned to Martha and said, "I couldn't help overhearing. The pumps you mentioned before. I know someone in Ferrington who's been a shoemaker and cobbler for nigh on fifty years. What he doesn't know about footwear is nobody's business. He just might be prepared to make you a special pair of pumps, if you are serious about running a race." Mort knew about Martha's intentions to run in a hill race and didn't see any reason why a fit and healthy young woman couldn't compete in such a race against men. Apart from, that is, the rules that prevented females from competing in the type of competition Martha intended to race in.

Martha's eyes widened and a beaming smile crept across her face. Her mother and Sarah kept silent at Mort's comment, more out of a sign of respect for the decorated war hero than any other reason. Martha opened her mouth to speak and, quite unlike Martha's usually quick and sharp response, spluttered out, "Are, are you, you being serious, Mr Johnson? No, you're having me on aren't you?"

"No, I'm not, Martha. I'm serious. If you intend running in a hill race you need a sturdy pair of pumps with a good grip. In fact,

6

more than pumps; you need racing shoes especially for running downhill."

Ruth commented, "That's all well and good, Mort but females can't run in those sorts of races. It's against the rules and not very lady-like if I may say so."

"Times are changing, Ruth. And if you don't push at the boundaries they won't move back," Mort stated philosophically.

She gave Mort a glancing look and said, "It will take ten years for times to change in these parts in comparison to London. That's where fashions and rules are made, so if the rules for girls weren't changed ten years ago for women running in men's races they won't be changed around here now."

Martha interrupted, "Mother, the rules for hill running aren't made in London. They're made here in the north, and some are made for local sports so if I get a petition up to change the rules, we might be able to change the minds of those old fossils who make the hill running rules round these parts."

"Well you go ahead with that, Martha; I'll be the first man to sign it."

"Not quite, Mr Johnson, my father will be, but you can be the second!"

"That will do me; I'll do just that. Let me know when you have the petition ready."

Ruth rose from her chair and said, "Come on, girls, it's time to catch the bus. Goodbye Mort, as always the tea and cakes were delicious. I'll see you on Wednesday when I come down for my groceries."

Both the girls said goodbye to Mort. Sarah held the door open for her mother, and Martha followed her out. It had stopped raining. They walked to the bus stop where there was a short queue. Ruth stood behind Teddy Moore – one of the young men from the village. He turned round and looked straight past her and trained his eyes on Martha.

"Hello, Honey, fancy seeing you here. Are you going to the dance tonight? If you are I'd be delighted to have a dance with you – preferably the first one, and the last one, and all those in

CHAPTER 1

between."

Ruth interrupted him. "You can take those eyes of yours off my daughter, Edward Moore. She's too young for you."

"I'm only two years older than her, Mrs Hunney, and there's nothing wrong with me asking her for a dance anyway."

Sarah said, "Why Teddy, have you got the hots for my sister?"

Martha and Teddy both blushed. Sarah realised that there was some chemistry between them and seized the chance to repay her sister for what she had said in the café earlier.

"Well, Teddy, if Honey's not interested in dancing with you, you can have a dance with me instead."

Teddy blushed even more, but plucked up the courage to say, "No thank you, Sarah, it's Honey or no one."

Mrs Hunney, now irate, commanded, "Now you can stop that, Sarah; you're causing everyone to look. I'll be glad when that bus comes!"

Across the street from the bus stop, Harry Smith was listening to the conversation. When it went silent for a moment he shouted, "I'll have a dance with you, Sarah, that's if lover boy over there isn't interested."

Sarah blushed and said nothing. Martha giggled, and their mother looked skyward, rolled her eyes and said, "Lord, give me strength."

The bus arrived and they all got on, the sisters and their mother sitting on the long back row seat, Teddy sitting as near the front as possible. Harry Smith sprinted across the road, jumped on the bus platform at the last moment, swivelled clockwise round the hand pole twice, and sat next to him. He swept his hair back with his left hand to rearrange it as he thought in James Dean style, who he believed he looked like. Harry glanced around in Sarah's direction. Mrs Hunney, with a serious expression on her face, promptly pointed her right forefinger at him spun it round in a circular direction and stabbed it forward. Harry instantly turned forward and didn't look back again for the rest of the journey.

Ruth, as she sat between her daughters, placed a hand on each one of their knees and said quietly, "I know you're both going to the dance this evening, but you do know that you have to be home at eleven – prompt!"

"Yes, Mother," they both replied which was their stock answer when they knew their mother was serious.

Sarah continued, "It's the Sabbath tomorrow and we are, as usual, going to be prim and proper, and in best Sunday voice for the praise and worship in chapel." She said this seriously knowing any form of sarcasm or mockery would bring the wrath of her mother down upon her.

"That's right, Sarah, 'Six days shalt thou labour and the seventh rest'. If it's good enough for the good Lord it's good enough for us, and good enough that we thank him for all his goodness toward us," continued her mother.

"That's why I don't go running on Sunday; I need a rest. It's a rest day and the days after are for working," Martha concluded.

"Right, well that's understood then, girls, and no shenanigans with those young men. Your father will be serving behind the bar like he usually does at the village dance." Ruth lifted her hands from her girls' knees. They knew just what she meant, and both said simultaneously, "Right, Mother," as they normally did in such circumstances.

Martha and Sarah were twins, although to look at them you would never have thought so. Martha was tall, slim, narrow hipped and comparatively flat-chested in comparison to her sister. Sarah had a voluptuous figure; she was not quite as tall as her sister – an inch shorter in fact, although Martha looked quite a lot taller because of her willowy appearance. Their likeness as twins lay in their humour and their uncanny knack of saying the same thing at the same time in response to almost any question they were asked.

It was as though they had built-in radar, but that's where it ended. Martha was the distance runner; Sarah was most definitely not. She liked her home comforts such as they were in that era. She helped her mother with most of the housework, and enjoyed sewing and completing jigsaws. Martha was an outdoor girl and was no stranger to getting her hands dirty. She liked to help her

CHAPTER 1

father during her work holidays, in fact, any opportunity she got, Martha would help her father but not on Saturday mornings – those were reserved for training on the hills and moor.

Chapter 2

The bus entered the terminus in town and before Teddy and Harry disembarked, Harry executed a precise double spin anti-clockwise around the hand pole, pointed at Sarah and shouted, "See you at the dance tonight."

"Don't take him on, Sarah, that lad's too fresh for my liking."

"Oh, I think he's rather cute, and harmless, Mother. He's all show. If you talk to him on his own he's shy."

Teddy and Harry made their way to the Saturday afternoon matinee at the Palace picture house on the corner of the Sunken Gardens Esplanade. They were going to watch James Dean in the film '*Rebel Without A Cause*' for the fourth time.

Ruth and the twins made their way to the shops on Sweet Street. The dressmaker's was situated between the ironmonger's – which had its wares spilling out onto the pavement as well as hanging above the jamb stones at either side of the open doorway – and Slinger's Butcher's, adorned with rabbits, hares and an array of fowl hanging to the left and right of the entrance; a few had been caught by the local poacher.

"Right, you two go into Ava's shop and have a good look at the material for your wedding frocks. No falling out either and be sensible in your choice and style. I'm going to get some meat from Slinger's. What would you like for your Sunday dinner: meat or fowl?"

"No rabbit or hare, please, Mother," Martha replied. "The last hare was full of pellets." She queried, "I thought Priestley the poacher snared his rabbits anyway?"

"Let's have duck for a change, Mother. I liked the last one you

CHAPTER 2

got from Slinger's, and Father did too."

"How do you know that, Sur, are you Father's confidante now?" quizzed Martha.

"No, Martha. Father doesn't talk when he's really enjoying his food, so that's how I know."

"Sarah's right – duck it is. I enjoyed the last one as well. Majority rules, Martha. Okay?"

"Yes, Mother. Duck it is!"

The girls went into the dress shop and said a polite hello to Ava, the proprietress.

Ava was a refugee from a Polish concentration camp who used to be a seamstress in Poland before the war. She was now firmly established in her Sweet Street dressmaker's shop. This was not without a great deal of hard work, patience, endeavour, and a shrewd business mind. Now in her forties, she was a spinster, although rumours suggested that she had been engaged to a Polish coalminer before the occupation. No one knew for sure, and no one knew how the rumours began. The real facts were that Ava was quite a gregarious woman but apart from her polite and engaging demeanour kept herself to herself in private matters. She knew all about the rumours associated with her and the Polish coalminer and was faintly amused by them. Some said he joined the résistance and fled to Switzerland when it finally succumbed to the occupying forces. Others said he was killed in a mining accident. The truth was that there was no Polish coalminer, only mistaken rumours.

Her mother, father, and brother had perished in the concentration camp she was liberated from, and this was a constant sleep-depriving agony for her.

"Now, you two lovely young ladies," Ava said in her strong Polish accent. "What can I do for you on this warm and pleasant afternoon? It is afternoon isn't it? Yes, it is," she answered herself.

"Only just, Miss Fleischmann," replied Sarah. "We're going to our Cousin Matilda's wedding in three weeks, and we both need a wedding frock in time. Ones we can wear for Sunday best after the wedding if you don't mind, Miss Fleischmann."

"Please, you call me Ava. You are young ladies now and very pretty as well if I may say so. I expect for you to call me by my Christian name, Ava, please."

Martha commented, impishly, "Thank you for your compliment, Miss. I mean, Ava. It's not often that Sarah gets called pretty though."

"I don't know that is why. Some of the young men in the village must say sweet things to you, Sarah," remarked Ava, missing Martha's sarcasm. "Should perhaps I call you 'Sarah' like your sister or would that be too forward of me?"

"Please call me Sarah, Ava," she replied, relishing the thought of being on first name terms with a forty-something-year-old woman, and more to the point being called 'Sarah' by her.

"Should I call you 'Honey', Martha or is that for the young man only? I have heard the young man in town calling you 'Honey', two weeks ago. Is that for him only, or is it for me also?"

Martha blushed and replied, "Please call me Honey, if you want to. I like that name – it's sweet!"

Ava missed the slight witticism and said, "Okay, I will do that." She continued, "Right, now let me see what I can show you two lovely girls the materials I have. And I have a catalogue of material which I can acquire in good time from the mill."

Then quite unexpectedly, and to the astonishment of both girls, she said, "I too am coming to your village dance this evening. I am being escorted by Mr Mortimer Johnson. What do you think about that, lovely young ladies?" Ava didn't give them time to answer; she carried on in her husky Dietrich-like Polish/English accent, "An old spinster like me stepping out with a handsome war hero like Mr Johnson! He asked me last week and I accepted without thinking. On a whim, without a thought; what do you think about that then?"

"Oh, you are hardly old, Ava," Martha quickly commented, remembering to be informal. "You're young – although I don't really know how old you are – and we will look forward to seeing you this evening, won't we, Sur?"

"Of course, we shall, and we'll look forward to seeing you

CHAPTER 2

dance with Mr Johnson, in a frock that you've made for yourself."

"You are perceptive, Sarah. I don't need to tell you I have a new frock which I have made especially for the dance. You must not tell Mr Johnson though. He might think I have made it to impress him." Ava giggled girlishly and blushed slightly as she said this. "What do you think of these materials, ladies?" she continued, changing the subject. "They are good quality dress materials and very good value for money."

"Can I look at the catalogue please, Miss Fleischmann? There is some lovely material that we've been making at work, and I think it will be just right for my frock," said Martha excitedly.

"I quite like this material with the small rose petal print. It's colourful but I hope Mother doesn't think it's too colourful for the chapel."

Ava went into the back room for the catalogue samples.

Tugging at her sister's coat sleeve, Martha quickly commented in a low whisper, "Miss Fleischmann's a dark horse isn't she, Sur? And what about Mort – you'd never put the two together, would you?"

"Oh, I don't know, Honey – Polish refugee and English war hero! There might be more to it than meets the eye; especially when Father told me Mort and him were both in Poland at the end of the war with the Yanks."

At that moment, their mother walked through the door. "What's that you said about your father?"

"Shush, Mother, I'll tell you later," whispered Sarah as she placed her right index finger to her lips, and pointed to the door leading to the back room where Ava was looking for the catalogue.

"Oh I see," said Ruth, "Mum's the word," and she placed her right index finger on her lips, mirroring Sarah.

"Here we are, ladies," said Ava, waving the catalogue chest high with both hands. "Hello, Ruth, your girls are going to look at this catalogue. It has the different patterns of the material made at the mill. It is quality material from that place, but of course, you know this with your two girls working there. They are lovely young ladies, Ruth; quite different in many respects but quite identical in others."

Hearing such comments from Ava, Mrs Hunney felt very proud of her daughters. She thought Ava was very intuitive and had read them well. She took a sideways glance at them both and thought, 'Yes, Ava is right; they're so different and yet so much alike'. As if to prove Ava's observations, the twins simultaneously placed their right hands on their hips and held their chins with their left hands while tapping their noses with their forefingers. They were looking at the material that Martha was contemplating choosing for her frock.

"I definitely think so," Martha said eventually.

"I do too," said Sarah.

"What do you think, Mother?"

Feeling the material, her mother replied, "This is just made for you, Martha; I really like the pattern and as long as it's made into a sensible style, with enough material being used, it will look wonderful on you." Her mother was making it clear that there would be no low cut bodice and above-the-knee frocks for either of her daughters.

Ava commented, "Quite right, Ruth. Ladies should not show off what lustful young males want to see – and more if they get a chance. No, keep yourselves covered up, young ladies. I believe there was enough of that sort of thing going on when those American airmen were in this country during the war. Of course, I was not here then, but I know all about them."

Ruth was quite taken aback by Ava's comments, and for a moment was stuck for words. Martha thought what Ava had said was quite funny, although she didn't agree with the notion that she should be dressed like a nun. Sarah stood there wondering where the American airmen came into the equation.

"You need to decide on the style of your dress, Martha and then Miss Fleischmann can measure you for it." Ruth then asked, "Sarah, have you any idea which material you would like your dress made from?"

"This is the one, Mother," fingering the material she had been looking at earlier. She said, "I'm having this one with the small

CHAPTER 2

primrose print; do you like it?"

"It's exquisite, Sarah; you'll look beautiful in the right style of frock made from that material. Not that you're not beautiful anyway."

Sarah blushed and said, "Oh thank you, Mother," giving her a hug. Her mother placed her hands gently around her daughter's waist and gave her a little squeeze.

Ruth rarely used her girls' shortened names. She thought Sarah was a friendly name but secretly liked Martha being called 'Honey' by her friends because they used it as a term of endearment, not because it sounded like her surname. Ruth thought her Honey was sweet.

Ava measured the twins and after they had agreed on the style of frock each had chosen, a date in two weeks' time was arranged for the first fitting. This would allow time for any alterations that were needed. After exchanging pleasantries with Ava, the Hunneys made their way to the café which was next-door-but-two to the hardware shop. The shop between the café and the hardware shop was the greengrocer's where Mrs Hunney called in for the weekly vegetables plus some apples and bananas. The bananas were for Martha. She said that they were good for energy. Oliver, her older brother, enjoyed one now and again but Sarah couldn't stomach them and Mr and Mrs Hunney much preferred a tasty Cox's Pippin apple.

Martha usually ate four bananas every week; one for each day she trained. No one really knew why Martha was training or took her seriously when she said she was going to run a hill race – that is, apart from her Father and Mort. They knew she meant it, and she was resolute that one day she would run a hill race. Her father wouldn't prevent her; in fact, he had told her he would do anything he could to help her achieve her ambition.

Martha and Sarah waited in the café for their mother, Martha ordering a pot of tea for three.

Mrs Hunney entered the café with three brown carrier bags in her hands; the sort with string handles that cut into the hands when there is too much weight inside. As usual, there was. Five pounds of potatoes in each of two of the carriers, with broccoli and lettuce on top of the potatoes, then apples and bananas, with a few tomatoes, in the third carrier. She placed the bags near the chair she was going to sit on and rubbed both palms with the tips of her fingers to get some feeling back.

Martha remarked, "You should have asked one of us to help you, Mother."

"It's okay, Martha," she said, looking at her hands. "Have you ordered yet?"

"No, Mother, only a pot of tea. We thought we had better wait to see what you wanted to eat."

"I'll have my usual, Martha, since it's your turn to pay; a cheese salad with two slices of bread and butter and no celery."

"I'll order it now. What would you like, Sarah, some of that Hungarian Goulash that's really potato pie, or fish, chips and peas?"

"Just salad, same as Mother, Honey, but with celery and radish if they have any. I suppose you'll be having a runners' meal of, um let me see: potato pie, chips, peas and gravy. Am I right, Honey?"

"You most certainly are, and two slices of bread and butter."

"You need to stop working with your father, Martha. He has you clearing drains, digging holes and goodness knows what else when you're with him. And he most certainly has got you into the habit of eating like a builder."

"It's okay, Mother, I'll run it all off on Monday when I get home from work. I'm starting a new training schedule and I'll need lots of energy food for that. I'm aiming to do a race and need to be very fit for it. Besides, Father works hard and he's as fit as a fiddle. He needs that sort of food."

"I know he does, Martha, but you need to keep your figure trim if you're to do what you say you're going to do."

A fleeting light came on in Martha's mind. 'Did I really hear what Mother has just said, or am I dreaming?' she thought. She pinched herself and her bubble burst.

Sarah interjected, "Yes, it's surely going to be a gruelling wheelbarrow race at the works' sports' day in a few weeks. Oh,

CHAPTER 2

and you're doing the three-legged race with Teddy Handsome, aren't you, Honey?"

Martha was instantly riled by her sister's statements and retorted, "I suppose you will be doing the ten-yard dash, Sarah, because that's just about as far as you can run these days!"

"We'll just see about that, Martha. I used to beat you at sprinting at school and I'll finish in front of you in the works' sports' eighty yards – like I did last year."

"Well, you'll have to strap your bosom down to stop you falling over if you are going to do the race."

Mrs Hunney snapped sharply, "Martha Hunney, what have I told you about that sort of talk? There's no need for it. What is it with you, cafés and your sister's chest? Now just stop it."

Martha rose from her seat and with head down looked at her sister saying, "Sorry, Sarah" in a low voice. She walked to the counter to order the food, talking to herself as she walked between the tables placed haphazardly in the main eating area.

She ordered the food and as she walked back to the table spotted Harry Smith standing outside the café. He tapped on one of the panes of glass in the shop door, and as Sarah and Ruth turned along with half a dozen other diners, he blew kisses at Sarah, and she instantly blushed.

Watching this exchange as she walked back to her seat, Martha tripped over the local policeman's size thirteen boot, went sprawling, and narrowly missed falling onto both Sarah and her mother.

Sergeant Fredrick looked at Mrs Hunney and commented, "Not those two young fellows again, Ruth. It's every Saturday alike; they always get up to some sort of mischief in town. I'm not chasing after them to give them an ear-bashing now. I'll catch them at the village dance tonight. Are you okay, Martha?"

"Yes thank you, Sergeant Fredrick. Is your foot alright?"

"Of course it is. You don't think a waif of a lass like you would damage these big hooves, do you?"

"I suppose not," Martha mumbled, not really liking being called a waif.

Mrs Hunney looked at Sergeant Fredrick and said, "Jim, those boys will be on the bus on the way back home. I'll have a word with them, make no mistake."

"Oh Mother, they were just having a bit of fun," stated Sarah. "You know what Harry is like! He's always showing off. He isn't hard to read, so you know where you are with him, and he is kind of cute," then she blushed again, realising what she had just said.

Martha came to her sister's rescue, "Yes, Mother, Sarah's right, he's basically a harmless fool," and then giggled.

Sarah scowled at her. At that moment, the waitress brought their food to the table, nearly tripping over Sergeant Fredrick's boots as she walked delicately past him with three plates of food balanced on a large tray.

"I think I'll get going before I cause any more accidents," remarked Sergeant Fredrick. He clambered out of his seat and made his way to the door, tripping over his own feet as he went. He opened the door, stooped his six-foot-four-inch frame, and narrowly missed banging his head on the door-casing. Placing his helmet on his head, he set off walking down Sweet Street towards the police station, whistling cheerily.

"You wouldn't think Sergeant Fredrick and his wife used to be national ballroom dancing champions, would you!" Both of her daughters giggled at their mother's comment and continued eating.

Leaving the café they walked to the bus terminal just in time to catch the bus back to Stippley Common. Teddy and Harry were sitting in the same seats as they had been on the outward journey. Mrs Hunney gave Harry a stern look and told him to behave himself in front of her daughters. He apologised, which he was rather in the habit of doing. Apologising was a way of life for Harry due to his many misdemeanours throughout the town and village; nothing serious, just mischievous antics that tended to irritate his victims.

The journey was uneventful – that is apart from the driver swerving to miss a fox slinking across the narrow road. Ruth lurched sideways and fell onto Sarah who in turn fell onto Martha, who was squashed beneath them both.

"Are you okay, Sarah?" asked a concerned Ruth, not realising Martha was underneath them both. She heard a muffled shout.

"Never mind Sarah, Mother. What about me? Get off, Sur, you're crushing me," cried Martha, not realising her mother was on top of her sister.

"I can't get off you and I'm not that heavy either."

Teddy, seeing what had happened, lurched his way to the back of the bus and grabbed hold of Martha's left arm, trying to pull her from under her sister and mother.

"Get off, Teddy, you big oaf, you're hurting my arm."

"Sorry, Honey. I'm only trying to help."

Ruth managed to lift herself off Sarah, and Martha wriggled out from under her sister.

"Are you okay, Honey?" Teddy asked in a concerned voice. Their eyes met – just for a moment.

"Yes, I'm alright, Teddy. Sorry for calling you an oaf," Martha said in a soft voice. Looking up into his face, Martha noticed his piercing dark brown eyes and experienced a very peculiar feeling. Nothing like she had ever experienced before.

"I'm alright as well, Teddy. Thanks for asking," commented Sarah, sarcastically. Teddy didn't hear Sarah; he had set off for the front of the bus again slightly embarrassed at his own gallantry but at the same time glad to have been so close to Martha.

The driver managed to reverse the bus out of the shallow ditch it had landed in and the conductor picked up the money that had spilled from his satchel when the bus swerved.

Ruth commented, "We'll have to be sharp getting home, girls, it looks like we're in for one of those heavy showers again and I don't want these carrier bags getting wet."

"I'll go and pick my bicycle up from Pringle's garage and meet you back at the house. Are you going to rest for a while when you get home, Mother? I'll peel the potatoes for tomorrow and Martha will do the veg, won't you, Honey?"

"Of course I will. You get your feet up, Mother. Father will have had his tea by the time we get in. He's to be back in the village for half past six to set the bar up. I wonder if he unblocked Mr Ritson's drain."

"More to the point I hope he's taken his work clothes off before he goes in to have a wash. They smell something awful when he's been on a job like that, and yes, girls, I will put my feet up for half an hour."

Ruth and Martha set off walking up the lane to their home and Sarah walked to the garage to pick her bike up. When she reached the garage Harry was waiting for her. He had run across the road and along the back alley to avoid Ruth. "How about tonight then, Sarah; will you have a dance with me or not?"

Sarah wasn't surprised in the least to see Harry. She exclaimed in a teasing tone, "You'll just have to wait and see, Harry Smith, won't you!" She straddled her bicycle which had been propped against the garage side entrance wall and rode off up the lane leading home. As she went she glanced back momentarily. Harry saw the glance and knew right then that he would be dancing with Sarah later in the evening.

After she had ridden two hundred yards it started to rain. It was a heavy sudden downpour and despite wearing her raincoat and hat she was drenched but there was no point in sheltering. She could see two figures in the distance who she knew were her mother and sister. They looked to be bending over and searching about near to the ground. As Sarah reached them she realised the carrier bags full of fruit and vegetables had been saturated in the downpour causing the bottoms to fall out. The potatoes had spilled all over the road and one of the bananas had been squashed after Martha stood on a potato and tripped over.

Sarah parked her bicycle and helped them pick up the groceries. Fortunately, Sarah had a basket on the front of her bicycle and a saddlebag on the back so they were able to cram all the fruit and vegetables into them. She cycled on while Ruth and Martha squelched their way home behind her.

Chapter 3

Ted Hunney was ready to go out to the village hall by the time the saturated threesome arrived home. As they came through the door he commented, "I see you got caught in the heavy downpour, Ruth. Martha and Sarah, you two look bedraggled; go and get dried off before you catch your death."

"Yes, Father," both replied simultaneously. They trudged upstairs, rainwater still dripping from their clothes.

As she rubbed her soaking hair with a towel, Ruth commented wryly to her husband, "Yes dear, we did get caught in the downpour. Have you had something to eat before you go out?"

"I've had a beef and beetroot sandwich, love. That'll keep me going until the potato pie supper later this evening. I'll get going now to set the bar up. I won't be late; not after eleven anyway." He walked out of the kitchen and as he slammed the front door shouted, "I'll make sure the girls get home safe. I don't want them missing chapel in the morning."

As she took the fruit and vegetables out of the basket and saddlebag to store them in the pantry, Ruth mumbled to herself, "I wish that husband of mine wouldn't keep slamming that door. He'll have it off its hinges one day." When she had finished putting the groceries away she continued to dry herself off and then went upstairs to change her clothes.

Martha was the first to get herself ready for the dance so she started to peel the potatoes. Sarah came down from upstairs and worked with her sister until they had finished preparing the food for their Sunday dinner.

Sarah had to go back upstairs for her cardigan and on the

way down slipped off the second bottom tread of the stairs and fell onto the hallway floor, knocking a vase of flowers off the small oak table. Fortunately, the vase stayed intact but the water splashed onto Sarah's cardigan which she had thrown on the floor as she fell. Martha rushed from the kitchen and helped her sister get up from the floor. Hearing the noise, their mother called from upstairs, "What's going on down there, are you two falling out again?"

"No, Mother. Sarah's fallen down the stairs and it looks like she won't be dancing tonight."

Sarah replied sharply while rubbing her ankle, "Oh yes I will, even if it's only on one leg."

Ruth rushed downstairs and asked sympathetically, "Are you alright, love? Here let me have a look. Is it your foot?"

"No, it's my ankle, Mother."

"Hold on to me and then see if you can put your weight on it. Move, Martha and give your sister a bit of room."

Martha jumped quickly out of her sister's way, and commented, "I don't think you will be dancing tonight, Sur, it looks swollen even from where I'm standing."

"Yes I will," Sarah shouted forcefully.

"Martha, stop annoying your sister. Put your foot on the floor, Sarah. Nice and gently does it."

Sarah gingerly placed her left foot on the floor and her mother let go of her gradually.

"How does it feel, love?"

"Sore," she replied after hobbling a few short steps down the hallway.

"Go into the living room and sit on the settee. I'll have a good look at it."

Ruth had been a nurse before the war and only stopped working after her first child was born. Sarah hobbled into the living room followed by her mother and Martha. "Will you move out of my light, Martha and then I can have a good look at your sister's ankle." Martha sat on her father's armchair near the fireplace.

"Now let's have a good look at it. I can feel that it's not broken.

CHAPTER 3

It is quite swollen, though. You will have to put it in a basin of cold water to help take the swelling down. And then I'll rub some of that ointment on that your father has for his sore back."

"No, Mother, that stuff stinks. I'm not going to the dance with that on me."

"Harry might think it's your perfume, Sarah," commented Martha, giggling.

"Very funny, Martha," retorted Sarah, as she screwed her face up and stuck her tongue out at her sister.

Ruth snapped, "Don't be ridiculous, Martha. Anyone can tell it's not perfume."

"Sorry, Mother. It was only a joke really."

"Do go and get a basin of water for your sister to soak her ankle in. We need to get the swelling down if we can before you both go out. Hurry up, Martha. The longer Sarah soaks it the more the swelling is likely to go down."

Martha came back with a tin basin three-quarters full of ice cold water from the well outside at the back of the cottage – enough for Sarah to soak her ankle and foot in. It was much colder than the tap water. Martha knew this because a few weeks earlier she had twisted her ankle while running from Wickelton Pike on her way down from the moor, and had had to hobble home. She had used the ice cold water from the well and after two sessions of soaking her ankle in it, the swelling had gone down.

"It's not as swollen as mine was, Sarah. Can you remember when I went over on my ankle and thought I wouldn't be able to run for weeks? This water should cure yours in one go. I think you will be dancing tonight after all. Harry will be pleased."

Her mother gave her a stern look and Martha got the message – no more comments regarding Harry Smith and her sister. Sarah placed her foot into the ice cold water and quickly lifted it out, splashing Martha's shoes as she did so.

"Don't be soft, Sur, get it back in. If I can stand it so can you."

Sarah looked at her sister and said nothing then forced her foot into the water again, splashing Martha's shoes once more.

"That's very bright of you, Sarah. Now I'm going to have to

change my shoes and I've only got my work shoes and pumps I can wear." Martha looked at Sarah and pleaded, "Unless I can wear your second good pair?"

"I'll think about it, Honey," remarked Sarah, intending to keep her sister in suspense.

"Keep your foot in the water for ten minutes, Sarah and then take it out and dry it off with this towel." Ruth handed Sarah the towel she had brought downstairs from the cistern cupboard.

After Sarah had taken her foot out of the basin, she dried it and immediately stood up with both feet on the floor. She walked across the living room in her bare feet and, to the amazement of her mother, promptly announced, "I'm cured!"

Martha knew differently and said, "I told you how good that water from the well is. It's what's known as 'efficacious'."

"Well let's not tell everyone, Honey, otherwise we'll have crowds stretching back to the village wanting to bathe in the water," commented Sarah.

"Now, Sarah, don't talk silly. Are you sure your ankle is mended?"

"Of course I am, Mother. I'm that cured I'll let Martha borrow my shoes," she said standing on her left leg and lifting her right one off the floor. "See."

"Oh thanks, Sur," commented Martha excitedly and then, giving Sarah a hug, she kissed her on her cheek. As she did, Martha commented quietly, "If you're lucky you might get one of those off Harry tonight."

Sarah blushed and said quietly in Martha's ear, "I hope so." They both giggled.

Their mother informed them, "I'm going round to your gran's in half an hour for a couple of hours. She could do with some company now that she struggles to get out with her broken wrist."

"We'll both pop in to say hello to her on our way to the dance, won't we, Sur? And I'm going to spend some time with her when she goes home from here after dinner tomorrow."

"I'll come with you, Honey and we'll stay for tea if Nan wants us to."

CHAPTER 3

Soon the home was empty, apart from the cat sleeping on the settee and the dog in its basket. At last, Ruth could finally put her feet up for a while, before going to visit her mother-in-law.

Martha and Sarah called in to say hello to their grandma on the way to the village dance. Their mother, as was her rule, had reminded them to behave in a ladylike manner and they had simultaneously replied that they would. After leaving their grandma they continued walking down to the village hall, Sarah hobbling slightly. They talked about the usual things: boys, work, Martha's favourite subject – running – and their brother Oliver who had gone back to continue his National Service in Cyprus.

Chapter 4

As usual there was an eclectic mix of people at the dance; Tom Proctor, at ninety-six, was the third oldest person in the village and still able to take the floor for the barn dance. Admittedly the five-piece band and regulars at the fortnightly dance had to keep pace with him rather than him with them. On the occasions that Tom decided to take part, chaos usually reigned and the dance would become a hilarious farce. It was all in good fun though and no ill feeling was aimed in his direction. In fact it was quite the opposite. Ted Hunney would offer Tom his pick of the drinks from behind the bar and then pay for it himself – it was usually a tot of rum, a drink Tom had imbibed since his navy days, sixty years in the past.

The music varied from the old traditional dance style to modern jive and swing. The younger folk enjoyed the modern stuff more than traditional music, but they took part in most of the dances anyway.

Teddy and Harry were always first to their feet when jive music was played and they didn't need female partners either; they danced separately, each performing their own rendition of the one-man bop. The girls would look on for a few moments before they coupled up and danced with each other. After a few more moments some of the other young men would politely ask those girls still sitting down if they wanted to dance, which, naturally, most of them did.

There were usually twenty to twenty-five younger folk, most of them from the village. Four or five came from the nearby farms and hamlets, and sometimes two young Irish lads from

CHAPTER 4

Middleview Farm would ride over on a motorbike. They came to meet Bryony and Bridget – two Irish sisters who had settled in the locality with their widowed mother. She had taken work in service to Lord Letherby at Letherby Hall Estate.

The sisters had met them – Patrick and Shaun – on the boat while travelling from Ireland and by coincidence had discovered they were all destined to work for Lord Letherby – the sisters at Letherby Hall with their mother. The young men both worked as farmhands at Middleview Farm, which was situated on Letherby Hall Estate. Patrick Murphy was an excellent cross-country runner and had been the Irish Schoolboy Champion only a few years earlier. Shaun McMullan was the All-Ireland Eating Champion, as could be deduced by his voracious appetite and rotund stature!

Sarah and Martha arrived at the village hall at seven forty; the dance floor was empty but the chairs were full. The five-piece band hadn't turned up yet so everyone was engaged in conversation about one thing or another. The bar was busy and Ted had to ask Mort to help him serve the farming community who were always first to quench their thirst. Bob Stokes was the other regular barman. He was an expert at opening bottles and pouring the contents into a glass with one hand. Unfortunately his right hand had been blown off during the war along with his right leg.

The hall door swung open and through it struggled Sofia Reynolds carrying a big bass drum. She shouted across the room to Ted, "We're a threesome tonight, Ted, unless someone here can play the saxophone and piano."

"No problem, your honour," shouted Shaun McMullan with a high-pitched County Killarney drone. "We'll be right on it, won't we, Patrick?"

"No problem, to be sure," Patrick replied. "We'll play it – you sing it, dance to it, do what you want with it. We'll have a gradely old Ceilidh to be sure, sir."

Shaun walked over to Ted and continued, "Murphy will play the piano and I will play the sax if that's all right with you, sir, and no one else would like to play?"

Ted shouted over the room to Sofia, "These two young Irish

fellows will give it a go if that's okay with you? That is unless someone else would like a go. How about you, Miss Benton, would you like to play?"

"No, thank you, Mr Hunney, I'll save my playing for chapel tomorrow. Let these two young fellows show us what they've brought with them in the way of talent from across the waves."

"Come on then, boys, help us in with the instruments – they won't carry themselves in, you know," shouted Sofia, who for some reason known only to her, was still standing half-way through the doorway holding the bass drum. Patrick and Shaun helped the musicians set up the host of instruments that were to be played during the evening's entertainment. The quintet always used the village hall piano.

Cyril Squire, who played guitar or trumpet depending which music was being played, turned to Patrick and Shaun and said, "I hope you two can read sheet music."

Patrick replied, "We can, sir, and we can both play by ear as well." He nodded towards Cyril's head and commented nonchalantly, "By the way, sir, your wig piece has slipped a wee bit, to be sure." Grimacing comically, Cyril rushed to the gents' toilet and straightened his toupee, as he struggled to see himself in the cracked mirror hanging askew on the wall. He came back to the stage after composing himself and started tuning his guitar.

Meanwhile, Shaun and Patrick were having an impromptu jam session, playing jive and folk music and both of them singing. Shaun in his high-pitched Irish brogue – not unlike Josef Locke, the famous tenor at the top of a note – and Patrick in a deep toned bass. Their singing styles complemented each other well and a few of the young women gathered around the stage to listen to them. With a cheeky wink, Shaun acknowledged what he perceived to be an admiring glance from Beatrice Cloister and she promptly blushed and giggled, whispering to her friend Delwyn Williams, "I think he's rather cute, Del, don't you?" To which Delwyn replied, "I rather think the tall, lithe one is the cutest, Beatty. Look at those handsome features and the way he stands when he's playing the piano. He's gorgeous!"

CHAPTER 4

After a short discussion by the makeshift band culminating in which music was to be played and which songs were to be sung, the dance proper finally got underway. And as usual, Harry and Teddy were first to their feet as the music flowed from the instruments in perfect harmony. On this occasion though, the band started with a barn dance so the boys quickly made their way over to Martha and Sarah, who duly obliged when asked to dance.

Most of the married couples were soon joining the other couples, and a number of young men asked single girls to dance. No one was refused and soon the floor was full of couples dancing in sequence. Tom Proctor decided to sit the barn dance out and was content to sip half a pint of stout and watch the dancers circumnavigate the floor in formation.

After a few traditional dances, the band played swing and jive music. The floor was packed with the younger folk and there were some very nifty dance moves to be seen. Harry and Teddy were in their element dancing with Sarah and Martha and luckily Sarah's ankle didn't trouble her at all. It was as though she had never fallen down the stairs. In fact she and Harry were dancing so well together, the rest of the dancers formed a circle around them, and cheered and clapped as the couple 'strutted their stuff'.

A bit later in the evening Sofia asked Martha if she and Sarah were in the mood for singing with her in a trio. They had done so at past dances and had been very popular.

"Come on, Sarah, let's sing 'Boogie Woogie Bugle Boy' with Sofia."

"I hope those two Irish fellows are up to it," Sarah exclaimed.

"No problem, sweetheart," Shaun announced. "We'll swing this place around, don't you worry, love. You sing like larks, we'll keep the tune. Isn't that right, band?" To which each musician nodded and mumbled the affirmative.

"I think that young fellow's kissed the Blarney Stone, Mort. What do you think?"

"Most definitely, Ted. Most definitely, without a doubt," Mort replied and then commented wryly, "I'd better go and sit with

Ava, or she'll think she's come to the dance on her own. I escorted her here and I need to pay her some attention before old Tom steps in!"

"Right you are, Mort. Carry on."

The band swung into action and played harmoniously with enthusiastic gusto. The songstresses sang like nightingales, in complete accord. There was such a flurry of action on the dance floor the village hall seemed as if it was being jived off its foundations. The evening was turning out to be a great success.

Later, Sergeant Jim Fredrick and his wife Mildred danced the quickstep to rapturous applause. Martha questioned Sarah, "How is it Sergeant Fredrick can dance like that and yet he can't stay on his own two feet when he's at work?"

"I don't know, Honey; it's one of life's big mysteries to me," she replied.

Toward the end of the evening the music slowed and couples danced cheek to cheek. Mort and Ava danced closely and a few of those who were watching nodded approvingly.

Martha and Sarah sat the cheek-to-cheek dancing out while Harry and Teddy danced with each other in mock affection. Bridget and Bryony sang 'Danny Boy' to rapturous applause and the dance came to a close after the band played the National Anthem.

Everyone left the hall by ten thirty and Ted had locked up inside by ten forty-five. His daughters waited for him outside with Bryony and Bridget. He made sure Bryony and Bridget arrived home safely at the end of the dance. He had promised their mother he would do this as a pre-requisite of the girls being allowed to go. Patrick and Shaun, sitting astride their motorbike, were chatting to the four girls. Ted locked the front door and said, "On your way now, you young fellows, then I can get these young ladies home."

"Right you are, sir, and thanks for having us play in the band. It was a grand experience to be sure," replied Shaun.

Ted replied, "You did a good job; you young men can play really well. Maybe you could play again sometime and these

CHAPTER 4

young ladies could sing along. We'll see anyway. Be on your way now." Patrick kick-started the motorbike and sped off up the lane back towards the farm.

"I don't think we'll be catching those two up," Ted muttered to himself. After everyone was settled in his vehicle he took the two sisters home to the Estate and saw them safely inside, with a nod of acknowledgment from their mother who was waiting at the front entrance of Letherby Hall.

"Right, now let's get you two back home; it's chapel tomorrow, you don't want to be late up for that. We don't want Reverend Boniface giving us his famous glare if we walk in after he's started, and besides you're both singing tomorrow; you can't be late for rehearsal before chapel starts!"

"Yes, Father. We'll be ready in time, Father," the girls said simultaneously.

Chapter 5

Sunday morning arrived and the choir started singing the first hymn at Bethesda Chapel, the congregation joining in with great passion, "Oh Lord my God as I in awesome wonder consider all the works thy hands hath made…"

Reverend Boniface began his sermon. "In consideration of that wonderful Russian hymn we have just sung, I am obliged to say this:

"Let no one doubt that God was the instigator of how this Universe came into being. Some might tell you it came with a big bang. If that's the case then who, might I ask, instigated that bang? Some might tell you, no one, or nothing. Well if that is seen as the truth, would it not take greater faith to believe that something was made from nothing, without anything being there in the first place? I ask you to consider this – all you of little or no faith – if not God, then who or what was the agent that caused this idyllic planet with all its order? This planet earth we dwell upon on this beautiful Sabbath morning. Ask yourselves this and consider it well…"

And so the Reverend Boniface proclaimed his powerful sermon.

Following the service the Reverend Boniface stood outside the chapel entrance and shook hands with those who had a mind to talk to him after his sermon. This was his custom. Very rarely would anyone challenge him concerning the contents of his sermon but one such person was Isaiah Allbright; he was the local astronomer and a scientist of renown.

"Good sermon that, Reverend. It must have been, it kept Tom Proctor awake most of the time, although old Jack Snead was

CHAPTER 5

sound asleep and snoring," teased Isaiah.

"I get your point, Isaiah. Keep looking at those planets and stars and consider well how they came about."

"Right you are, Reverend. I'll do that."

Surprisingly, and for the first time, Bryony, Bridget and their mother, Orla, attended chapel that morning. This was because Patrick and Shaun had been present on the previous two Sundays and had advised the sisters to try the chapel.

Orla Rowley was a striking looking woman, tall and elegant with beautiful facial features and strong bone structure. She had long, thick, tousled auburn hair tied back in a ponytail with a silk turquoise ribbon which helped to promote her facial features. In short she was a woman who could make a fallible man drool.

Not so Reverend Boniface. He looked Orla full in the face, not ignorant of her beauty, and said, "It's good to see you at chapel on this fine Sabbath morning. How long have you lived in these parts, or are you visiting?"

In her sensuous Irish accent Orla replied, "It's good to be here and no, we are not visiting, we live up at Letherby Hall." Pointing at Bryony and Bridget, she continued, "Those are my two daughters over there making small talk with those two fine young men. We all came over on the same boat, so we did, three months ago."

"I hope we will see you again then Mrs..."

"My name's Orla, Orla Rowley; and, to be sure, you will see us all again, Reverend Boniface," and then she said, "I noticed your name on the chapel notice board. You are Reverend Boniface, I take it?"

"Yes, Mrs Rowley, that is correct. Goodbye, and do have a pleasant Sabbath day."

"Goodbye, Reverend." Orla then called for Bryony and Bridget. "You two girls come and say goodbye to the Reverend Boniface." Bridget said goodbye and thanked him for the service. Bryony smiled at him and then they set off walking back to Letherby Hall.

Martha walked back home with her mother and sister. "I am quite certain that Reverend Boniface is correct in what he says about the beauty of this Earth. I can see it on the hills and moors when I'm out running. Yes definitely, God's done a wonderful job," she proclaimed.

Sarah stated, "I agree, Honey. This place didn't happen by chance. Look at these bushes and hedges, how pretty the blossoms are," and as she sniffed a hedgerow flower, she declared, "No, definitely not an accident and it didn't just happen. It was God for certain." Mrs Hunney looked at her two daughters and thought how fortunate she was to have them, with the outlooks on life that they possessed she was proud of them.

"We'll call for your grandmother on the way home. The dinner is near enough ready. We can have it as soon as your father gets home from mending that latch on the Reverend's door."

Reverend Boniface had left the front door of his home open because the latch had stuck closed, and not being a practical man he couldn't release it. Ted was going to fix it for him which he was certain was not going to take long.

Ted and Reverend Boniface had arrived at the Parsonage. "Let's have a look at this latch of yours, Reverend."

"I've told you before, Ted, you can call me James when I'm not in my official capacity."

"It doesn't seem right, Reverend Boniface. Anyway, I thought you were always in your official capacity."

"My wife calls me James. And if it's good enough for her, then it's good enough for you."

"Okay, Reverend, I mean James. I'll just get a couple of tools from my van and a drop of oil." He gave the latch a squirt of oil to lubricate it, tapped it with his pin hammer and the latch sprang free. He locked it, unlocked it, locked and unlocked it again and nodding his head said to himself, "Another good job done well by Ted Hunney Esquire."

"Thank you, Ted, how much do I owe you?"

"Have it on the house, James." Ted laughed at his own pun but the Reverend missed the wisecrack altogether.

"No, I need to pay you for your work."

"Not at all, Reverend Boniface, the job only took five minutes

CHAPTER 5

and it was on my way home anyway."

"I insist," Reverend Boniface said in an authoritative manner.

Ted knew he wouldn't get the better of him, so he said, "I'll write a bill out for you and drop it off on the way to work on Tuesday."

"Thank you, Ted, and thank you for the work you have done."

As Ted was arriving home, Ruth saw him through the parlour window. "Your father's here. Set the table, Martha. Sarah, help me finish off in here."

"Is there anything I can do to help, Ruth love?" Ruth's mother-in-law asked.

"You can brew a pot of tea, Bessie, but watch you don't scald yourself. You know you're a bit shaky on your feet after your fall."

"Can you hear your mum, girls?" said their grandma. "It doesn't seem long ago that I was doing the organising and handing the orders out. Now I'm on the receiving end of them; my goodness time does fly, I just don't know where it goes."

Martha remarked, "It goes into history, Nan, that's where it goes. Never to be seen again. Yesterday's gone, and last week, and come to think of it, tomorrow will go as well."

"Have you heard this one, Ruth? She's quite the philosopher. She'll be off to Cambridge if she carries on talking that way!"

"Not me, Grandma. We'll leave that up to Sarah, she's the brainy one; in fact, she should go to university. I'm a runner, not a scholar. Anyway, I'm going to get married and have two babies once I've achieved my running ambitions."

Sarah shouted from the kitchen, "Not me, Honey. I'm staying at the mill; going riding my bicycle with Lydia Burton; getting married; and having three babies. Did you hear, Martha? Three, not two."

"Will you harken to your girls, Ruth, they've got their lives well and truly mapped out."

"Well Nan, the Reverend Boniface says you should always make your plans God willing, and if you do that and try to succeed, that's all you can do."

Ted had walked into the room while Martha was talking and

exclaimed, "That's my girl, it's good to make plans God willing. Am I right in thinking you are still intent on running in a hill race, Martha? Against the men?"

"No, Father. Not just running – racing and beating them. Maybe not all of them, although I don't see why not. Women play football and play very good football. They've beaten male teams. That Dick Kerr ladies team, for instance, they have, and I've read that some men's teams won't play them because they're scared of being beaten by women. So I don't see why a woman can't beat a man at running, Father, do you, Nan?"

Her Grandma took a moment and answered, "Probably, but a good man will always beat a good woman at sport."

"Well, I think if we train harder and are more dedicated to our sport, a good woman can beat a good man."

Ted remarked, "That's all well and good, Martha love, but you have to get past the powers-that-be in that hill running sport, and you know that it's a male-dominated sport. Anyway, that's enough talk about sport on the Sabbath. Is the dinner ready yet?"

Ruth had been listening to the conversation while finishing the cooking but had said nothing. She started filling the plates with the freshly cooked food brought from town the previous day.

The family all sat down to eat after Sarah had finished setting the table and the food was in place. Ted said grace and mentioned how tasty the duck was. There was very little conversation at the table apart from a comment that Bessie made: "Your father used to like duck, Ted, God rest his soul and all those poor souls who were slaughtered in those wars." She started to weep. Ruth placed her arm around her shoulders.

"Now, now, Bessie don't be upsetting yourself again."

"Well, I still miss my Albert terribly after all these years. Forty-three years in July. What a waste of life. And I miss our Thelma – what a sad life for her and such a tragic end for her and baby Mara. Oh dear me, terrible. "

Sarah reached across the table and placed her right hand on her Nan's left hand and gently stroked her wedding ring saying, "Oh Nan."

CHAPTER 5

Bessie looked at Sarah, "I know, love. I know you all care for me. But you don't know the heartache unless you go through it yourself. I thank God that he spared your father in the second war and you girls; for your mother's and my sake. I couldn't have beared another loss." Casting dark wet eyes on Ruth, she said, "I wouldn't have wanted you to go through what I've gone through, Ruth, it was bad enough waiting for Ted to come home but he did, thank God."

Chapter 6

The Monday before the wedding arrived and the twins had been working for two hours at Bradshaw's textile mill.

"When you've finished sewing that stack of napkins, pack them in those boxes and take them down to the warehouse. And don't idle about down there, or you'll get your pay docked."

Martha replied, "Yes, Mr Garvan, I'll get back up here as quick as I can. Is it okay for me to go to the toilet on the way back?"

"If you must, but you must wait for brew time in future, Miss Hunney. This mill isn't a charity, you know, it's a place to earn your wage."

Not many people at the mill took to or associated with George Garvan. He was a firm's man and would say or do anything to stay on the right side of the mill owner. He was also an incorrigible womaniser and would use his position as works' manager to molest young and vulnerable females who worked at the mill.

"He's at it again," Martha said on the way past her sister who worked three machines down from her. "Just keep an eye on him and see if he comes past you. If he does, make sure you let me know. I don't want him following me down to the warehouse and trying to grope me. He tried it on with Lucy Lister last week and she's still a nervous wreck after her encounter with him."

"Alright, Martha, I'll whistle if he starts coming down there. You want to kick him right where it hurts if he comes near you."

"Only problem with that, Sur, is that I'll get sacked for assaulting him. Mr Donald won't believe me against Mr Garvan. It's about time someone sorted him out though and then he wouldn't try it on again with any of us."

CHAPTER 6

Martha continued walking down to the warehouse carrying the three heavy boxes of napkins. When she arrived George Garvan was waiting for her. He had slipped out of the side entrance at the far end of the building and walked down the ginnel entering the warehouse from the opposite side of the mill. He walked over to her and stood at her left-hand side.

"Now let's have a look at this top box, Miss Hunney, and see what we have in there. What's this then? A tablecloth! What's this doing in here? You weren't thinking of stealing this, were you?"

Shaking and anxious, Martha replied, "I didn't put it there, Mr Garvan and I certainly wasn't going to steal it."

"Well who did then?" Garvan demanded in a low, menacing tone. He had manoeuvred himself around to face Martha and started to move his left hand towards her left thigh. "Maybe we could come up with some—" but before he could finish speaking, Martha kneed him in the groin, side-stepped him and ran back, wide-eyed, to her sister.

Her voice trembling, she shouted, "He's tried it on and I've done it! I've kneed him where it hurts and now he's crumpled up on the floor. The groper. I'm sure to be sacked now. I know I am."

Sarah stood up and grabbed hold of her sister. "What did he do, Martha?"

Sobbing, Martha replied, "He was going to grope me, I know he was, he was right on to me and his hand was moving towards me. He accused me of going to steal a tablecloth that was in one of the boxes I took down to the warehouse. I didn't put it there."

"Alright, Martha. Mr Donald would prefer to believe Mr Garvan than you because you're easier to replace than him and he's worth more than you to the firm, and that's that. When we get home tell Father. He'll know what to do."

At that moment Garvan came staggering up from the warehouse shouting, "Get out of here, Martha Hunney, you're not working here anymore. You're too violent; just like that father of yours. Get out!"

"Come on Martha, I'll come home with you."

"If you go with her, Sarah Hunney, you can say goodbye to your job as well for deserting your workplace for no good reason."

The women working at their machines started muttering among themselves.

"Shut up you lot and get on with your work," Garvan demanded aggressively.

The sisters grabbed their coats and belongings, rushed out of the mill and made their way to the bus station.

Mortimer Johnson was in town, having visited Ava Fleischmann, and noticed the girls dashing by. "You two young ladies are in a hurry – is there a fire or something?" shouted Mort as they rushed past him.

Martha spun round quickly and sobbed, "No, Mr Johnson, we've been sacked and we're getting out of the way of Mr Garvan."

"Stop right there, girls, this can't be right. What's he been up to? As if I didn't know."

"I can't tell you, Mr Johnson, it's too embarrassing," sobbed Martha.

"Well, I had better get you both to your mother right sharp then. I'll get my van and run you home straight away. You can tell her what's been going on at the mill."

Sarah said, "Thank you, Mr Johnson, we need to get Martha home sharpish, she's in a right state. Come on, Honey, we'll go home with Mr Johnson and you can tell Mother what Garvan has been up to." Then she let slip, "The pervert."

"So he's been up to his old tricks, has he?" observed Mort. "Well, I wouldn't like to be him when your dad finds out what he's been up to. And as for you both being sacked, your dad knows Donald Bradshaw and I'm quite sure he'll be round to see him, don't you worry about that."

Martha continued sniffling all the way home. Sarah comforted her, wrapping her arms around her sister's shoulders. As soon as Mort's van arrived in the hamlet, Ruth opened the front door. She didn't see her daughters at first. "I thought I recognised your engine, Mort – what are you doing here?"

Sarah quickly jumped out of the passenger side of Mort's van followed more slowly by Martha. As soon as Ruth saw them both

CHAPTER 6

she asked, "What are you two doing here at this time, and what on earth is up with you, Martha, what's happened, love?"

Martha rushed over to her mother and grabbed hold of her round the waist.

"What's up, Martha love?" Ruth asked, very concerned as she stroked Martha's long black ponytail. "It's not like you to be like this at all."

Sobbing, Martha blurted out what had happened at the mill. Sarah stood next to her sister gently stroking her left arm and her back. Mort stood by his van without saying a word.

"Come inside, Martha love," said Ruth. "Thank you for bringing them home, Mort; will you come in for a cup of tea?"

"I will, Ruth; I'll hang about for a while, but will have to get back for two. I'll call up a bit later though just in case."

"If you could, Mort, it would be much appreciated," said Ruth anxiously.

"Ted's on a job up at Minsum and won't be back until about six. Will you put the kettle on, Sarah? Do you want a nip in yours, Mort?"

"Just a drop would be nice," said Mort glancing at Ruth with a half-smile on his gaunt face.

Sarah made a pot of tea and poured out four cups, tipping a drop of whiskey into Mort's cup. As was customary in the Hunney household she placed homemade biscuits on a plate for their guest to enjoy. Mort picked one off the plate and dunked it into his tea and then swallowed it in one gulp. This brought a short giggle from Martha, who had now regained some composure. Mort looked at her and gave her a half-smile and winked with his left eye. He was blind in his right eye as the result of a wound suffered on the day before the end of the Second World War. Nobody would know that he was blind in that eye unless they looked at it for a long time although it never blinked but stared all the time.

Martha asked what seemed to be a very strange question considering what had happened to her a short while ago. "What was it like for you and Father in the war, Mr Johnson? Father never talks about it, never ever. He's never mentioned it, has he,

Sarah?"

"No," Sarah quickly said, thinking that her mother would say something, but Ruth said nothing. Mort looked across the table at Martha and Sarah.

Mort said, "I'll tell you it was horrific and no more, apart from the fact that your dad's a hero. If he wants to tell you, he might do some day but don't go pressing him on it." Mort then repeated himself, as though at a distance, "Ted might tell you one day, that's all I've got to say."

"Now, girls, take heed of what Mort has said. Your father will tell you, and Oliver, when he's good and ready. Okay, girls?"

Martha and Sarah said simultaneously, "Yes, Mother."

Martha then said, "I'm going for a run, Mother. It'll help me clear my head. I'll take Shep with me but I'll make sure he doesn't round any sheep up on the moor."

"That's alright, Martha, if that's what you want to do, but don't go on one of your long runs; I'll only be worrying about you."

"Forty minutes maximum, Mother, and I'll be back."

"I'll come with you, Honey if that's alright with you," volunteered Sarah with a smirk on her face.

"And you will last until the gate, fifty yards up the field, and then after that will be you gasping for air. So I don't think so, Sarah," laughed Martha.

Martha changed into her running kit, thanked Mort for bringing her home and set off through the door shouting, "Come, Shep," as she went. Shep followed her and immediately picked up a stick dropping it at Martha's feet. "None of that today, Shep, we're just running." The dog took no notice of her, picked the stick up and dropped it at her feet again. Martha carried on running, ignoring the dog, and arrived on the fell-side after ten minutes of easy running.

Martha had a very long, graceful striding action on even terrain. When running on uneven terrain, she adjusted her action accordingly. For someone who was quite tall and slim, she was an extraordinarily strong uphill runner, no matter what the conditions underfoot were like. Martha's balance was impeccable

CHAPTER 6

when in full flight on a steep descent, whether on grass, over rocks or through mud. She would have been a cross between a mountain goat and a gazelle in the animal world.

On reaching the fell-side, Martha ran effortlessly down to Foxbridge Beck, striding out and leaping over the rocks and boulders strewn across the rough track. She waded ankle deep through the beck and continued the climb up to Wickelton Pike. The first three hundred feet were easy running for Martha. She had to shorten her stride on the steepening gradient but kept up a good running pace. There followed an abrupt increase in the gradient that always caused Martha to slow to a jog, and then the final quarter mile towards the top of the climb, before the run to the Pike, she had to walk with hands on knees due to the severity of the climb. The final stretch to the Pike was undulating but easy underfoot – no rocks or mud, only gravel, shale and moss.

Martha reached the Pike, touched the memorial plaque as was the custom, then set off across the moor to Beckhead Farm, negotiating the clumps of Turk's Heads with consummate balance. After bypassing the farm, she sped down the bridleway back towards the hamlet with Shep running on in front of her.

She didn't see anyone at all until the end of the run and was glad of the solitude. She had had the day's events running through her mind during the early part of the run but as soon as she started the long climb to Wickelton Pike her thoughts reverted to how she might be able to run in a competitive race. Martha knew there was a fell race at each of the three country shows based in nearby villages: two in August and one in September. She had thought about disguising herself as a boy and talking with an Irish accent. She was not sure that she could get away with the disguise or the accent although she had been practising her Irish in the privacy of her and Sarah's bedroom.

Towards the end of her run a voice said, "Oh to be sure, it's Marta," as she collided with Patrick Murphy turning the sharp corner before entering the hamlet at the end of the bridleway.

"Sorry," she spluttered out as she bounced back off his strong figure.

"I might start running myself shortly and run one of them there fell races at the shows."

Martha was taken aback with Patrick's remark. She asked him, "How do you know about the races?"

"Oh, I'm interested don't you know. I used to run back in Ireland, and I was quite good, if you will forgive my modesty."

"Well, you should start running again then, and do one of the races. I'm going to race one myself."

"I thought they didn't let girls run in the rough races. Aren't they more for farmers and shepherds and miners and that sort?"

Martha added sharply, "Yes – and mill girls if I get my way!" She thought for a moment then continued, "Well, I can run up and down to Wickelton Pike and run fast, so I can't see why I can't run in 'rough races' as you call them and I don't see why I can't run against the men."

A wide smile appeared on Martha's face and she giggled, "I watched the race at Ellington show last year and Rowley Thompson finished nearly fifteen minutes behind the winner and the race was only two and a half miles. Mind you, Rowley is sixteen stone if not more, so I could definitely beat him. That's why I should be able to run in a race."

"You've convinced me; I'll be on your campaign trail and no mistake, Marta. Anyway, I'll see you around, I've got to get back to the Estate. Next time you might just see me gliding across the moor right past you."

"And I might just re-pass you, Patrick Murphy." They both laughed and parted company.

Martha walked the last hundred yards to her home and entered the backyard. She took her pumps off and propped them up against the coal shed. It was a hot afternoon and Martha's face was moist with sweat. She strolled into the kitchen and swilled her face under the cold tap water, bent her neck round and put her mouth under the tap, taking a big gulp of water.

Ruth entered the kitchen and seeing Martha shouted, "Martha Hunney, that's not very ladylike. I've told you before about drinking from the tap like that."

CHAPTER 6

Martha gurgled, "I couldn't wait, Mother."

"You could have reached to the cupboard and got a cup, I'm sure. Anyway, how are you, Martha love?"

"I'm jobless, Mother but otherwise, I'm okay. I'll not allow what Mr Garvan did to get me down. I'm going to see Mr Donald and tell him all about Mr Garvan and his perverted ways. That's what I'm going to do, Mother."

"Martha, leave it to your father. He'll know what to do. He knows Donald Bradshaw. He was your grandfather Hunney's commanding officer in France. He was with him when he was killed. Don't mention I told you that. Your father will tell you all about what went on when he's good and ready."

"I won't, Mother. You and Father know what's best. But I still intend running a fell race this autumn at one of the shows. That's for sure, Mother. I will. I'm good enough and that's all that counts as far as I'm concerned. Don't you think so?"

"Martha dear, women have been struggling for equal rights with men for donkey's years, and will continue to do so. Women like Emmeline Pankhurst, God rest her soul, helped win us the right to vote. If that's what you want to do, I'll not stop you, but I still think it's a bit un-ladylike. Mind you, so is smoking and women have been doing that for years as well."

"I bet Lydia Burton can beat the men in cycling races and she can't compete against them either," commented Martha in frustration. "She's a really good cyclist. Our Sarah says she would beat the best of men." At that moment, Sarah walked into the kitchen. Martha said, "Isn't that right, Sur?"

"Isn't what right, Honey"?

"Lydia could beat the men at cycling," Martha replied.

"Of course she could. Lydia rides with Barry Edelstone and he's the best round here. She beats him easily on the hills, and finishes fresher than him on a long ride. When we go out together she has to wait for Meg, Mary and me at the top of each hill and she's really fearless riding downhill. They won't let her compete against men though and that's a pity because she'd beat most of the men in the country I reckon."

"There you are, Mother, another reason for women being able to compete against men, don't you think?" said Martha.

"If you insist. Now go and get a wash and freshen yourself up; your father is taking you and Sarah to Ava's this evening for your final fitting. She's staying open especially for you two so you need to be ready when your father gets home. He said he'll call at the chip shop in town for his tea while you're with Ava."

"Are you coming, Mother?" the girls asked simultaneously.

"Of course, I'll be there to make sure everything is okay with the fitting of your frocks. Don't forget, I'll be telling your father what happened at the mill today, so neither of you say anything. Leave that to me. I know how he'll probably react so I'll have to make sure he doesn't go looking for George Garvan. Or else there will be real trouble for him and make no mistake."

"We won't, Mother," the girls both said.

Chapter 7

Ted Hunney arrived home earlier than expected.

"You're home early, Ted. Did the job go well then at Minsum?"

"It is going well, Ruth, but I need a special fitting. I've picked one up from Evans but it's too late to go back. I've fixed the leak for now but will have to go and finish the job off tomorrow. I've the pointing to do anyway so I'll be there for at least three days more." Ted turned to his two daughters sat next to each other on the sofa and said, "Hello you two, have you had a good day at work?"

Before either could answer Ruth tugged on Ted's shirt and whispered, "Come into the backyard; I need to talk to you."

Ted could tell that his wife was upset and concerned about something. He walked outside with Ruth following and said, "What's the matter, Ruth, you sound upset?"

"It's not me, Ted, although I am upset. It's the twins." Wringing her hands together and with tears in her eyes she said, "They've both been sacked and that's not all. George Garvan has tried it on with Martha."

Ted stared at his wife and said, "He has, has he? Well that's the last thing he will ever do to my girl and any of those girls at the mill. I'll swing for him, the nasty pervert." He strode into the front room and faced the girls who were still sitting side by side and said, "How are you, Martha?" and before she could answer he continued, "Don't worry, my girls, I'll sort this out for you both. George Garvan won't bother you again, Martha, I'll see to that."

Martha quickly responded, "I'm alright, Father; don't do anything you will get into bother for. He's not worth it."

Ted said, "Don't worry, I won't." He then motioned to them with both hands and said, "Come here, my girls." They sprang from the sofa and he gave them both a hug and then said again, "Don't you worry, I'll sort this out for you both."

Simultaneously they said, "We know you will, Father." And both gave him a kiss, Martha on the left cheek, Sarah on the right cheek.

Ted walked into the kitchen. "What time do you have to be at the dress shop this evening, love?"

Ruth replied, "They have to be there at quarter to seven. Ava is staying open late so the girls can have their final fitting. With the wedding being on Saturday, she can do any alterations by Friday, so the frocks will be ready to wear in time. If you want to go earlier, I'll phone Ava up and see if we can go down sooner. What do you think, Ted?"

"That's okay by me, Ruth. I'll have my tea at Blenkinthorpes – they do a good mix there: chips, peas and gravy and a couple of slices of bread… what more could a man want?"

Ruth phoned Ava to arrange an earlier time for the twins to go for their fittings and luckily was successful. Six o'clock was the rearranged time.

"We'll have to set off at half past five, Ted. I arranged with Ava for six. You girls go and get ready. Martha, you need to wash that mud off your legs. You don't want your wedding frock spoiling before you've worn it!"

"I'll do it right now, Mother. Are we going to have something from Blenkinthorpes as well, since we haven't time for any tea and I'm hungry and Sarah's always hungry?"

"I am not, Honey, you cheeky thing. You eat enough for two yourself and you're still a skinny thing."

"Well, that's because I'm in training. You just eat for the sake of it, Sarah, don't you?"

"Now now, girls, that's enough. Go and get ready. I need to have a wash and get changed as well, so be quick about it and no falling out up there."

Ted asked, "Will you all be having something from the chip

CHAPTER 7

shop, Ruth or have you made something?"

"Yes, I suppose so. I intended making a potato pie for tea. But never got round to it with what's gone on. Curse that George Garvan; I've a good mind to take a knife to him myself. But as the bible says, 'Vengeance is mine, sayeth the Lord, it is mine to avenge' so I'll have to leave it to the Almighty to sort out."

"That's right, Ruth dear," commented Ted.

When everyone was ready they set off for the town and Ava's dress shop. They duly arrived, on time, at six o'clock. The twins and Ruth made their way to Ava's while Ted parked his van on Sweet Street just below the ironmongers. He walked round the corner to go to the chip shop and as he did he saw George Garvan coming out of The Shoulder of Mutton.

The pub was Garvan's usual drinking den after work. He would call in and have two pints of beer before walking home. He usually took a short cut round the back of the mill, unless it was dark. He wasn't married and lived with his widowed mother, who had waited hand and foot on him all his life.

Ted decided to wait in the doorway down the back alley until Garvan came out of The Shoulder of Mutton. He knew about the shortcut Garvan made on his way home from the pub because he had walked home with him on certain occasions to say hello to Mrs Garvan, his mother. Her husband had fought alongside Ted's father in the Great War and they were both killed at the same time by enemy machine gunfire while trying to capture a strategic village on the Somme.

George Garvan came stumbling out of the pub and walked along the cobbled street towards the back alley. He spotted Ted and turned to run, but he was too slow. Ted grabbed Garvan's jacket sleeve and spun him round into the doorway. In one swift manoeuvre Ted grabbed hold of Garvan's throat, squeezed it tight, kneed him in the groin and hit him in the stomach. Garvan gasped for air, groaned and slumped. Ted held him up by the throat and said in a calm whispered tone, "If you ever touch my Martha again, or Sarah, or any other girl in that mill, it will be the last thing you ever do. Have you got that, George? It's only because of your mother that you're standing upright now. Do you understand, George?" He then hit Garvan in the stomach again and said, "Come on, I'll see you home and say hello to your mother. I hope you've got the message, George – for you and your mother's sake, I wouldn't want her mourning over you, as much of a skunk as you are." George Garvan groaned and staggered towards his home with Ted holding him up.

At the end of the back alley, Sergeant Fredrick was standing just around the corner, whistling and looking into the second-hand bookshop window, reading the titles. One in particular caught his eye: 'How to Stay Young and Succeed'. He was musing about what the contents could be when Ted and George Garvan walked past him. He turned and asked, "What's up with you, George, one too many again?" Garvan groaned.

Ted quickly said, "I'm seeing him home, Jim. He's a bit under the weather as you can see!"

"You need to take a bit more water with it next time, George. Don't let me see you in that state again at this time of day or you'll be down the station, sleeping it off in the cells."

Ted helped Garvan get home, had a short conversation with Mrs Garvan, and then set off walking back to Ava Fleischmann's dress shop. He walked along Bright Street instead of using the back alley, catching up with Sergeant Fredrick on the way. "George was in a bit of a state," the Sergeant commented.

"Yes, but it wasn't what it seemed, I have to admit," replied Ted. "He had had a couple of pints but he wasn't drunk. George Garvan has been up to his old tricks again and unfortunately for him, Jim, he picked on the wrong girl – my Martha – and I'm not having any of that. I gave him a good talking to and a bit more." Touching his nose twice with his left forefinger, he looked straight into Sergeant Fredrick's eyes and said, "You know what I mean, Jim. No, he picked on the wrong girl this time. He's sacked Martha and Sarah, saying that Martha assaulted him..."

"Just a minute, Ted," interrupted Sergeant Fredrick. "You've given him a good hiding?"

"Not exactly a hiding but a taste of what he will get if he tries

CHAPTER 7

anything like that again."

"Ted, it's not the Wild West round here, you know, you should have reported it."

"You know as well as I do, Jim, he would have got away with it. He made sure that there were no witnesses to his perverted act. Just like the other times he's been reported and got off with it – mill girl against mill manager; no contest without any witnesses present. Martha wouldn't make a story like that up and he's not getting away with what he's done, I'll see to that. Martha and Sarah need their jobs back and I'll make sure they get them."

"Alright, Ted, I get the picture. But you should have come to me. I wouldn't be surprised if he puts a complaint in about you assaulting him."

"He's no witnesses, it's his word against mine unless you are going to stand up in court and testify against me, Jim. Would you do that, knowing what he's like?"

"You know I wouldn't do that. You know me better than that Ted; give me a bit of credit."

"Sorry, Jim, but this has wound me up to the hilt and I'm concerned for my girls. They are my first priority and I don't want them upsetting like he's done to them. He's sacked Sarah too, you know, for leaving work before she was supposed to. Sarah was seeing her sister home and he sacked her for that. He's a nasty man; I should have left him in that hell-hole for the rats to eat."

"Come on, Ted, settle down. You don't want to be having one of your turns and going into a depression..."

Ted interrupted Sergeant Fredrick, "I'm not going to do that, Jim. I just need to sort this work situation out for my girls."

"I know one thing, Ted. You would never have left anyone in that hole who was breathing. You're not that sort of man. That's why you received that medal, Ted; you're a hero round these parts. We'll get your girls their jobs back. I'll make sure of that. I'll be paying George Garvan a visit and talking some sense into him, don't you worry."

At that moment Martha came jogging down the street and demanded, "Father, where have you been? We've been looking all over the place for you," and then politely said, "Hello Sergeant Fredrick."

"Hello Martha, how are you?"

"I'm fine, thank you."

"Have we finished, Jim?" asked Ted.

"Leave things to me from now on, Ted. Don't be doing anything you'll regret. Call round to the station on Thursday and I'll give you a progress report."

"Right you are, but I want my girls to get their jobs back – will you sort that, Jim?"

"Like I said, Ted, leave it to me." Sergeant Fredrick looked at Martha, raised his police helmet and said, "Have a pleasant evening, Martha. See you, Ted. Be good." He walked off whistling 'Colonel Bogey' as he turned and walked down the back alley of the mill.

Martha tugged Ted's arm and said, "Come on, Father. Mother and Sarah are waiting at the chip shop. I called in there and Bobby said you'd walked straight past. He said he thought you went in The Lamb. I called in there and they said you hadn't been near. Where have you been, Father?"

"I had a bit of business on, Martha, and then I bumped into Sergeant Fredrick. I told him what went on at the mill, so he's going to sort things out if he can. How did the dress fitting go anyway?"

"Oh, everything's okay. There's just one small adjustment on Sarah's frock. She has to call in on Thursday, and then if it fits right, we can pick them both up on Friday. I'm really looking forward to Matilda's wedding. Are you looking forward to giving her away, Father?"

"Of course I am." Ted shook his head slowly and said, "It's a terrible shame that her Father can't be there to do it but that's what happens in war, Martha love."

Ted's sister Thelma had married Jack Spriggs who was a pilot. He had been shot down over the English Channel during the War – his body was never found. Thelma was six months pregnant with twin girls, Matilda and Mara, at the time. Tragically, baby

CHAPTER 7

Mara died of polio at six months old. Thelma did marry again ten years later but her second husband left her for a younger woman. At the time it caused a great deal of heartache and upheaval in the village and feelings still ran high five years later as a result of the sordid episode.

Some in the village said Thelma had died from a broken heart after the loss of her first husband, her baby, and the circumstances of the breakdown of her second marriage.

They walked back to the chip shop with Martha linking her father's arm and leaning her head on his shoulder. They didn't speak again. Suddenly a cold sweat came over Ted but gently gripping Martha's arm he forced himself back to the present. He smiled at Martha and she smiled back pushing her head onto her father's shoulder a little harder. She had no idea the terrible thoughts Ted Hunney had just been experiencing and for that he was grateful.

"Where have you been, Ted?" asked Ruth. "We've been waiting for ages, love."

"Father's been on business, Mother," Martha replied.

"Come on; let's get our tea from the chip shop. We can listen to the wireless tonight. There's a good play on after the Archers. I wonder if Dan Archer has got out of that mess he's been getting into. He's always putting his foot in it that fella," stated Ted.

"I'm going to make sure all my clothes are ready for the wedding on Saturday – well apart from my frock – when I've had my tea," stated Sarah. "I suppose you'll be leaving yours until Friday evening, Honey, won't you?"

"How did you guess? I know where all my stuff is, and it won't take me four days to sort them out like you, Sur. A good hour should do it."

Ted and Ruth laughed. Sarah pulled her face at her sister and Martha reciprocated.

Chapter 8

"Are we going for that bike ride, Honey or are you still planning the downfall of the male domination in fell running?"

"You can be sarcastic all you want, Sur, but if you don't have a plan, you fail. Fail to plan, plan to fail. Perfect planning and preparation lead to success. Being slap happy does not."

"Have you been reading that philosophy book of Father's again?"

"No, that's what the Reverend Boniface says. He should know. He planned to play for England, and then he did! So if it's good enough for the Reverend, it's good enough for me. Anyway, I'll only be five minutes. We'd better take our waterproofs just in case. It looks quite overcast."

"Okay, we'll go up to Paynters Point. It's a good sixteen miles there and back, the way I'm thinking of going. Do you think you're up to it, Honey? I'll wait for you on the hills, don't worry."

Martha laughed. "I think it's going to be the other way round. It's a good job you've lost those five pounds you say you have, or you'd never keep up with me. Although I have to admit you do look good in your wedding frock. I think Harry Smith will be paying you quite a bit of attention at the wedding, Sur."

"Well maybe so, but there'll be other boys too, you know."

"Ah, Sarah Hunney, you hussy; I've never heard you say anything like that before. You'd better not let Father hear you or he'll be tethering you to where he can keep an eye on you!"

"Honey, I'm only kidding you, and you know that very well, so stop making a song and dance about it. Mind you, I think Patrick Murphy is rather handsome. Anyway, he won't be at the wedding.

CHAPTER *8*

At least, I don't think so."

"Oh, I think he's taken anyway. I heard Delwyn Williams telling Beatrice Cloister, she thought he was cute. And if Delwyn gets her claws in him, well that's it – he'll be snared. Oh, but on second thoughts, Sur, he's on about running in one of the fell races, so he'll be training and won't have time for courting. He told me he was a top runner in his school days and that means he's got some talent."

"You seem to know a lot about him, Martha Hunney. Do you want to tell me anything?"

Martha laughed and remarked, "Not particularly. Anyway, I only have eyes for Teddy. But when I bumped into Patrick on the way back from my run the other Monday, he told me that he was thinking of running in one of the races and was going to do some training, so what do you think about that then?"

Sarah stood with hands on hips, eyes wide open, and smiled, taking in everything that Martha was saying. "Well good for him, that's what I say. I hope Patrick beats that big head Arthur Beardsworth if he does do the race. For the last two years, Arthur's said that he'd win the Rivestone Pike race only to come in limping near the back of the rest of the runners complaining that he's twisted his ankle. No such thing! Sam Kendal told me, Arthur had set off too fast and run out of steam both times."

"Yes, and I hope I get the chance to beat all of them," Martha said haughtily.

"Dream on, Martha. Come on, let's get on our way."

"You see if I don't," retorted Martha.

The sisters set off on their bicycle ride, with Martha pushing on in front. She knew that Sarah wasn't as fit as the last time they had gone for a ride together and that was when Sarah left Martha on each hill climb. Sarah wasn't as natural a cyclist as Martha was a runner, but could be strong on the hills when she cycled regularly. She wasn't as focused and nowhere near as competitive as her sister; Sarah was definitely more laid back. She knew which buttons to press when she wanted to avenge her sister though. This was usually when Martha had annoyed her over some petty incident, such as whose turn it was to peg the washing out or fill the coal bucket, two of the many tasks they did in their daily routines.

On Martha pushed, hoping that Sarah would drop off at some stage of the ride. Sarah shouted exasperatedly to her, "Will you slow down, Honey? You're not doing the Rivestone Pike you know, racing against Sam Kendal – not that you'd stand a chance against him. You know I'm not as fit as last time we went for a ride."

This only spurred Martha to speed up on the hill they were approaching. Exasperated, Sarah pulled up at the side of the lane half way up the hill and rested her bike against an oak tree saying to herself, "Blow it! She can carry on if she wants, I'm having a rest."

Martha reached the top of the hill without realising Sarah wasn't behind her. She sped down the other side of the hill half expecting Sarah to fly past her. When she reached the bottom, Martha turned her head round to find out where her sister was but couldn't see her. She pulled up and waited for a short time and then said to herself, 'I hope Sarah hasn't had an accident, like the time she broke her arm and collar bone'. She turned her bike around and set off back up the hill. Reaching the top and freewheeling down the other side, Martha still couldn't see Sarah. Eventually, she spotted her sitting on the grass verge. "I hope she's alright," she thought then shouted, "Are you okay, Sur?"

"Not really," Sarah replied.

"You haven't broken anything like last time, have you?" Martha asked anxiously.

"No, I haven't. And I haven't had an accident either. It's you, Martha," Sarah answered angrily. "Why do you have to be so competitive with everything you do? You know I'm not as fit as you. You've been training hard all year. Can you not take it easy for once and enjoy the ride with me instead of riding me into the deck?"

Martha stared at Sarah then got off her bike and dropped it next to her sister's. She walked over to her, knelt down, placed her

CHAPTER *8*

arms around Sarah's shoulders and kissed her on the cheek. "Oh Sur, I'm so sorry. I've no excuse. It's just that I'm obsessed with doing a fell race; it's on my mind all of the time. I'll try to curb it." Martha looked Sarah full in the face and insisted, "But I'm still going to do one."

Sarah hugged her sister and stated, "I do believe you are, Honey. Yes, I do believe you will run a race and I'll help you all I can."

"Thanks, Sur, you're the best sister in the world."

Sarah laughed and said, "By the way, Martha, I'll still beat you in the works' sports' day sprint – if we ever get back working there."

"Well, you'd better get in training then, Sur." Martha laughed and pushed her sister on the arm. Sarah reciprocated and they got back on their bicycles, riding to Paynters Point at a leisurely pace, chatting as they went.

Sarah asked, "What do you think will happen, Martha? Do you think we'll get our jobs back or will we definitely be sacked by Mr Garvan?"

Martha turned to her sister, nearly falling off her bicycle in the process, and stressed, "We have been sacked, Sur. Mr Garvan has no intention of taking us back to work at the mill. If we ever do get our jobs back, I know one thing for sure – if he tries it on with me again he'll get more than a knee in the groin. I'm not putting up with that sort of thing. I'm hoping Father will sort it out for us to go back. He knows Mr Donald really well and will go to see him. Anyway, Father's had a word with Sergeant Fredrick and he'll sort something out, I'm sure. He'll go and see Mr Garvan and tell him off."

They reached Paynters Point just as it started to rain. A torrential summer downpour and a strong wind blowing, the girls sheltered in an open sandstone cave in the hillside waiting for the severe weather to pass over. The cave was shallow but watertight. They sat down on a large stone that had been rolled in by workmen who had been resurfacing the road a few years earlier. Sarah pushed her bicycle into the cave and took some sandwiches out of the saddlebag.

"Here you are, Honey, get one of these sardine butties inside you."

"Oh, thanks, Sur. I'm glad you put some butties up, I'm feeling really hungry. I should have had more breakfast after my run this morning."

"Well, that's not like you. You usually have lots of food after a run. As you say you've got to put back in what you take out."

"I did have some but obviously not enough. Anyway Sur, I was busy making my plans wasn't I?"

Sarah changed the subject. "I'm really looking forward to Matilda's wedding on Saturday. I hope Reverend Boniface has got rid of his cold and sniffling nose by then or we won't be able to tell what he's saying! Can you imagine, Honey?" Sarah pinched her nose with her index finger and thumb and spoke down her nose making a ridiculously unpronounceable muffle of words.

Martha laughed so much she fell off the stone and banged her head on the cave wall. "Ooh, that hurt," she blurted out and then carried on laughing at her sister's antics.

The downpour stopped and the sisters stepped out of the cave. The water from the rain was still flooding down the road and the girls decided to wait for a few minutes before they set off for home. As they were waiting, a figure appeared in the distance running off the moor and heading towards them at speed.

"Flippin' 'eck," shouted Martha "Who's that? He's shifting!" She stared in amazement as the figure approached them, and then she gasped, "I don't believe what I'm seeing. It can't be, can it, Sarah? It is, isn't it? It's Roger Thompson or what's left of him; he's about four stones lighter!"

Sarah laughed at her sister's astonishment and then shouted, "Is that you, Roger?" as the figure approached.

"It sure is. I can't stop; I'm in serious training for the fell races." He slowed down slightly and continued, "No last place for me this year!"

Martha shouted as he passed, "Roger, I'll see you on the starting line."

He didn't understand that Martha meant as a competitor in

CHAPTER 8

the races, he thought she would be a spectator. He shouted back, "See you, Martha, see you, Sarah. I'll see you at the wedding on Saturday," then sped up as he crossed the road and headed over the rugged moorland toward Plotley, the hamlet where he lived.

"The way Roger's shaping up he'll not be last in this year's races. He looks quite trimmed down and he's moving like a proper runner. A good one at that. Yeah, I don't think he'll be last this autumn," Martha enthused.

"I'll bow to your vast expertise," Sarah commented slightly sarcastically and then said, "Come on, let's get home before it starts pouring down again."

It was an uneventful return journey home. The sisters rode side by side and chatted mainly about the forthcoming wedding – who would be there, who would be wearing what, and who would be with whom. Sarah and Martha were going to sing a duet at the ceremony, with accompaniment on the piano by Miss Benton, the chapel pianist and village school teacher. Arrangements had been made by the bride and groom for Patrick Murphy and Shaun McMullan to renew their successful village dance band partnership, with Sofia Reynolds and Cyril Squires to play later in the afternoon at the wedding reception in the village hall. Martha and Sarah were also looking forward to singing at the reception with the makeshift musicians.

The sisters arrived home in time for them to help their mother make the tea. "Your Father will be late home tonight, so he's said for us to have our tea. He'll have his when he gets home, and before you ask, Martha, he'll be home when he gets here. I don't know where he's gone; he never told me."

Martha replied, "Father's probably looking at a job. That's what he's usually doing when he gets home late or calls at The Lamb for a pint."

Ruth stopped stirring the broth with a large wooden spoon and looked sternly at her daughter. "He only calls for a drink once in a blue moon, Martha, and he always tells me if he's going for a drink and that's usually work related anyway."

Sarah observed, "Maybe it's something to do with the wedding,

Mother."

"Well, he would certainly have told me about that. Anyway, let's get on with making the tea. Are you going down to see your Nan later, Martha? You said you would, remember?" Ruth turned round after receiving no answer and asked Sarah, "Where's your sister gone? For goodness sake, she's whippet quick that girl." She then shouted in a high-pitched voice, "Martha."

Instantly, Martha appeared after thundering down the stairs. "Yes, Mother?" she asked.

"How can you disappear so quickly, Martha Hunney?"

"Training, Mother. It's what you call 'speed training'. I've got to be fast as well as having stamina for when I race the fells this autumn."

Her mother looked at her with eyebrows raised and said, "You've a one-track mind. You're intent on doing a fell race against the men, aren't you?"

"You know I am, Mother."

Sarah interjected, "Well, we'll see how fast you are at the works' sports day, won't we, Honey? I'll blast you off the track, and you'll be eating humble pie after I've finished demoralising you."

Pulling her tongue out and pushing her sister sideways with her elbow, Martha retorted, "Yes, well, unless something happens we won't be running will we? And you've no chance of beating me anyway."

"Sarah beat you last year if I remember rightly," said their mother and then asked Martha again, "Are you going to your Nan's?"

"Yes, Mother," she replied and then wandered off into the living room, sulking.

Her mother called her back and said, "Set the table, Martha and stop sulking. You take this sport business too seriously – someone wins and all the others lose; that's a fact of life. When your sister beat you last year and finished second in the race all the other girls who ran hugged each other. But not you, Martha Hunney. Oh no; no, you sulked."

"I did congratulate Bonny Parker for winning and I said to our

CHAPTER 8

Sur 'well done' didn't I, Sur?"

"Oh yes she did, Mother; about two weeks later!" exclaimed Sarah, and then started laughing.

Martha laughed mockingly, and said, "There's no such thing as a good loser anyway."

Sarah retorted, "Give it a rest, Martha. If you do ever run against men, you won't win anyway, so you'll have to get used to losing now."

"That's different altogether. I'll just be glad to compete in a fell race against them. That's my aim, although I will try to beat as many as possible."

Her mother gave her a 'get on with it' look, pointed to the cutlery drawer and motioned with her hand to the table. Martha started setting the table for tea.

Chapter 9

Ted Hunney strode into the police station. He didn't have time to say anything before Sergeant Fredrick, who was on desk duty at the station entrance, announced, "I've had a word with George Garvan, Ted, and he said it was a big misunderstanding between him and Martha. He's willing to accept that she probably misunderstood his intentions toward her and is willing, under the circumstances, to reinstall her and Sarah to work back at the mill. As a gesture of goodwill toward the girls, he's willing to pay their wages for the time they've had off."

"Well that's very big of him I must say," remarked Ted, sarcastically. "Who does he think he is? A misunderstanding indeed. Martha and Sarah need an apology from him, Jim."

"I wouldn't push it too much, Ted. He's a slippery character and could make trouble in the long run. You know how close he is to Bradshaw. No, leave it now, Ted."

Ted took a long hard stare at his friend Jim Fredrick and, after weighing the pros and cons of his war comrade's suggestion, he replied in a low, cool and collected tone, "Yes, you are right, Jim. I'll leave it be." He turned and walked towards the exit.

"Have a good afternoon, Ted."

Ted turned toward Sergeant Fredrick, smiled, and answered, "The same to you, Jim. Good afternoon."

However, as far as Ted Hunney was concerned, it wasn't the last encounter he would be having with George Garvan regarding his daughter Martha and the sordid incident at the mill.

He set off home driving slowly, thinking about Martha, the wedding on the coming Saturday, the job he was finishing on

CHAPTER 9

Friday, and not really concentrating on the road. Suddenly a figure appeared from nowhere, as it seemed to fly over the wall and land in the country lane right in Ted's path. Ted swerved as fast as he could but as he did so he heard a dull thud. He pulled his van up onto the grass verge at the side of the hedgerow, quickly opened the door and climbed out. He could see a figure sprawled out on the side of the lane. He suddenly felt sick in the pit of his stomach and his heart started racing.

'Oh no, not this again,' he thought, and his mind flashed back for a moment to being in a convoy of vehicles in France during 1944. Ted had been driving at the rear, there were infantrymen walking to the fore and side of the convoy. One stumbled and fell on the hard and rutted frosty ground under the front wheels of Ted's vehicle. He had stopped instantly but the damage was already done, the soldier's legs were crushed. Much to Ted's distress, he later learned that the soldier had lost both his legs in the incident. It was of no comfort whatsoever to Ted that he was absolved of all blame at the inquiry into the accident.

Coming to his senses, Ted rushed over to the prostrate figure on the ground and was about to ask if they were hurt. He was amazed and mightily relieved at what he saw next. A young man rolled over on his stomach and leapt to his feet. No sooner was he upright than he promptly keeled over again. Ted's heart sank into his boots.

Then, in a rich Irish accent, the young man said, "I think that I'd better take a mandatory eight count."

It was Patrick Murphy – he was out running and had leapt over the five-barred gate leading from a field belonging to Lord Letherby.

"Is that you, Patrick?" asked Ted.

"To be sure it is, Mr Hunney, and how are you on this fine day?"

"Never mind me, Patrick, how are you?"

"I've never felt better, sir. In fact, I'm in training for the fell races this autumn. I'm going to do all three – work permitting. I hope I haven't damaged your van, sir."

"The van's okay, Patrick, but are you sure you're alright?"

"I'll let you know on Saturday. I could stiffen up a bit but I'll be right for playing the old joanna for the wedding do." Patrick wriggled his fingers and declared, "No fingers broke, Mr Hunney. I'm sure to be okay! Are you looking forward to the wedding yourself, sir?"

Ted didn't answer Patrick's question but forcefully insisted, "Come on, let's get you to my home where you can have a brew and I'll ask Mrs Hunney to check you over. I'd hate to think you might have some internal bleeding or concussion or something else."

"Okay, Mr Hunney, anything you say, sir."

Ted said light-heartedly, "Patrick, you don't need to keep calling call me 'sir', I haven't been knighted, well not yet anyway! But we better get home soon – if I'm much later than I am already, Mrs Hunney will crown me. Here, let me help you up."

Patrick rose to his feet aided by Ted and walked gingerly over to the van. They travelled to Ted's house chatting about nothing in particular apart from Patrick asking if Ted thought Martha would be able to run in one of the upcoming fell races. Ted's response was to tell Patrick, "A female has never competed in a fell race against men in these parts, but knowing Martha, she will move heaven and earth to be the first to do it!"

Ted parked his van and climbed out, "Steady on," Ted ordered as Patrick climbed out and tottered a few paces. "Are you sure you're okay? You look a bit pale to me. Here put your hand on my shoulder and I'll help you in."

"Right you are, Mr Hunney. I'll not argue with you, sir."

Ted quickly replied, "I've told you – not yet."

Patrick looked at Ted, puzzled. "I haven't been knighted yet, Patrick," Ted reiterated.

"Oh right you are. I forgot, but I'll remember in future, that's for sure, no problem with that, your honour."

Ted shook his head in frustration and said, "Come on, or else I will be getting crowned and not in the way I would want to be."

CHAPTER 9

Sarah had heard her father's van and made her way from the kitchen to the front door. She opened it just as Ted was about to turn the doorknob. She looked at Patrick leaning on Ted's shoulder and asked mockingly –to hide her delight at seeing him, "What's up with you, young-fellow-me-lad?"

"Now, now Sarah, this young fellow has been involved in an accident and got himself injured. Go in and put the kettle on."

"Yes, Father," she instantly obeyed and rushed back into the kitchen shouting, "Medical emergency at the door, Mother; Patrick Murphy needs your assistance."

Ruth rushed to the front door but not before Martha could push in before her. She took one look at Patrick and said sympathetically, "I guess that's you out of the fell races this autumn."

"Oh no, Marta, it's just a slight blip on my road to glory."

"Well in that case, if it's glory you're after, you had better stop messing about and get some real training done. My father's not going to assist you on three miles of rough fell ground! Anyway, what have you done?"

Before Patrick could reply, Ruth ordered her husband to take the young fellow through to the kitchen and sit him away from the table at the kitchen sink. "Is that blood I can see trickling down your leg, Patrick? I can't tell with all that mud there."

"That's not mud, Mrs Hunney, that's pure Lancashire peat from off the tops near the Pike," he replied. "If it is blood, I've done it myself when I jumped over the fence and ran onto Mr Hunney's van bumper."

"Have you run him over, Ted Hunney?" Ruth gasped disbelievingly.

"No, he didn't, Mrs Hunney, it's more like I ran over the van and came off the worst. Mr Hunney tells me I haven't damaged it though, thank goodness."

Ted insisted, "Ruth, it was just one of those freak incidents that seem to happen once in a blue moon."

Sarah had made a pint pot of tea for Patrick. She asked, "How many sugars do you take, Patrick? I've made it nice and strong for you."

Patrick looked at her with a smile on his face that melted her heart, "Oh, that's gradely, just the three teaspoons, that should do the trick, thank you very much."

Sarah blushed as she passed Patrick his tea. Her blush didn't go unnoticed, especially by Martha who stored the moment up for a later date.

"Here you are, Father, a nice pot of tea for you as well." Sarah handed the pot to her father handle first, so he wouldn't scald himself.

As he took hold of the cup Ted's hands were shaking and he knew it was down to the war and the frightening memories he had no control over. He would say to his wife in private, "This is what I brought back from the war, Ruth," and he would hold out his hands which trembled uncontrollably. They didn't always shake, just in times of stress, and when he had a flashback to those terrible war years.

"Thanks, Sarah love," Ted said gratefully. "What do you make of this young fellow's leg, Ruth?"

Before Ruth could answer, Patrick chirped up, "It's really nothing, Mr Hunney, a mere shallow flesh wound to my thigh. It didn't happen when I jumped on to your vehicle. I caught it on the top of a cam stone, leaping over a wall coming off the moor. It's only a graze, to be sure."

"I'll be the judge of that, young man," said Ruth, looking sternly at Patrick. "I'm the nurse in this home; I'll say whether it's a mere flesh wound, as you call it. Roll your shorts leg up and let me have a look."

Sarah stood watching with a glint in her eye until her father said, "You two girls go into the front room while your mother attends to Patrick."

Martha had already left the kitchen when Sarah remarked, "We'll never learn about nursing unless we stay and watch Mother at work."

"This examination isn't for your eyes, Sarah love, now do as you're told."

"Yes, Father." Sarah traipsed slowly into the front room,

CHAPTER 9

glancing back to see if she could catch a glimpse of Patrick's muscular thigh. She was disappointed, though; her mother was masking her view of Patrick as she prodded carefully at his injury.

"Well, Patrick, your diagnosis is correct; it is a mere flesh wound. Take yourself out the back and give your legs a good wash in Martha's miracle water. Ted, will you show Patrick the well, and give him a clean cloth."

Looking at Ruth, Patrick announced, "Only the good Lord can work miracles, Mrs Hunney. I don't think Marta's water can cure the pain instantly."

"It's just a figure of speech, Patrick, but you might be surprised. Be off with you, and you can stay to tea when you're done."

"Oh, I can't do that, Mrs Hunney, thank you very much but I've work to do at the farm, and I have the beasts to milk."

"Another time then. Ted, will you take Patrick to Middleview Farm when he's done washing?"

"I will, Ruth, as soon as the boy's ready."

After Patrick had washed his legs and Ruth had smeared some ointment over the superficial wound, Patrick glugged down the dregs of his pint pot of strong tea and made ready to leave.

"Thanks for your hospitality, Mrs Hunney."

Ruth replied, "You can call again whenever you like and next time, stay to tea."

"I will, to be sure," Patrick cheerfully replied.

Sarah had been hovering near the front door and when her father and Patrick appeared from the kitchen she asked, "Is it alright for me to come with you, Father? For the ride and some fresh air, I mean."

"Do you mean you want me to drive with all the windows open, Sarah?" Ted teased.

"It's a warm evening, so why not?" Sarah replied innocently.

"Don't hang about talking at the farm, Ted," Ruth cautioned sternly. "You know what you're like when you and Charlie Danson get together."

"Well I can't very well ignore him if he's there, can I?" Ted turned to Patrick and asked, "Does Charlie come up for milking, still?"

"Not on Thursdays, he says he goes to choir practice."

Ted laughed and turned to Ruth, "Did you hear that, Ruth? Patrick says Charlie goes to choir practice on Thursdays."

Ruth replied sardonically, "He's more likely to be in The Lamb, and the only singing he'll be doing is on his way home – drunk."

Ted set off for Middleview Farm with every window on the vehicle wide open, just as the evening was beginning to cool. As she nudged him and pointed to the window-winder, Sarah asked Patrick if he would close his window, rotating her right hand clockwise by way of demonstration.

"I thought you wanted some fresh air, Sarah?"

"It's getting a bit chilly, Father."

Ted laughed, and thought to himself, 'Fresh air indeed; more like Patrick-itis.'

Back at the Hunney household, Martha and her mother were talking. "What do you think, Mother?" Martha asked as they walked back into the kitchen, "I don't think it was fresh air or a ride in Father's van that Sur was interested in."

Ruth, knowing what her daughter was intimating, replied, "Well, I don't know how she feels about Patrick but I think Harry Smith will have his work cut out if he intends courting Sarah."

"And I think Delwyn Williams will have her work cut out if she intends making a play for Patrick, especially when Sarah starts using her feminine charm on him."

"Well, that's one way of putting it, Martha. I know for definite, your father will be keeping a very close eye on the situation to make sure there's no impropriety. You know what happened when he caught Billy Briggs making overtures toward Sarah. I don't think Billy has even looked at Sarah, never mind spoken to her, since that day."

"Yes, Mother, but Sarah was only fourteen at the time and Billy was eighteen – it's no wonder Father went spare and frightened the living daylights out of him. I think Father should start trusting us both a bit more now though. There are young women married at our age after all. Look at Mary Glassen, she's younger than us

CHAPTER 9

and she's on her second baby now."

"A bit too young if you ask me, Martha. Your father and I were both twenty when we married."

"I'm certainly not thinking of getting married yet, Mother. I don't think Sarah is either. But it would be nice if we could do some courting if the right man came along. What do you think?"

Ruth had thought for a while that a conversation along this line would crop up sooner rather than later, and even though Sarah was more forward in these matters than her sister was, it was Martha who would always be more forthright in bringing up the subject of relationships with the opposite sex. And if the subject did crop up, their mother would also be forthright in explaining in detail what her daughters needed to know.

"I've certainly no objection to either you or Sarah courting with the right young man. It's possible that your father thinks the same as I do because we have only recently discussed it. But don't you forget, Martha, I saw how you and Teddy Moore looked into each other's eyes when he rushed to the back of the bus to help you."

Martha blushed. It was the first time that her mother had shown any inclination that she knew Martha had an interest in the opposite sex, and Teddy Moore in particular.

Martha fumbled about with the cutlery on the table and said, "So are you saying, Mother, that if Teddy asked me to go to the pictures with him it would be alright and Father wouldn't mind? Is that what you mean?"

"Yes, that's what I'm saying. He seems a decent enough young man. I'm not saying Harry Smith isn't, but he is a bit of a show-off. Anyway from what I've heard, Harry won't be in these parts for much longer."

Although Martha was overjoyed with what her Mother had said about Teddy Moore, she was perplexed by what Ruth had said regarding Harry Smith.

"Why, where's Harry going, Mother?"

"To join the Air Force. I know he's passed the test and the medical and according to his mother he will be leaving for the training base in three weeks' time. He's following in his father's footsteps I suppose."

"Sarah might not be happy about that."

"I don't think she will be a quarter as bothered as you would be if it was Teddy Moore who was joining up!"

Martha's heart sank at the thought of it, and at that moment realised just how much Teddy meant to her.

Chapter 10

Ted pulled up in the farmyard. Standing in the shippen doorway, agape with a pork pie in his hand, was Shaun McMullan.

Patrick laughed, "Will you look at that fella McMullan? He never has food far from him. I wouldn't advise you to invite him home for tea, Mr Hunney; he'll eat you out of house and home, to be sure. I hope there's plenty of food on tap for the wedding otherwise you'll have to tie that fella up."

Ted shrugged his shoulders. "Don't worry, Patrick, there will be plenty for everyone; mind you, he does look well looked after and well nourished."

Ted climbed from his van and as he walked around to the passenger side he waved to Shaun, asking, "How are you doing there?"

"Oh, I'm fine and dandy, your honour."

"It's okay, Shaun I'm not a judge – not yet anyway."

"Right you are, Mr Hunney, sir."

"As I have told Patrick, I haven't been knighted yet either."

"Right. I've got your message, Mr Hunney. Is everything set for Saturday?"

"I'm sure it will be. Anyway, enough of the small talk, Shaun. Patrick here has had an accident and–"

Shaun shouted to Patrick before Ted could finish, "I hope you're alright for milking, Murphy. There's only me and you and thirty beasts, and Charlie's on choir practice."

"Stop fretting, McMullan, and finish your pie. I've only got a scratch, but thanks for asking me how I am anyway."

Sarah climbed out of the passenger side and Ted walked around to help Patrick out, but before he could reach the door, Patrick slid across the seat and jumped out.

"Well, Mr Hunney, either the ointment that Mrs Hunney has rubbed on my leg, or the water from the well has done the trick; I can't feel a thing."

"It will be the water, Patrick," stated Sarah as she looked at him and thought how handsome he was. "It made my ankle right after I'd fallen downstairs and twisted it. Yes, it's definitely the water."

"Sarah does have a point; Martha uses it when she hurts herself out running and it seems to mend her quite quickly. Anyway, come on, Sarah we had better get back home, I'm hungry, and we have things to prepare before the wedding on Saturday as well," remarked Ted.

"Come on, Murphy," shouted Shaun. "Get your skates on; we've music practice tonight with Sofia, Cyril-the-wig, and the girls."

"Which girls are those, Patrick?" questioned Sarah, feeling a sudden pique of jealousy.

"Oh, that would be Bryony and Bridget," shouted Shaun, using his sonar radar.

"They're going to be singing with us, and they both play a mean fiddle. I hope you and your sister are going to be singing with us at the wedding do. It went down a real treat at the dance the other week."

Sarah climbed back into the van without saying anything else to Shaun. She said goodbye to Patrick in a low trembling voice.

He nodded back at her and said, "Thank you, Mr Hunney," to Ted, who was already in his van and ready to drive off.

Ted replied, "We'll see you on Saturday, and don't be overdoing it on that leg of yours. We could do with a fresh winner in the fell races. Sam Kendal needs some competition after winning all of them for the last couple of years. So get yourself right and give him a race, Patrick."

"Will do," Patrick replied.

Ted drove off through the open farm gates and back up the stony track that led to the road. It was a scenic journey from

CHAPTER 10

Middleview Farm to the Hunneys' home. The hedgerows were full of blossom with a sprinkling of common figwort, burdock and hogweed. Two yellowhammers and a goldfinch fluttered in and out of the hawthorn. A few hedge sparrows fought for the abundant seed and a fledgling robin hopped in and out between bracken fern as Ted drove past.

There was silence for a short while then Ted commented excitedly, "I've just seen a wood mouse scurry into the banking, Sarah. You don't see those little critters often."

"What about the butterflies, Father? There's lots of them about this evening. There's plenty of Red Admiral and Peacock butterflies this summer. They look beautiful, especially when the sun catches them right."

As Ted turned off the narrow track onto the lane leading to home, Sarah suddenly banged her hand on the dashboard and shouted, "Stop!"

Ted jammed on the brakes and shouted, "What the blazes is up, Sarah?"

"There are legs wearing trousers sticking out of the hedgerow just back there on this side; I think it's a man."

Ted slammed the gears into reverse and sped back thirty yards, until Sarah cried, "Stop," again.

He jumped out of the van and walked back a few more yards, and, sure enough, there was a man with a bloodstained head, sprawled face down, half in the hedgerow, half in the narrow ditch. Ted bent over to get a closer look and whispered to himself, "I don't believe it." It was George Garvan. He could see that Garvan was breathing but unconscious. He walked back to the van and told Sarah who it was.

"We can't leave him here, Sarah. It looks like he'll need hospital treatment, he's been knocked over or someone has given him a beating and dumped him here. I'll get him in the back of the van and take him to the hospital. I'll drop you off at home first, and then you can tell your mother where I've gone."

Ted loaded Garvan into the van and drove home. The only conversation they had was Ted saying, "It looks like he's got his come-uppance one way or another."

Sarah just nodded.

They arrived home and Sarah jumped out of the van, running inside to tell her mother what had happened. Ted sped off to the hospital.

"Mother," Sarah shouted urgently.

"What on earth are you so excited about, child?" said Ruth, thinking her daughter was about to tell her something about Patrick Murphy – maybe he had asked her to go to the pictures!

"Guess what? Father has just taken George Garvan to the hospital!"

A feeling of panic came over Ruth. She knew what her husband could be like and was dreading what he might have done to Garvan. She kept her composure and asked, "Why, what's happened, what's up with him?"

"We don't know, Mother. I spotted him lying by the roadside. His head is covered in blood and he's unconscious. Father's taken him straight to the hospital; so it must be serious."

Martha, who had been listening, commented, "Well it serves him right, he's a dirty old man and he deserves what he's got," and in a low whisper said to herself, "although I wouldn't want him to die."

Her mother, who hadn't heard Martha whisper to herself, replied, "That's enough of that talk, young lady. I hope your father doesn't get into trouble for this."

"Why should Father get into trouble?" the sisters asked simultaneously.

"Never you mind. But your father and George Garvan have a chequered past, and with what's happened to you at the mill, Martha, some folk would put one and one together and make three."

"Well they shouldn't be such gossips and busybodies, those sort of folk," remonstrated Martha angrily.

"Martha, you know very well that people talk about this and that, and one thing and another; usually not coming to the right conclusion and adding stuff to a tale, like what happens in Chinese

CHAPTER 10

whispers. You know most of us are guilty of that."

"Well, it shouldn't be at my expense. I don't want folk thinking bad things about me." Martha burst into tears. Her mother moved swiftly to her and gave her a hug. "There, there, Martha love, there's no need to get upset, everyone around these parts knows that you're a good girl."

Sarah, echoed her mother's sentiments saying, "Everyone knows, you're snow white, Honey. I heard Fred Cowper call you the 'vestal virgin of the village', once."

Martha burst into tears again.

Mrs Hunney momentarily lost her temper and shouted at Sarah, "That's enough, Sarah Hunney. There's no call for that sort of talk; leave your sister alone."

Sarah immediately apologised to her sister in a quiet timid tone and moved to place her arms around her, but Martha moved backwards and pushed Sarah's hands down and away from her.

Ruth quickly intervened, realising that the situation could escalate like it had a few years previously when she had had to separate her daughters from fighting, both of them ending up crying and being sent to bed.

"Sarah, get your coat on, and go to your Grandma's and see if she needs helping with anything. You can have a sandwich and something else for your tea there."

Glares were exchanged between the sisters, and not one word was spoken in those fleeting few moments. It took Sarah thirty seconds, and she had thrown her summer coat on, rushed out of the back door and was riding her bicycle at speed to her grandma's home.

"Martha, we'll have our tea now. Your father will have to have his when he gets back, whenever that's going to be. I don't know what's going on, what with all this upset happening. I'll be glad when you two are back at work, then things can get back to normal."

"I'm sorry, Mother, it's my fault all this, isn't it? I should have kept out of Mr Garvan's way and none of this upset would have happened."

Ruth grabbed hold of her daughter, hugged her and said, "You must never think any of this is your doing. It's down to George Garvan and his lustful ways; he's the reason for this upset. All the same, I hope he recovers whatever has happened to him. Now come on, Martha love, let's have our tea; there are things to get ready for Matilda's wedding. We need to be ready for that. We need your father settled as well. I don't want him having another of his turns before the wedding. That's what the War does for a soldier, only the good Lord knows what goes on in your father's mind when he's in one of his black moods."

"We'll all have to make sure that Father is alright, Mother. He needs to be able to give Matilda away and then do the speech during the celebrations. Do you think Reverend Boniface would have a word with him? Just to calm him down what with all that's gone on."

"No, Martha, that might not help. We're better just leaving things as they are. We'll just have to pray about it. You never know, if the Lord wills it, he will sort your father and this situation out for the good."

"I hope so, Mum; we don't want Matilda's wedding spoiling because Father can't do his speech."

Chapter 11

Detective Inspector Alfred Loncton had stopped Ted for speeding.

"What's the hurry, sir?" the Inspector asked.

Ted pointed to the back of his van and said, "I need to get this man to the hospital as soon as possible, he's badly injured."

"Oh, and what's happened to him, sir?"

"I found him at the side of the road, or rather my daughter spotted him, and I helped him into the van."

"Where is your daughter now?"

"I took her home. Look, George is badly injured and he needs to see a doctor straightaway."

"Open the back doors please, sir," DI Loncton commanded.

Ted climbed out of his van and swiftly opened the back doors.

The Inspector peered inside. "There's a lot of blood here. Get back in your vehicle and follow me."

Alfred Loncton climbed into his car and sped away with his siren bellowing out; Ted followed him at a distance. They arrived at the hospital and as the police inspector had called for assistance along the way, two ward orderlies with a stretcher and a doctor were waiting at the front entrance. As soon as Ted pulled up, he quickly jumped out of the van and opened the back doors. The doctor climbed inside and then motioned the orderlies to bring the stretcher.

"He's in a bad way; we need to get him inside as soon as possible. Do you know how this has happened, Ted?"

"Sorry, Dr Richardson, I didn't recognise you for a moment. No, I don't know how it's happened. I found him at the side of the road in this state." Ted pointed to Garvan. "He's called

George Garvan and he lives in the village." He turned to Inspector Loncton and said, "You will know Sergeant Fredrick, won't you, Inspector Loncton? He's the local bobby."

"Yes, I know him well. We go back a long way, Jim and me."

"Get him inside to the High Dependency Ward," Dr Richardson commanded the orderlies, interrupting Ted and Loncton's conversation. He turned to the inspector and said, "I can give him a thorough examination in there."

"How long will it be before I can interview him?"

"How long is a piece of string, Officer?" Dr Richardson replied brusquely. "Leave matters with me, Inspector. I will let you know as soon as he is fit and able to converse."

"Okay Doctor, but I do need to talk to him as soon as I can. I need to find out whether he has been assaulted or not. Although looking at him, he hasn't done this to himself." Inspector Loncton turned to Ted and said, "I will need your particulars and I'll need to speak to you in the near future. Do you live locally?"

"About twelve miles back towards and through the village. I'm working all day tomorrow at Shripton Manor – do you know where that is?"

"I know it well, I caught the burglars who stole the silverware from there," the Inspector boasted proudly.

"And on Saturday, I'm at a family wedding in the village chapel and then in the village hall after the service. That is if you haven't been to see me in the meantime." Ted gave Inspector Loncton his particulars and then set off home.

He arrived home and as soon as he walked through the front door, Ruth said, "Sit down, love, and I'll get your tea. I plated it up not five minutes ago, and put it on the oven over a simmering pan to keep it warm for you. I thought you might not be too long. Corned beef hash in juicy gravy – your favourite, Ted. How's George Garvan?"

"I've had to leave him in the capable hands of Dr Richardson, Ruth. He's in a bad way though. He might have a fractured skull. It looks like he's had a right going over by someone, or been knocked down. I can't see that though. What would he be doing

CHAPTER 11

out near Middleview Farm? Garvan's hardly the outdoor type. In fact, his main activity these days is walking to work, or The Lamb, and back home."

Martha walked into the kitchen from upstairs, sat down at the table next to her father and smiled at him. He nodded and smiled back at her. "How's Mr Garvan, Father? Sarah said he was in a right state and lucky to be alive."

"I've been telling your mother, Martha, he's in a very bad way, but he's in the capable hands of Dr Richardson." Ted then said something that both his wife and daughter had never heard him say before, "If the good Lord wills it then he will live. Let's hope he does." Changing the subject he asked, "Where's Sarah – is she upstairs getting her stuff ready for the wedding?"

"No, Ted, she's not upstairs, Sarah's at her Grandma's."

"What's been going on then, have you two been falling out again, Martha?" Ted knew that when one of his daughters was at their grandma's at that time in the evening it was usually because they had to be separated; something would have gone on between them, and usually, a fight ensued. The safest course of action was for one of them to be out of the way of the other until tempers had settled down. It happened rarely now that the twins were older, but when it did it was generally because of what one had said to the other.

"Sarah's helping her Grandma get her clothes ready for the wedding, Ted," Ruth interjected.

"Could she not have done that tomorrow?" Ted asked sharply, knowing that his wife was playing the matter down between their daughters.

"The twins are going to help prepare the village hall tomorrow since they are off work now. Matilda isn't sure about the decorations at the village hall, so Martha and Sarah can help Ava and Miranda there, while I help her and her mother with floral arrangements at the chapel."

Ted knew that something had happened between his daughters and thought his wife was covering up whatever it was. But the twins never held grudges with each other for long and it would soon blow over so he let the matter go. There had been enough upset in the household during the week and, as far as he was concerned, it was time for his family to focus their thoughts on Matilda and Jacob's wedding.

"A police inspector may call here tomorrow, Ruth. I've told him where I will be working, but he might want to have a word with Sarah about George Garvan. He said he needs to speak to me again and as soon as Garvan comes round – if he does, that is – he will be asking him questions as well. I don't think Garvan will be at the wedding. I know he's invited because he's Jacob's uncle, but he'll be in no state to be there. I suppose that should ease any tension there would have been under the circumstances."

Ruth stated anxiously, "Well, this accident or whatever it is will be a blessing in disguise then as far as I'm concerned. If George decided to drink like a fish – as usual – at the wedding, and then he had one over the top, anything could have happened."

"Oh come on, Ruth love, not on Matilda's wedding day. He wouldn't ever dream of upsetting her on that of all days. No, not ever, believe you me. The girl's had enough upset in her lifetime at such a tender age." Ted stood up from the table and placed a burly arm gently round his wife's slim waist. He looked into her eyes, gave her a kiss on the cheek and said, "Anyway, love, as I said, he won't be there."

Martha, who was not used to seeing her parents in such an affectionate embrace, was embarrassed and made a soft coughing sound to catch their attention. They looked at her and both laughed.

"I'll carry on getting my wedding clothes ready if you don't mind." Martha skipped out of the kitchen and ran upstairs commenting to herself, "Martha Hunney reaches the top of Ecklberry Pike first!" She punched her left arm into the air, leapt into her bedroom and flopped onto her bed, announcing in a deep manly voice, "First and in a new record time – winner of the fell running title – Miss Martha, Honey, Hunney."

Chapter 12

"Don't forget, Ruth, if that policeman turns up I'll be up at Shripton Manor but I shouldn't think he'll forget, he wrote it down in his little black notebook. You never know though, he's only human. Sarah, don't forget to tell him exactly what you saw and know."

"Only thing is we won't be here. We are going to the village, Father, to help get things ready for the wedding."

"Oh yes, I forgot."

Before Ted could say anything else, Sarah stated, "I'll leave a note for him on the front door telling him where I am, and where you are. Then if he wants either of us he can find us."

"That's my bright girl." He turned to his wife, kissed her on the cheek and said, "I'll be home at six at the latest, love."

"OK, but don't forget to practise your speech for the wedding. You know how forgetful you can be."

"I've got it written down in my materials book so I'll practise it at dinnertime and if I get time for a brew."

Martha came downstairs in her running clothes and said, "See you, Father. Have a good day at work. I'm going for a five mile run up over the moors."

"Yes, well, don't go too hard. It's getting very warm already and it's only seven. It looks like we're in for a heatwave, and it's going to be hot for the wedding tomorrow."

"I'll take it steady, Father but if it's hot on the day of the race, I'll be flat out and no messing."

"That's if there is a race for you to do, Honey," Sarah remarked.

"Now you two, don't start anything today; no falling out. We want a peaceful run-up to the wedding. Do you both hear what I'm saying?"

They answered simultaneously, "Yes, Father, no falling out."

Ted got into his van and set off to work, wiping his brow with a piece of cloth as he pulled out onto the country lane.

"We'll be setting off for the village at nine sharp, Martha; I hope you will be washed and ready by then. Have you had something to eat this morning?"

"Yes, Mother. I've had some cornflakes and a pot of tea. I put some cold water in that, it was too hot, and I'll have a drink of water before I set off."

"OK, take the dog with you and make sure he drinks water at the stream and the beck. Otherwise, he'll run his-self silly."

"Mother, Shep's barmy to start with, he never stops; up and down, up and down all the time. If I had his natural abilities, I'd be a world beater, and have more medals than Fanny Blankers-Koen, and that's a fact. Now she was a runner, four gold medals at thirty, and two children to look after."

"Go and get your pumps on, Martha, and be on your way." Then her mother said something that Martha found very heartening. "By the look of those shorts and shirt, you are going to need some new running clothes shortly. We'll see Miss Fleischmann about measuring you up for some. If you are going to continue running, we don't want you looking like a rag-a-muffin all the time. No daughter of mine is going to look like a scruff-pot on the start line." Her mother gave her a hug as she said, "Be on your way and don't forget what I've said about the dog."

Martha went through the kitchen and out into the back yard, pulled her plimsolls on, shouted for Shep, and then set off for Wickelton Pike.

She had gone no further than the first stile into Low Meadow when she turned back, much to the dog's consternation. "It's okay, Shep, I'm only going back for my hat, come on." She entered the back door, and shouted, "It's only me, I've come back for my hat."

No one had time to reply – she was back out of the door as quick as a flash.

CHAPTER 12

Martha patted the dog on his head, and whispered, "Come on, Shep, I can feel a good run coming on. You will just have to make your own entertainment and throw and chase your own sticks and stones. No trying to trip me up to get my attention, either." She set off running, commentating to herself as she did on these occasions, "This is Raymond Glendenning with live commentary at the Letherby Autumn Country Show, where history is about to be made. A young local girl is shortly to compete as the first ever female in a fell race. Yes, you did hear me correctly, listeners. A young woman is about to race in the most arduous, dangerous, and strenuous of all male-dominated sports. This has never been allowed before, but because of her sheer persistence, she has finally broken the resistance of the powers that govern the sport."

Martha continued her running commentary on the run out to Foxbridge Beck, easily negotiating the rocks and boulders strewn across the sheep track. Breaking her commentary for a moment she called, "Come on, Shep, get yourself a drink," not realising the dog was already lapping the cool water furiously. She bent down and cupped her hands, scooping a drink from the flowing water. The beck hadn't dried up in five years which was when the last long, hot, dry summer had caused a drought in the area. The chances of it drying up again were high, especially if the hot weather continued, but for the time being there was plenty of water flowing down off the moor above to feed into the local village and hamlet wells.

As soon as Martha started the ascent to Wickelton Pike, the commentary began again, but the words didn't flow as fluidly as earlier and were interrupted by her gulping for air. "Looking through my binoculars I can see three or four have broken away from the rest of the field of runners with a lone runner about twenty yards adrift of the leaders, and about the same distance from the chasing pack. Unless my eyes deceive me, I do believe it's the lone female competitor and she looks to be closing the gap between herself and the leaders with every step she's taking, on what seems to be a fast part of the course. We will have to see how she gets to grips with the steep climb she is about to be confronted with."

Eventually, the commentary stopped as Martha concentrated on the steepest part of the slope. As soon as she reached the Pike, the commentary started once more. "The athletes have been out of binocular range for a few minutes, listeners, but now I can see three runners moving swiftly away from the tower. Two more are chasing them, and I can't really believe what I'm seeing, but is it the distinctive, long loping style of who I think is? Yes, it is. It's Martha Hunney, the lone female runner. How remarkable!"

"Who's that you're talking to, Marta? Do you have a leprechaun with you, or one of those invisible friends that only you can see? Sure, you're going at it fifty to the dozen. Did you not notice me coming up the hill behind you?"

Martha stopped in her tracks, turned around and sure enough, just as she thought, it was Patrick Murphy. "Oh it's you – you didn't half startle me."

"Well, I've been throwing stones for your dog for the last five minutes, and a fine dog he is too; did you not notice he wasn't with you?"

"I'm in a world of my own up here. Shep would have caught up with me. He sometimes chases a rabbit, so I didn't really notice he was gone."

"So who were you talking to, Marta?"

She started laughing. "Oh, believe it or not I was doing a race commentary on my first fell race. I was Raymond Glendenning, the sports commentator."

Patrick looked at her with a perplexed expression and then asked, "Well, how were you doing then?"

Laughing, Martha replied, "Not too bad as it happens. Where are you running to anyway?"

"I'm heading back to the farm for milking. Shaun is expecting me in ten minutes. Do you think you can make it in that time?" Patrick then set off like a startled hare.

Martha shouted after him, "You bet I can," and set off in hot pursuit, commentating as she ran. Shep ran at her side hindering her in her pursuit. "Go on, Shep, forward, you're getting under

CHAPTER 12

my feet." The dog was obedient and instead of impeding Martha, it was now Patrick's turn.

"Coming through," Martha shouted as she sped past Patrick on a gentle, stony slope.

"Get out of the way, dog," Patrick shouted in his deep Irish accent. Shep took no notice and carried on running at his side, stopping momentarily. Patrick picked up a stone and threw it as far forward as he could. Shep sprinted after it and by the time he had retrieved the stone, Martha heard the Irishman breathing down her neck.

"You're not getting away from me that easily, Marta." He went past her with consummate ease and pulled away from her on the long descent to the fields approaching the farm.

Martha was impressed at Patrick's ability as he descended the hill. She chased him hard but by the time he had reached the stile leading into the first field after the descent he was at least fifty yards in front of her. The distance lengthened to seventy yards and Martha marvelled as, instead of climbing over the stile, he leapt the five-barred gate with the elegance of a gazelle. Once she was also over the stile, Martha started to gain on Patrick, and as they approached the penultimate field before Middleview Farm, she had more than halved the distance between them. Another prodigious leap over a ditch and he was fifty yards in front once more. However, Martha moved swiftly and before they had reached the last field, was shoulder to shoulder with Patrick. She realised he was flagging badly.

"Is that the best you've got? What about the finish?" Martha mocked.

"Oh don't you worry about that, girlie, you've only had a glimpse of what I might have. You don't show your opponents everything you have, or did you not know that, Marta?"

Martha didn't reply; she started striding out again, commentating to herself. "I don't believe it, that young stripling of a girl is actually raising a sprint finish and is going to complete this gruelling race. Surely this male-dominated sport should be open to females now."

Patrick let her go, he was on his cool down now, and wasn't fazed by Martha's finishing speed. Martha reached the farm where, standing near the shippen, was Shaun, bacon sandwich in one hand and a pot of tea in the other. "Hello Marta, would you like a drink of me tea or bite of me butty? I've just made them, they're both fresh. Before she could answer he asked in his high pitched voice. "Would you look at that fella? He looks like he needs an ambulance. What have you done to him, Marta? He looks like he's been run ragged." He shouted across the farmyard, "What's up with you, Murphy? Couldn't you keep up with the girl, you big Nelly?"

Patrick jogged towards Shaun, bent over, placing his hands on his knees and gasped out, "Carry on filling your face with that butty, Shaun and give it a rest." He looked at Martha and said, "There isn't one reason in this world why you shouldn't be running in one of the fell races this year. You're very capable, to be sure. Do you want a drink before you go?"

"Well, Shaun offered me a drink of his tea, but I'd rather have water if you don't mind, and thanks for your comments, Patrick, they're much appreciated."

Shaun interrupted, "I can tell you something, Marta, this fella might look all in, but wait until he races on one of those fells, it'll be a different kettle of fish then I can tell you. He's only had about four runs in four months. I've barely started training him yet."

"That's a laugh, McMullan. You train me? I'd rather have one of the cows in the shippen train me," said Patrick, starting to laugh.

Shaun laughed too and patted Patrick on the back. "Oh, you're a fine broth of a boy so you are, Patrick Murphy. I'll get you and the dog a drink now, Marta; do you want one, Murphy?"

"Fetch me a bucket-full, I've got a raging thirst, so I have," he replied.

Martha drank her water, splashing a few drops onto her sweating face before setting off across the fields to her home.

Patrick shouted across the farmyard, "See you tomorrow, we'll talk running and so on then if we have time. Will Sarah be at the

CHAPTER 12

wedding?"

She shouted back, "All right then. Yes she will. See you. See you, Shaun."

"You will so," shouted Shaun in reply.

As she entered the first field, Martha thought to herself, "Yes Patrick, we will talk running, that's if I can manage to see you before Sarah, Delwyn or for that matter, Beatrice, get their claws into you."

Martha slowly jogged the half mile back home. She was pleased with her training session. The dog was still full of energy and had picked up a stick. He dropped it at Martha's feet. "I'm going to throw it four times for you Shep and then that's your lot. You'll be asleep all afternoon in the shade while I'm decorating the village hall. Go on away with you."

Martha had a strong left arm and threw the stick precisely four times as they reached the final field before home. Martha commanded the dog, "Home, Shep." He set off back home, and by the time Martha had reached the backyard, he had slurped a bowl of cool water and was lying down on the kitchen floor, panting.

"Come on, Martha, where have you been?" her sister asked.

"Oh, I've been spending some quality time with your prospective boyfriend, Sarah."

"And who might that be then?" asked Sarah, knowing full well who Martha meant.

"Why, Patrick, of course," said Martha in a teasing manner.

"Right, stop it right now you two before you start. You've got work to do this afternoon and I won't have you falling out," Ruth interjected quickly.

"Sorry, Mother," they said simultaneously.

"Martha, go and get ready. I'll make you a sandwich. That should put you on until dinnertime. We'll meet at Mort's at half past twelve and I'll treat you both to some dinner. Now go, Martha, and be quick about it."

Martha had a drink of water and then rushed upstairs into the bathroom. Even though it was very warm, she had stopped sweating and was able to have a tepid wash and was dressed and downstairs in ten minutes.

"Are you doing anything with your hair, Honey?" asked Sarah.

"No, I'm going for the natural look. It will all fall into place anyway."

"Yes, and be a tangled mess."

A sharp glare from her mother, and Sarah said no more. Martha saw the glare, and whispered to Sarah, "I'm not taking you on! I have better things to do, like eating my sandwich."

Martha strode over to the dog and said to him, "Can't take the pace, eh Shep?" and reached for her sandwich. "Thanks for making my butty, Mum; what's on it?"

"Jam."

"Oh thanks a million, there's plenty of energy in jam. That's what I'm going to eat before I race the men this autumn."

She touched the dog gently with her left foot and said, "Lazy bones, you won't be doing much today, will you?" Shep lifted his head slightly off the kitchen floor, looked at her with one eye open, the other half closed, and then dropped his head back down to the floor. Martha bent down and stroked him gently. "You are just the best training partner, Shep, aren't you? Well, that's when you're not nearly tripping me up."

"Are you two ready to set off yet? I need to be at the chapel at half past nine, so if you aren't ready I'm going to set off now anyway."

"I'll be ready in five minutes, Mother. I don't know about Martha, though. She seems to be in a world of her own at the moment; she's talking to the dog like he's human, expecting him to answer back!"

"I'm ready now, Mother but I'll wait for slowcoach Sarah and walk down with her. What time are the others going to be at the village hall?"

"The same time, half past nine. Don't forget to meet me at Mort's at half past twelve, sharp, okay?"

"Yes, Mother," they both replied.

As she closed the door before walking to the chapel, Ruth reiterated, "And don't forget what I've told you both. I'll see you

CHAPTER 12

later."

The twins replied simultaneously, "Yes, Mother. See you, Mother."

"Why aren't you ready yet anyway, Sarah? You are usually the first, so what's going on?" asked Martha.

"You know, Honey!"

"No, I don't, what are you on about?"

"Come on, let's get going and then you can tell me all about Patrick."

Martha looked at her sister, smiled and thought to herself, 'Here we go, the grand inquisition. Twenty questions time, most of which I won't be able to answer. It's the same every time she gets a crush on someone.'

Martha made sure the back door was locked, and that Shep was okay, then they set off for the village hall.

Before her sister could ask any questions, Martha asked in a languid voice, "So, what's your first question, Sarah?"

"Is he spoken for, has he got a sweetheart?"

"Don't beat about the bush, Sur! I've absolutely no idea. It's not something we discussed when we were racing each other off the Pike."

"Oh, so that's where you've been, with Patrick is it, Martha Hunney?"

"Don't start, Sarah. I was out running on my own, well not exactly, I had Shep with me..."

Sarah interrupted, "Very funny, I know the dog was with you!"

"Let me finish, Sarah, then you can get the full picture. I had just passed the Pike when Patrick caught me up – he was out for an early run before milking time. Anyway, we didn't really say much, apart from him asking me if I could get back to the farm in ten minutes. He set off like a world-beater down the hill, quite impressive really! I chased after him, and then burned him off across the fields to the farm."

"Very modest I must say. Did he ask about me?"

"Why should he?" Martha asked, feigning no interest.

"Don't be rotten, Martha. Answer the question and I won't ask any more."

"As a matter of fact, he did. He said 'do you think your sister will dance with me tomorrow?'."

"No he never did, did he, Honey?" Sarah asked excitedly, pushing her sister.

"No, he didn't," Martha replied and then laughed. "No, he said 'is Sarah going to be at the wedding?' as if he didn't know you would be, and he had a smile on his face a mile wide, and a glint in his eye when he asked. Now no more questions."

Sarah was about to ask a million questions when they heard a roaring noise that got louder and louder every second until it suddenly stopped. It was Shaun and Patrick on their motorbike.

"Hello girls, off to the village are we?" asked Shaun.

Sarah stood with her mouth wide open. Martha smiled. She thought how ironic it was that at that moment Patrick, in particular, would appear on the scene.

"Yes, we're going to decorate the village hall for tomorrow, so don't go telling anyone; it's a surprise for Matilda and Jacob."

"Oh to be sure, we won't say a dickie bird, will we, Patrick?"

"Oh not at all," and then to everyone's astonishment – even his own – Patrick looked at Sarah, who was still standing with her mouth wide open, and asked, "Will you be having a dance with me tomorrow then, Sarah?"

She was so flabbergasted she couldn't answer. Her sister nudged her and then deftly kicked her on her right ankle as if to say 'this is your chance, answer him'.

Sarah regained an inkling of composure and answered, "Maybe," her nervousness betraying her.

Shaun, sensing this, started the motorbike, turned to Patrick and shouted, "Looks like you have got yourself a dance there, Murphy, and maybe a snog too for later!"

"Oh be quiet, Shaun," Patrick shouted above the noise of the motorbike. He couldn't believe what he had just said, but thought, 'it's done now and I meant it'.

The boys set off, and waved as they went. Shaun shouted, "See you then." Patrick said nothing.

CHAPTER 12

"What about that then, Sur? It looks like one of the Irishmen has got eyes for you!"

"He's only asked me for a dance, Martha, not to marry me. Mind you he is handsome; he's the most handsome Irishman I've ever seen."

"Well, from where I'm standing, Sarah Hunney, Patrick Murphy is very interested in you. And anyway as far as I know you've only seen two Irishmen in your life, and they both just rode down the road on a motorbike!"

They laughed, pushed each other gently, linked arms, and carried on walking slowly.

"What about Shaun, then, Honey?" Sarah asked teasingly.

"What about him?"

"You know."

"Sarah, you know very well I only have eyes for Teddy, so don't try to pair me off with anyone else. Teddy is my sweetheart. Even though he doesn't know it yet. But he will know, and he will be, just you wait and see, Sarah."

"Honey, you don't have to convince me. But you had better start working some feminine charm on him before Beatrice or Delwyn get their claws into him."

"Don't you worry, Sarah, I know Teddy, he looked me in the eyes and that said it all to me. We are made for each other. Those two have no chance with Teddy, but you had better watch out for them getting their claws into Patrick."

Chapter 13

When the twins arrived at the village hall they were quite thirsty after their walk in the warm morning sunshine.

"A cup of tea before we start, ladies?" enquired Ava. By common consensus it was decided this is what they would have, that is apart from Martha.

"I'll have a cool drink of water before we start please, if you don't mind, Miss Fleischmann."

"Please, Martha, call me Ava. I feel more comfortable with that you know. You are a young woman and I am not your senior, well only in age, so please, 'Ava' if you don't mind, and you too, Sarah."

"Yes, Ava," they said in unison.

She gave them a rather peculiar look, and wondered if they were by any chance telepathic, having noticed they quite often said the same thing simultaneously.

"By the way, Sarah dear, how do you know if your dress fits you for tomorrow? You didn't call by yesterday evening to see if the alteration I have made was correct. Don't forget to collect your dresses this afternoon, young ladies. I'll be in my shop at four o'clock. You can see if it fits you then, Sarah and if not I'll make another alteration and then both dresses will be ready for you to take home."

Sarah was shocked that they had forgotten about the fitting and that their mother had not mentioned it. She replied, "I'm sorry about that, Ava. We've had such a difficult time the last few days. I know we shouldn't have forgotten. Thank you for reminding us."

Martha echoed her sister's apology and then said to Sarah,

CHAPTER 13

"How could we have forgotten something so important?"

"Well, we have, and Mother has as well – I can't believe it. That's not like her at all."

"Never mind, ladies, come to my shop and you will have your frocks, which you both will look so lovely in," Ava reiterated.

Miranda, who had volunteered to prepare the drinks, came from the kitchen and offered them round. "We'll have the drinks and then get started. Ava and I have a plan and if you girls can do as we ask, we should be finished by about two."

"We are meeting our mother at Mort's at half past twelve if that's alright. She's treating us to some dinner," said Martha.

"Of course, that's okay. We are going there ourselves anyway. So perhaps we can all go to Mort's together. What do you say, girls?"

The sisters looked at each other and both replied, "That's okay by us, Miranda."

Miranda was the village postmistress and was to be Matilda's chief bridesmaid. Her father was looking after the post office on the day of the wedding, assisted by Miranda's betrothed, Jack Seymour.

Miranda and Jack had been engaged for three years with no visible sign or notion when they would name their wedding day. The main drawback was Jack's occupation as a merchant seaman. He was away from home three months at a time, and on leave for a maximum of only three weeks, which, according to Miranda, made it very difficult for them to be married and set up home. She would rather Jack left the merchant navy to work in the mill but he was always telling her he 'wasn't ready to work in one place, under one roof' and not until he had passed forty would he consider it. Miranda had accepted this but really longed for him to settle down with her. It was because she loved him so much that she was willing to wait for the day he would give up life at sea.

When the drinks were finished, the women started to decorate the hall with bunting and Union flags. Being more agile, Martha and Sarah fixed the bunting and flags both inside and outside the hall. Sarah passed the materials to Martha who attached it anywhere she could tack a nail into the woodwork, and at the same time arrange it into an aesthetic uniform pattern.

Ava and Miranda set the tables out that had to be ready for the food and drink: plates of buffet sandwiches; assorted confectionery including cakes and sweets; and savouries, provided by Mort in conjunction with Slinger the Butcher, which would be delivered shortly before the wedding guests arrived. Copious jugs of lemonade, ginger beer and apple-juice were to be prepared by sisters Delwyn and Scarlett Williams, and would arrive early in the afternoon at the same time as the food.

At precisely ten fifteen, Charles Smythe, a retired civil servant from the local government office, arrived with flowers from his allotment. Dahlias, sweet peas, roses, and chrysanthemums were just a few of the flowers he had hand-selected from his well-populated plot. Ava and Miranda were to arrange the flowers to adorn the hall. The two women had already made posies up for the bride and bridesmaid, as well as a bouquet for Jacob's mother, which would be presented to her after the customary wedding speeches.

Charles was quite a gossip and anyone was prey for his flowery tales. "I say, ladies, have you heard?" He waited until they stopped working and he had their full attention. "Old Garvan has copped for it. He's had a right going over."

Sarah pushed Martha gently on the hip with her forearm and both girls looked at each other, carefully saying nothing.

Ava, not really believing him, asked in an exaggerated Marlene Dietrich accent, "Why, what has happened, Charles? Is it the end of him?"

"Not exactly, old girl, but he's in quite a bad way in the hospital and the police are looking for his assailant. Someone who has a grudge against him I shouldn't wonder."

Miranda spurted out, "Well he's a pervert – groping girls at the factory. Someone had to give him a good thrashing sooner or later; it was only a matter of time. I say good for them – whoever's done it – what do you say, girls?" She mumbled without being very coherent.

CHAPTER 13

"Well if he dies and they catch the blighter who has perpetrated this crime, then it's the noose for them. Unprovoked attack, what! Yes, it'll be the short drop for certain!"

"Stop it, Charles," Ava shouted authoritatively. "Can't you see you are upsetting Martha and Sarah, they've both gone deathly white. No more I tell you."

"Terribly sorry, girls, I did not realise that sort of language upset you. My sincere apologies." He left the hall abruptly, pointing at the flowers and mumbling, "Lovely those, what?"

Ava shouted to him in a conciliatory way, "Thank you for the flowers, Charles, they are most beautiful and such an array!"

Charles raised his left hand without turning around, acknowledging Ava's comments but feeling somewhat deflated after what he thought would be a juicy conversation piece had been brusquely curtailed.

Ava's intuitive nature got the better of her though and in a low melodramatic voice she asked, "What do you two lovely young ladies know about it, eh? You do know something, I think. I am correct, am I not?"

"Yes, Ava, you are, but it's best not to talk about it. Our mother and father wouldn't want us to, would they, Martha?"

Martha was very abrupt with her answer. "No," she said, and that was the end of the conversation.

"Well, we had better get on then," commented Miranda.

Martha and Sarah continued dressing the hall with bunting and Union flags while Ava and Miranda started arranging the flowers. The conversation between the two sisters was rather muted although Martha raised Sarah's spirits when she mentioned Patrick and the possibility of him being in Mort's café at dinnertime.

"Shaun is quite funny, don't you think, Martha? He seems to not have a care in the world and comes out with some very odd things to Patrick. I think they could be on the stage as a double act – a bit like Laurel and Hardy! Mind you, they look nothing like them. Well, Shaun does look a bit like a young Oliver Hardy without the moustache, but Patrick looks nothing like Stan Laurel."

"Oh, I don't know about that, Sur, he does have a look of him,"

Martha teased. She looked at her sister and pulled one of her funny faces making them both laugh.

"Don't be ridiculous, Honey, he looks nothing like him. He's got more of a look of that film star, Clark Gable. Now, he's a very handsome fellow."

"Don't let Father hear you talking like that, Sur, or you will be in for it. You know what he thinks about us two and boys anyway, so I don't know what he'd think of you talking about mature men like that!"

"I don't look on Patrick as a boy, Martha, he's a young man, and I'd never dream of talking like that in front of Father anyway."

Miranda, who had been earwigging, chipped in with, "Oh, he is very handsome indeed."

Both girls looked at her astonished.

She turned to Sarah and said, "Oh, I mean Clark Gable, of course, not your young man."

Much to the twins' and Miranda's utter amazement, Ava commented, "I think he is the most handsome man in the world – apart from Mort, that is."

They didn't know whether to laugh, keep quiet or ignore her comment. After what seemed an eternity, Ava laughed loudly and said, "Don't be shocked, ladies, just because I'm a middle-aged lady doesn't mean I don't have certain opinions about the opposite sex – just as you have. Mortimer is very handsome to me, and a gentleman," and in a low tone as if talking to herself, "and I wish a bit more." She then walked to the far side of the hall and placed a vase of flowers on the right-hand side of the stage.

Martha whispered to Sarah, "Did I hear that last bit correctly?"

Sarah whispered, "A bit more!" The girls pushed each other and giggled.

Miranda was standing near to them and jerking her head back she commented, "Young ladies, indeed!" She then walked across the hall, and placed a vase of flowers on the left-hand side of the stage. Miranda's prim and proper comment prompted the twins to giggle even more.

Ava strode back across the hall, looked at the twins, smiled and

CHAPTER 13

beckoned to them, "Come on, young ladies, it is time for dinner. Please do not say things to Mortimer or any man. This conversation is for females only, and yes, you did hear me correctly, although it was meant for myself only." She then touched Miranda lightly on her shoulder and whispered, "Come, Miranda, it is time for dinner at Mortimer's place."

Ava pulled the door of the hall closed, and all four set off walking the short distance to the café.

Martha pointed across the street at someone sitting on the bonnet of an open-top sports car. "Who is that, Sarah? Oh, it is, isn't it?" Sarah had no time to answer but she knew instantly who it was. Martha shrieked, "It's Oliver!" and ran across the street, with Sarah a stride behind, and leapt at him with both arms open. "Oh, Oliver, you've made it. How was your journey home from Cyprus?"

"Steady on, Martha," was his reply. "You've nearly done me more damage than all the enemy put together!" The twins hugged their brother tightly. "It's good to see you both," he said as he returned their hug and then wriggled free. "I'm just waiting for Major Coulthurst. He's in the shop getting some cigarettes, and then I'm off to see Mother."

"No need to drive home, Oliver. Mother will be in Mort's at exactly half past twelve; we're having dinner there – Mum's treat," commented Sarah.

Oliver replied, "Nonsense. My treat." He then shouted across the street, "Hello Miranda, how are you, still not married?"

She walked across the street and pecked Oliver on the cheek. "Yes I'm fine, Oliver and yes, still not married."

Oliver who was quite outspoken, stated, "Jack's a fool, that's all I can say. A blithering fool," and then laughed.

Knowing Oliver's abruptness only too well, Miranda laughed. "Well, you know Jack. Only when he's good and ready."

Ava had followed Miranda and said, "You are looking healthy, Oliver. You have caught the sunshine I see."

"Lots of the outdoors, Miss Fleischmann, it's good for your

health."

"Please call me Ava, you are not even a teenager anymore and your lovely sisters call me Ava, please, you too."

"Okay, Ava it is from now on. Oh, here's Major Coulthurst."

A tall, supple figure appeared from the shop and strode militarily across the street. "I say, Sergeant Hunney, who are all of these lovely ladies surrounding you? You have kept this quiet. A small village adorned with such beauty! What a blessing. Major Michael Coulthurst, at your service, ladies."

Martha and Sarah blushed, Miranda ogled the handsome Major, and Ava, standing with hands on hips and her head held back slightly, commented haughtily, "You military men, you are all the same, womanisers, all of you. You must have caught it off those Americans."

"Oh no, my good lady, I can say it is all quite me, no bad habits off the Yanks. What is the point of keeping your thoughts hidden on matters of aesthetics? If you see beauty, you should admire it."

As Ava was about to respond, Martha saw her mother arriving at the café. "Oh, look Oliver, Mother's here." He set off like a whippet across the street and touched his Mother on her back as she was about to enter the café.

Startled for a moment, she gave a squeal of delight, hugged him, and then kissed him on both cheeks. "Oh, Oliver love, you've made it." She stood back and stared at him. "Let me have a look at you, you are tanned and you've filled out, I'm sure."

"It's wonderful to see you, Mother. How are you?"

"I'm happier for seeing you and looking forward to the wedding. Oh, I have lots of things to tell you, but in private. Who's this you're with, Oliver?" Major Coulthurst had walked across the street with Ava and was waiting to be introduced to Ruth. "This is Major Coulthurst, Mother. He has kindly come out of his way to drop me off."

"Thank you, Major Coulthurst, we were worried Oliver wouldn't make it back in time for his cousin Matilda's wedding."

"Please call me Michael, Mrs Hunney."

Ruth smiled. "Will you have dinner with us in the café,

CHAPTER 13

Michael?"

"Rather. It's been a long hot drive from the airfield and I am rather peckish. I've another eighty miles to home yet."

"Call me Ruth, please."

"My treat," interrupted Oliver.

"Nonsense, Sergeant Hunney, I'm pulling rank on you."

Ruth smiled and said, "No one will be paying if we don't get in the café because we can't eat out here."

All three entered the café. Ava had walked inside while the Major and Ruth were talking, and was soon deep in conversation with Mort. Martha and Sarah had squeezed past their mother and were busy rearranging some tables. Miranda, meanwhile, had decided to call in at the post office to see how her father and Jack were getting on with the morning's business.

Martha was sitting at the rearranged tables and noticed Mort's hand slide gently down Ava's back to her waist. She nudged Sarah, and nodded in their direction, whispering, "And I wish a bit more, indeed." The twins burst out in fits of laughter.

"What's going on with you two?" asked their mother.

"It's a secret joke, Mother, we can't tell you," answered Sarah.

Ruth looked at her daughters sternly saying, "Well, I just hope it's not at anyone else's expense. I've told you before about your secret jokes, as you call them. Now, let's order our dinners. Has everyone decided what they are having yet? Oliver, Major Coulthurst, what are you having?"

Oliver replied, "Well, Mother, since we only had toast for our very early breakfast, I'm going to have the works: bacon, sausage, eggs, chips, beans and three rounds of fried bread. And a pint pot of tea."

The Major replied, "Yes, I think that will do for me as well, Ruth, and if you don't mind, I will wander outside for a smoke. I believe you have a budding athlete in your family and I would not wish to hinder her performance due to her inhaling my tobacco smoke."

As he lifted his large frame out of his seat, he turned and smiled at Martha, saying, "You wouldn't think I once ran on the same

Iffley Road track in Oxford as the first sub four minute miler, Roger Bannister." And then he casually walked to the door, tapping a Capstan full strength cigarette on the cigarette packet.

Watching him walk through the doorway, Ruth commented, "Well fancy that! Running on the same track as Roger Bannister."

"Major Coulthurst was a very promising track athlete until he had to pack it in through injury," Oliver remarked. "When he does some training, he can still run the half mile in under two and a quarter minutes, despite him smoking those blasted cigarettes. I copped the full brunt of them once, in a shelter during a training exercise. Choked me they did!"

Ruth replied, "Well, at least he's had the decency to go outside and smoke anyway."

"I've told him all about Martha, Mother, and how she wants to compete in a fell race. He's all for it, and he's all for women getting more involved in activities within the Forces too."

Martha seized on the opportunity to keep her running as the focal point of conversation. "Do you think Major Coulthurst might know any influential people in the sport, Oliver? Any that might help me run in a fell race, perhaps?" she said hopefully.

Sarah interrupted her, "Running up hills and athletics are totally different things, Martha."

"No, they are not," Martha snapped back. "They are basically the same sport. One foot in front of the other – only, uphill and downhill, and even with some flat as well. It's just on different terrain, not track running, more like cross-country."

Hoping to put a stop to the onset of hostilities between her daughters, Ruth rapidly changed the conversation back to food.

"Right, girls, what are you having for your dinner?"

"I'll have the same as Oliver," Martha replied.

"So will I, except no fried bread, sausage or beans," was her sister's response.

"Well it's not actually the same then, is it, Sarah? I'm having the very same," stated Martha haughtily.

Oliver groaned irately, "I can see you two haven't changed much in the time I've been away. Give it a rest, will you, and have

CHAPTER 13

a day off."

His sisters laughed the same laugh, and said simultaneously, "Sorry, Oliver. Sorry, Mother."

All four of them laughed and the girls stuck their tongues out, pulling faces at each other. Ruth said, "Stop it off both of you, and you had better be on your best behaviour when Major Coulthurst comes back in. I don't want him thinking you are a couple of immature babies, so act sensibly." She looked at Sarah and, placing her hand on her daughter's forearm, said quietly, "Go and order the food, love. I'll have a corned beef sandwich with tomato and lettuce, and a cup of tea. You know what everyone else wants."

Sarah walked over to the counter and ordered the food and drinks. "It's good to see Oliver home, isn't it, Sarah?" Mort asked.

"Oh yes it is, but he's only home until Monday I think and then he goes back."

"At least he's here for the wedding and will be able to see most of your family in one place."

"I suppose so, but we'd rather have him home permanent, Mother says. She says there's been enough trouble with wars for our family without Oliver being called up for National Service. Anyway, he's only got four months left and then he's out for good, unless he decides to sign up full time." Sarah sighed and said, "I hope not, I agree with Mother."

"Well, let's hope he doesn't then. I'll send your drinks over in a couple of minutes; your food will be ready in ten minutes, tell your mother."

Mort took Sarah's order into the kitchen. "Scarlett, have you seen who's out there, it's–" Before Mort could finish, Scarlett Williams' heart jumped for joy – she knew by instinct what Mort was about to say. She rushed out of the kitchen, heart pounding, ran over to Oliver, and as he raised himself off his seat, threw her arms around his chest and kissed him full on the lips.

Ruth was flabbergasted. Martha sat with her mouth wide open and Sarah stared at the couple. Oliver did nothing to prevent Scarlett; in fact, he fully participated in the romantic encounter. At that moment, the door opened and in walked Major Coulthurst.

In his best parade ground voice he shouted, "Sergeant Hunney. Atten-shun!" But to no avail. Scarlett and Oliver were in a deep embrace and nothing could penetrate or shake their passion.

Luckily, Martha's quick wit seemed to lighten the situation as she joked, "I think a bucket of water should do the trick, Mother!"

Mort had made his way over to the couple; he coughed loudly and said in a loud, firm voice, "Scarlett, you have some food to prepare in the kitchen." He stood to one side with his left hand pointing towards the kitchen and Scarlett managed to prise herself away from Oliver, blowing a kiss from her hand to him as she made her way to the kitchen while walking slowly backwards.

Martha quickly said, "You kept that quiet, Ollie," and then teased, "when's the big day?"

Oliver, seemingly unperturbed by what had just happened, replied, "Not just yet, Honey."

"I should hope not either, Oliver Hunney. I didn't even know you were courting the girl!" exclaimed Ruth.

"Mother, we've been courting since our school days. Why do you think she came to our house so often? To play with Sarah and Martha? No, she didn't, Mother, she came to see me!" Oliver replied light heartedly.

"Yes, I know that, Oliver, but I thought she just had a schoolgirl crush on you."

"That feeling has always been mutual as far as I'm concerned. We will get married one day."

Major Coulthurst commented, "Well, good for you, Sergeant Hunney, I like a man who knows what he wants. Good for you, that's what I say."

"Thank you, Major."

"Does your father know about Scarlett, Oliver?"

"Of course he does, Mother. We men have to keep some things to ourselves, although he doesn't know my intentions towards Scarlett. But I suppose he will very shortly, now the cat's out of the bag."

Mort arrived at the table with the drinks. He set them in place and as he turned to walk away winked at Oliver and gave him a

CHAPTER 13

thumbs up sign. Ruth hunched her shoulders and glared at Mort. He smiled back at her.

After a little while longer, Mort and Scarlett brought the food out from the kitchen. Martha asked, "Are the drinks ready for tomorrow, Scarlett?"

Scarlett with her eyes focused on Oliver and smiling at him replied, "Delwyn is finishing them off; we'll have them at the village hall in plenty of time tomorrow."

Martha, feeling a little ignored, said, "I'm over here, Scarlett, not in our Ollie's eyes." Sarah burst out laughing at Martha's comment and that instantly piqued her.

Martha whipped around in her chair to face Sarah and then, as if changing her mind, turned around again and asked Major Coulthurst, "Do you have any friends in high places that can get me permission to race in a men's fell race, Major Coulthurst?"

Ruth Hunney rolled her eyes, looked up to the heavens, and said, "Please help me, Lord."

To everyone's astonishment the Major replied, "As it happens, I might just know a fellow who could set the ball rolling, Martha. Yes, it is a possibility, although by no means a certainty."

"Well, Honey, does that make things a bit better for you now? You never know, you might be running a fell race, after all," commented Oliver who had come back down to earth after the brief encounter with his sweetheart.

"No, Oliver, you mean racing in a fell race, don't you? I'm not going to turn up just to make the numbers up. I'll be racing and make no mistake!"

Major Coulthurst looked at Martha, smiled, and remarked, "That's the spirit! There's no point in merely taking part in any activity if you are not going to get the best out of yourself and test your opponents to the full."

Martha was delighted with the inspirational pep talk. She instantly decided her endeavour to compete in a fell race before the autumn was over would be redoubled.

After finishing their meals, Major Coulthurst said his goodbyes and set off home. He had arranged to pick Oliver up at 'six hundred hours' on the following Monday in the same place that they had arrived at – the village green.

Ruth had finished her work at the chapel, and after a brief conversation with Ava, and then buying some groceries, she walked home. Oliver waited, basking in the afternoon sun, until Scarlett had finished helping Mort clean the café after the day's trade. When they met outside, Oliver and Scarlett walked hand in hand on the riverbank before settling in a shaded spot under an oak tree. They were engrossed in each other's company as only lovers can be and for that short time it was as though nothing else in the world mattered.

Meanwhile back at the village hall, Ava and Miranda continued with the flower arranging, and Martha and Sarah finished off the bunting decorations. Ava mentioned, "We shall have a cool drink because it is so hot and then I think we can go to our homes, but only after you two ladies have come for your dresses. I have arranged for Mortimer to take us all to my shop, and we will make sure that your wedding dresses are the correct fitting. Then you can come back to the village and bring your dresses with you."

At precisely two o'clock, Mort took the twins and Ava to her shop. After a small alteration to Sarah's dress it fitted perfectly. "You both look absolutely lovely in your frocks, ladies. You will certainly be turning the young men's heads towards you tomorrow. What do you think, Mortimer?"

"Yes, but they mustn't upstage the bride, and spoil her day."

"Oh, Mort, we wouldn't think of it! We'll both stay in the background, won't we, Sarah? Matilda's wedding is the biggest thing that will ever happen in her life."

Nodding, Sarah replied, "I'm certain that Matilda will be the centre of attention, with her beautiful wedding dress. That's because you've made it, Ava!"

"I have no comment to make about her dress or Miranda's bridesmaid dress. You will have to wait and see for yourselves, and then form your own opinions. All I know is that you two lovely young ladies will be fighting the young men off."

CHAPTER 13

"I think Father will be keeping a close eye on us both; he is very protective of us. Anyway, apart from talking with Patrick about running tactics, I will be with Teddy, and I'll be asking him to take me to the pictures instead of him going with Harry Smith all the time."

"Martha Hunney, you're being very forward, aren't you?" Sarah remarked, genuinely shocked at her sister's statement.

"No, I'm certainly not, Sarah. It's Teddy who is being backward."

Ava looked at Mortimer and said to herself, 'And Teddy's not the only one'.

"What did you say?" asked Mort.

"Oh nothing, Mortimer. I was just thinking how wonderful young love is – Oliver and Scarlett; Matilda and Jacob; Martha and Teddy." Ava sighed and smiled at Mort.

"Oh and don't forget, Sarah and Patrick – that's if she gets her own way."

Sarah pushed her sister gently and they both giggled.

Mort thought it was about time they set off back. This sort of conversation wasn't within his comfort zone; he preferred discussing horse racing or football. Definitely not romance.

Mort dropped the twins off in the village, rather than take them home because they were going to visit their grandma. Sarah picked her bicycle up from the garage and, with Martha carrying their dresses, they set off on the short distance from the village to their grandma's house. As they were walking slowly along the narrow country lane in the late afternoon heat they heard the familiar sound of a motorbike roaring up behind them. They stopped and stepped onto the narrow grass verge where they were nearly camouflaged by the sprouting hedgerow.

"I thought it was you two," Shaun McMullan shouted above the noise of the motorbike in his high pitched voice. "Sorry, I can't stop the blasted thing; it might not start again if I do. Its firing is a bit off and that's why it's so noisy. Anyway, you two need to get right home – the police have been up to Shripton Manor and taken your dad. There were two of them. The one with the enormous feet was one of them."

Both sisters promptly asked the same question with trembling voices, "Where have they taken Father, do you know, Shaun?"

"According to Patrick, Mrs Rowley – that's Bryony and Bridget's mam by the way – was up at the Manor on some business for Lady Letherby and she said that the police were taking him to the local police station."

Martha said, "Thank you, Shaun. Come on, Sarah, we had better get home to see Mother, we can call at Nan's after that."

"No problem," Shaun replied. "I hope everything is alright for you both," and then he roared off into the distance.

Sarah mounted her bicycle and started to pedal with Martha running by her side. Breathing quite heavily she asked, "What do you think Sergeant Fredrick wants with Father?"

"It's fairly obvious to me, Sarah. It's to do with that George Garvan, that's what it is. They will have taken Father in for questioning since he was the one who found him. It wouldn't surprise me if they came for you next, Sarah."

At that instant Martha stopped and before Sarah could draw breath to reply to her sister, a police car drove past and stopped thirty yards in front of them on the long, narrow straight of the lane.

Sergeant Fredrick climbed out of the car and ambled up to the sisters, who for all intents and purposes were frozen to the spot.

"No need to be alarmed, Sarah, Martha. I take it you are on your way home?"

"We were going to Gran's before Shaun McMullan told us you had Father at the police station, but now we're rushing home to see Mother," answered Martha.

"There's really no need to panic, girls. I was on my way to see your mother, and you, Sarah. We would like you to come with your mother to the police station." Sergeant Fredrick sought to keep both Martha and Sarah calm. "And again I stress that there is no need for alarm, only some routine questions and that's all, nothing more. Come with me and I'll take you home."

"I'll leave my bicycle behind that gap in the hedge and pick it up later then." Sarah pushed her bicycle behind the hedge and

CHAPTER 13

then climbed into the police car.

Martha placed her hand on her sister's shoulder and whispered quietly, "I'll go and see Nan while you go with Sergeant Fredrick to get Mother and go to the police station. I won't tell her anything – it will only upset her. I'll make sure she has everything ready for the wedding and remind her what time the car will be coming for her. She's been really looking forward to the wedding for months so I don't want her having a sleepless night bothering about Father and you. I'll come with you to see Mother first though and we'll have to put our frocks away as well."

"Alright," a preoccupied Sarah replied.

"It looks like it's going to be another scorcher tomorrow for the wedding. You two girls will both have to wear your sun hats when you're not in the shade." Sergeant Fredrick's conversation had the desired effect and settled the sisters for the rest of the short journey home.

Chapter 14

As soon as Sergeant Fredrick pulled up outside their home, the twins jumped out of the car and ran towards the front door. But before either of them reached it, their mother was standing there with the door ajar, a solemn expression on her face. She was expecting bad news and knew it would be concerning her husband. Her stomach churned over as her girls raced towards her, non-smiling and heads drooping – she expected the worst.

"What's the matter? Is it your father?"

Before they had time to reply, Sergeant Fredrick had read the situation from a distance and bellowed, "There's no need to be alarmed, Ruth, it's just routine."

Martha quickly followed with, "Father's at the police station, and Sarah needs to go there as well."

Sarah burst into tears as she blurted out, "Sergeant Fredrick wants you to come as well, Mother. Will you come with me, then we can get Father home?"

Ruth grabbed her daughter gently round the waist and pulled her close. "Of course I will, love, I'm sure we can sort this out. Isn't that right, Sergeant Fredrick?"

"We'll do our best, Ruth. It's the big day tomorrow and you don't want to be upset for the wedding." Sergeant Fredrick motioned with his hand, pointing to his car, and said, "Let's go back to the station and sort it out, then when you get home you can get organised for tomorrow; that's if you're not already sorted out."

Martha asked, "If I'm not being too forward, Sergeant Fredrick, would you please drop me off at my grandma's on the way?"

CHAPTER 14

"No problem, Martha," was his reply.

"Right Sarah, give me your frock and I'll put it in the bedroom with mine."

Martha was up and down the stairs in a moment and then climbed into the front passenger seat. Sarah had stopped sobbing but was still snivelling. Her mother was sitting next to her on the back seat of the car and was still holding her. "Don't let this spoil your evening, Sarah; I'm quite sure there is nothing to be worried about." She then produced a handkerchief from her pinafore pocket and beckoned her daughter to wipe her tears.

"Well I am worried, Mother, what with what went on at the factory with Mr Garvan and our Martha, and Father and me being the ones to find him. I hope the police don't think me and Father have done it."

"Oh, Sarah dear, you're letting your imagination run away with itself. The police will only be trying to fit the pieces together to find out what has happened to George Garvan."

"Your mother's right, we need to know certain things to make sure we have the correct information. You and your dad can help us with some of that, so you don't need to worry, Sarah," commented Sergeant Fredrick.

After dropping Martha off at her grandma's, Sergeant Fredrick drove into town and parked the car at the front entrance of the police station. He climbed out and opened the back door for Ruth and Sarah. As they entered the front door they could see Alfred Loncton sat reclining in the office, with Ted Hunney sat diagonally across from him. There was no conversation between them; Ted was silently rehearsing his wedding speech for the next day, and Inspector Loncton was twiddling a pencil about in his fingers whilst conjuring up questions to ask Sarah. Ted smiled and waved to his wife and daughter who both tentatively waved back. Sarah managed a shallow smile, Ruth's face was impassive.

"If you both sit down and wait here for a moment," said Sergeant Fredrick pointing at a row of four chairs, "I'll just check to see if Sergeant Loncton is ready for you, Sarah." He ambled into the office and bending his huge frame whispered something into his superior's ear. Ted strained to listen but couldn't hear what Jim said, only the reply by Inspector Loncton, which was a short sharp, "No".

Sergeant Fredrick straightened himself up, turned to Ted, nodded and ambled back out of the office.

"I'm afraid you will have to wait here, Ruth. Sarah, will you follow me?" Sergeant Fredrick's voice had changed since meeting Martha and Sarah on the country lane, from being polite and sympathetic, to being more authoritative. Sarah was shocked by this and as she followed him she turned to her mother and managed a nervous smile.

"Don't worry, dear, your father's in there; you'll be okay."

"Will you leave the room, Mr Hunney? And you sit down in that chair, Miss Hunney. Then we can get on with sorting this matter out."

Sarah instantly felt sick in the pit of her stomach. Ted could tell by the look on her face that she was terrified. He smiled at her and said, "Don't worry, Sarah." He turned to Inspector Loncton and asked, "Is it alright for Sarah's mother to be with her?"

As he carried on twirling his pencil, Loncton looked up at Ted, managed a half smile/ half smirk and said, "Yes, there's no reason why Mrs Hunney shouldn't be present if your daughter wants her here. Do you want your mother to sit in with us, Miss Hunney?"

"Yes please." Sarah's spirits were lifted at what she thought was a concession by the Inspector.

"Sergeant, will you ask Mrs Hunney to come and sit with her daughter?"

Once more Sergeant Fredrick ambled out of the office then motioned for Ruth to enter. She left her husband sitting alone, followed the Sergeant into the room, and sat next to her daughter. Sergeant Fredrick sat next to Inspector Loncton. As Loncton was about to start questioning Sarah, Constable Abrahams knocked at the door and motioned Sergeant Fredrick to come into the corridor.

"Superintendent Ramsden has just pulled up in his car; I thought I'd better warn you just in case Loncton's not following

CHAPTER 14

procedure."

A large stocky figure suddenly appeared behind Constable Abrahams and in a strong Glaswegian accent bellowed out, "Why are you not manning the front desk, laddy? Anyone could walk in and start snooping about."

"Sorry, sir, I'll get right back there now."

"Aye, and be sharp about it, laddy. Now what's going on in there?"

"I'm not sure, sir," was the Constable's reply and then he hurried off to the front desk before the Superintendent could question him further.

Without knocking on the office door, Ramsden marched in, raising his hat as he saw the two females. He looked at Ruth, and smiling, said in a polite mellow voice, "Madam." He lifted his eyes to gaze at Sarah and carried on smiling.

Ruth nodded in acknowledgement of the Superintendent's courtesy and Sarah instinctively smiled back.

The Superintendent turned to Inspector Loncton and said, "Outside for a moment, Inspector."

Loncton sprang to his feet, opened the door and followed Inspector Ramsden into the passage.

"What's the situation here, Inspector Loncton?"

"There's been an alleged serious assault just outside the village and the young girl in there and her dad found the injured man. I've brought them in to answer some questions pertaining to the assault." Pointing at Ted he remarked, "He has a bit of previous with the injured man."

Ramsden raised his eyebrows and pursed his lips, observing, "Well, Inspector, we all have some previous with someone or another. Is that the father sat over there and the young lady's mother sitting with her?"

"That's right, sir."

The Superintendent commanded brusquely, "Well, let them go. You've no business questioning them here. If you need to ask them anything you can call at their home; there's no need for this heavy-handedness. That young lady looks petrified!"

"But, sir–" Loncton didn't get time to offer a reason for the questioning.

"Let them go. If they live any distance away and have no transport take them home."

Ted had heard the conversation and walked towards the men. "Would you be able to take me back to Shripton Manor so I can pick my van up, Inspector?"

The Superintendent turned to Ted and nodded. "Of course he will, sir. Right away. Inspector Loncton – step to it."

A chastised Inspector Loncton opened the office door and said, "Sergeant Fredrick, you can take them all home. Sorry for the inconvenience, Mrs Hunney, Miss Hunney," and then turned to Ted and repeated, "Sorry, Mr Hunney, for any inconvenience."

Ruth and Sarah followed Sergeant Fredrick out of the office and walked with Ted to the front entrance of the police station.

Sarah had completely regained her composure and as she passed the front desk smiled at Constable Abrahams and said, "We'll see you tomorrow, Noah; are you nervous about being your Jacob's best man?"

"Just a lot!" he replied.

Ruth, for the first time since leaving home with Sarah, smiled. "See you tomorrow, Noah."

"Yes, Mrs Hunney, Mr Hunney. I'll see you all tomorrow; the weather's looking good for Jacob and Matilda, well, all of us really."

"Let's get going, Ted. You could have done without all this interruption," commented Sergeant Fredrick.

"You can say that again, I've lost two hours this afternoon and all for nothing. I'll have to go back to the Manor to finish off tomorrow morning now."

"Oh no you won't, Ted Hunney. You'll have to go back Monday; it's the wedding tomorrow, and I'm not having you on the last minute when you're giving Matilda away."

Ted laughed, and then said, "Oh yes, I nearly forgot."

Ruth raised her eyebrows and walked out of the police station followed by Sarah. Ted looked at Sergeant Fredrick and Constable

CHAPTER 14

Abrahams, shrugged his shoulders and then motioned towards the door, saying, "After you, Jim."

Sergeant Fredrick took Ruth and Sarah home, and then took Ted to retrieve his van from Shripton Manor.

Back in the village Oliver had escorted Scarlett home and then called in to see his grandma Hunney where Martha was helping her to iron the frock she would be wearing for the wedding.

"Is that you, Oliver? Martha told me you were home. My, you do look brown. Come and give your Nan a hug and let me have a good look at you."

Oliver walked over to her and, because he towered over her, had to bend low to hold her round the waist and give her a gentle hug and a kiss on the cheek. He straightened up and as he did his grandma sat down on the sofa and gazed up at him. "Oh what a handsome young man you are, Oliver; you look just like your Grandad, God rest his soul. He was a handsome fellow just like you, and as tall as well."

"How are you, Nan? You're looking very well and I assume you're looking forward to Matilda's wedding tomorrow?"

"Well I did hurt my wrist, as you can see, but I'm having the cast taken off on Tuesday. I thought I might have had it off for the wedding, but never mind at least I can still go, and it's going to be warm."

"That's good then, Nan. Maybe we can have a dance together; that's if you're up to it, of course."

"You've no need to worry about that, Oliver. I wouldn't miss a dance with the most handsome young man in the village – and my own grandson at that. I'll look forward to that and no mistake. Don't tell your father what I've said though; I think he still thinks he's the most handsome young man in the village!" His grandma paused for a moment and then remarked, "But he may well be the handsomest middle-aged man, though."

Martha and Oliver both smiled. Martha observed airily, "I think you might be a little bit biased, Grandma. Not that Father isn't handsome, and Scarlett Williams will agree with you about Oliver, but really the handsomest man in the village is Teddy Moore. He's definitely the most handsome."

"Is there something you want to tell Nan and me, Martha?"

"Well, he doesn't know it yet but he's going to take me to the pictures, instead of going with Harry Smith all the time, and I'm going to ask him at the wedding tomorrow, or I'll be waiting forever!"

"Martha Hunney! That's not how it was done in my day. I think you are being a bit forward, don't you, Oliver?"

"No, not at all, Nan. Not for Martha, anyway. She will ask him and no doubting that. Personally, I feel sorry for poor Teddy." Martha tried to interrupt but Oliver raised his voice and stopped her. "If Martha gets her tentacles into him, I'm afraid he'll be caught hook, line and sinker. I know what she's like, and if she pursues him like she does with the fell running caper, I'm afraid he's caught already. He just doesn't know it, Nan!"

Martha, not one to lose an opportunity to talk about running said, "You're right there, Ollie. I'll be competing in a male dominated fell race this autumn if it's up to me and no mistake."

"Yes, love," stressed her grandma, "but it's not up to you, is it? Those men who run the sport make the decisions, not you. I don't want to put a dampener on your ambitions, but you will have a hard job convincing the powers that be if you are to run in one of those races."

"Like I've said before, Nan, there's something about our Honey that I don't see in other young women in these parts. Maybe, just maybe, she will run in one of those fell races."

"As I keep saying to other folk, Oliver, not just running in one, but racing against men on equal terms."

"Well, we'll see, Martha love, and I hope you do by the way. If us women can have babies and endure that pain I don't see why you can't stand the pain of running uphill for a couple of miles. When we were young before the First War your Grandad and I used to walk for hours on the moors and round-about. I could keep up with him as big and strong as he was, and me a slip of a lass – not unlike you, Martha, but not as tall. Oh, I could keep up with him alright."

CHAPTER 14

Oliver was getting concerned, he knew how upset his Nan could get and asked, "Are you alright, Nan? You know what you can get like sometimes when you start talking about Grandfather."

She smiled at Oliver. "Of course I am, love; fond memories of my husband and your grandad, that's what it is." She turned to Martha and smiled. "Maybe I'm the one you get your ability to run from, Martha. You pursue your dream and make it happen if you can, love," and then repeated herself, "yes, Honey, you chase your dream and make it happen."

It was the first time Martha had heard her grandma call her Honey and she was heartened to be called by her nickname. She walked home with Oliver in a jovial mood after they had said goodbye to their Nan. That is until he asked her, "Where's Sarah anyway? She's usually at Nan's with you."

"She's at the police station being questioned; Father as well." And then before he had time to ask why, Martha relayed what had happened to her at the mill, and described the state George Garvan was in when their father and Sarah found him in the country lane.

No sooner had Martha finished describing the last few days to Oliver than their father drove past and, pulling up in his van, he lowered his window and shouted back, "Come on, get in the pair of you."

They both ran the few yards to the vehicle and climbed in. Ted immediately set about easing Martha's worries. "Before you ask, Martha, everything's okay; there's nothing to fret yourself about. A Superintendent called in at the station and over-ruled that Inspector Loncton, he should never have got us in there in the first place. Your mother and Sarah are at home. Let's get back, get sorted out for the wedding, and settle down for the evening." He looked at Oliver and with a wide smile on his weathered face said, "It's good to see you again, Son. You look well. Are you looking forward to the wedding?"

"I am, Father..."

Before he could elaborate, Martha butted in, "He's more looking forward to seeing Scarlett Williams again, aren't you, Oliver?"

To save Oliver's blushes, Ted swiftly remarked, "Nothing wrong with that, Oliver; she's a pleasant young woman is Scarlett, always asks how you are when I call in at Mort's. Now I know why! You could do a lot worse than Scarlett, Son."

"Thanks, Dad, I'll bear that in mind, and yes, Martha, I am looking forward to seeing Scarlett tomorrow as well as going to Cousin Matilda's wedding. Are you looking forward to seeing Teddy Moore?"

Martha elbowed her brother and he laughed. "Have I hit a nerve with that, Honey; what are you blushing for?"

"Is there something you want to tell me, young lady?" asked Ted.

"I'm going to ask Teddy to take me to the pictures, Father," Martha replied sheepishly.

"Should he not be asking you, Martha?"

"He should, Father but he's wooden, so I'm going to take the initiative and ask him. In fact, I'll tell him."

"What's your mother think about this?"

"Mother's more bothered about what you will say, Father, not to mention what you might do."

"Well, I'm going to do nothing, as long as Edward Moore behaves himself; you have my blessing, only, can you not work it so that he asks you?"

"Leave that to me, Dad. I'll put Teddy in the picture. Don't you worry, Martha, I'll sort it out for you. Teddy will be down on one knee asking you to the pictures before you can say Jack Robinson!"

"Nothing too extreme, Son, just a quiet word in his ear, that's all. Martha doesn't want him running a mile." Ted looked at Martha, smiled and winked at her and said, "You just leave it to Oliver, lass."

"Right, Father, I will do, but you'd better not be rough with him, Ollie."

"Martha, stop fretting, he's alright is Teddy. I'll treat him with kid gloves and he'll be taking you to the pictures next Saturday." Oliver turned to his Father and said, "Anyway, Dad, I think if

CHAPTER 14

Teddy did run a mile, especially uphill, Martha would still catch him!" Ted and Oliver laughed; Martha raised her eyebrows and tutted loudly.

Chapter 15

Martha was out of bed, washed, and downstairs by six o'clock. Half an hour later she was out running after devouring a slice of toast and swilling it down with a cup of tea and a half pint of cool water. Martha put her plimsolls on in the backyard, peeped through the kitchen door at the wall-mounted clock and noted that it was exactly six thirty.

She took the dog with her and was in full flight after running half a mile along the country lane leading to Middleview Farm. Martha felt amazingly good for an early morning run; it usually took about half a mile before she got into her stride. She decided to push on and see what time she could do the run in. Climbing through the gap at the side of the five-barred gate she sped across the field, taking little notice of Shep as he continually dropped a stick a few yards in front of her.

"Not today, Shep, I'm on a time-trial and I'm not stopping." The dog seemed to understand and contented himself with tossing the stick into the air and then carrying it in his mouth for a few yards before tossing it up again.

Martha raced down toward Foxbridge Beck easily negotiating the rock and stony strata. Up toward Wickelton Pike, pushing and climbing harder than she had ever done before; even jogging the section she normally walked with hands placed on knees. Breathing deeply but not gasping for air, she had a singular momentary thought: 'If only I could feel like this in a race…'

In what seemed no time at all she had covered good ground and was headed back down toward Middleview Farm. Striding over the rocks and boulders in her path she ran on, negotiating around

CHAPTER 15

or stepping on and leaping off those too high to stride over.

Quite unexpectedly the sole on her left plimsoll suddenly started to flap. She looked down and thought, 'Blow it—you're not going to stop me now!'. Speeding along across the last two fields she burst through the back gate of the yard, flung the back door open and looked at the clock on the wall. "Twenty-three minutes and only a few seconds – three minutes faster than ever before," she shouted and punched the air with a fist.

"Oh you're back then, Martha; who are you talking to?" asked her mother.

"To myself, Mother; I've beaten my best time by three minutes. I'm getting fitter and faster with every run."

"It doesn't look like your training shoe is getting any fitter, Martha. Has the sole come loose?"

Martha slipped the shoe off, looked at the sole and stated, "I think it might have had it, Mother, unless I can get it stuck back down. Mort knows a good cobbler. I'll ask him about it at the wedding."

"Where's Shep, Honey?"

"He's having a drink outside, Mother."

Ruth opened the back door and shouted for the dog. He came sauntering through the backyard gate with his tail wagging happily. "Look at the state of him, he's dripping wet. Stay out there, Shep, until you dry off. I'm not having you in here dripping over everyone and spoiling our wedding clothes."

"He's not muddy, Mother. It's as dry as Ezekiel's bones on the moor and in the fields."

"He still needs towelling down. Get that old towel from under the sink and give him a rub down in the yard."

"Alright, Mother." Martha was still having positive thoughts about the progress she had made in her training run and wasn't going to grumble about having to rub the dog down.

"We have to be at the chapel at half past ten, Martha. Make sure you are ready for ten, fingernails and toenails painted; not that I advocate doing that sort of thing all of the time, unlike some young girls do, but on special occasions like weddings, it looks elegant." Ruth looked at her daughter's bare feet and pointed to them. "Besides, you're going to have your toes showing in those pretty sling-back sandals and that black toenail won't look all that pretty. I want you to look your best for Matilda and Jacob's sake."

"And Teddy," Martha mumbled to herself.

"I heard that, young lady. Your father told me about your intentions towards Teddy Moore. You just be careful, that's all I can say."

"Mother, with Father and Oliver standing guard, you don't think Teddy's going to try anything on, do you? Not that he would anyway – he's not Mr Garvan, you know!"

"He's a male, Honey, my dear. I'll say no more, you know what I mean, we've discussed this often enough. Go and get yourself washed before your sister gets in the bathroom otherwise you'll be waiting half an hour for her."

"I'll have a wash in the well, Mother, it'll be lovely and refreshing. All I need is my flannel and a bar of soap."

"Martha Hunney, you'll do no such thing! Go up to the bathroom. Now."

Martha gulped down a full mug of water and took another up with her to the bathroom. "Where have you been, Honey?" her brother asked as they passed on the stairs.

"Running up to Wickelton Pike," Martha replied, looking back at Oliver as he jumped off the third-from-bottom stair into the hallway.

"You should have called me; I'd have run with you."

Martha bragged, "I don't think so, Ollie, you wouldn't have been able to stand the pace. I took three minutes off my best time."

Oliver turned and looked up at Martha, who was standing on the landing. "Oh, and when did you do your previous best time?"

"Last November in a howling gale and pouring rain," was her reply.

"Well, have a think about it, Martha. Three minutes off your best time – that's all well and good, but have you taken into consideration the extremity of the conditions? Wet, windy and

CHAPTER 15

soggy underfoot versus warm, windless and dry underfoot. Have you really done that much better?"

With the wind taken out of her sails, Martha felt deflated after Oliver's summary of the two training runs. But she soon remonstrated, "Yes Ollie, but the one in wintertime was during a Saturday afternoon. The one I've just done was first thing in the morning so I think I have improved overall by about a minute and a half, taking into account the conditions." She went on to elaborate, "And also, the wind in November nearly blew me all the way back, so I could say that the second half of that run was wind assisted. Yes, definitely a minute and a half improvement, I'm saying, so there, Oliver Hunney." Martha tossed her head back and stood with her hands on her hips, glaring at her brother.

Oliver, in a sarcastic tone, replied, "If you say so, Honey."

Martha heard a door handle turning and instantly rushed into the bathroom knowing that a grumpy Sarah was about to appear on the landing from their bedroom. She slammed the door and locked it. Instantly the door handle rattled and turned. A groggy Sarah droned, "Who's in there?"

Martha putting a deep voice on replied, "It's the big bad wolf."

"Come on, Martha, stop messing about, I'm in no mood for your jokes." Sarah was not a morning person and was almost always reluctant to take part in any conversation for the first hour after getting out of bed. It was no different on this special wedding day.

"Go and have your breakfast and come back in ten minutes."

"I can't wait that long, Martha, I'm bursting, let me in."

"Well, that's all you're doing because you're not hogging the bathroom. I need a wash; I've been running hard and sweating like mad while you've been flaked out in bed."

"That's your choice, Honey, and for your information, I've been setting my clothes out from the wardrobe, not flaked out in bed. Now let me in before I burst."

"Well, I'm staying in. I know you; you'll lock me out and take over the bathroom."

"Oh, do what you want, Martha, just come on," Sarah

responded while jigging about on the landing, hopping from one foot to the other.

Martha opened the door and her sister burst in and in a flash was sitting on the lavatory with a groan of relief. Martha leaned against the window wall with her arms folded, tapping her foot on a creaky floorboard. "You can stop that, Martha," ordered Sarah.

"Stop what?"

"You know what. That foot tapping."

"I'm surprised you can hear me, the noise you're making. You sound like one of the cows off the farm."

"Don't be so horrible, Martha. That's not nice at all. If Father hears you talking that sort of coarse talk he'll give you a clip behind the ear, as old as you are."

A voice from the landing sent a shiver down Martha's spine and put a smirk on Sarah's face. "Come on you two or you'll feel the back of my hand." It was Oliver, who had crept back upstairs and was mimicking his father.

"Now you're for it, Martha. Father's heard you." Sarah knew it was her brother but Martha wasn't sure. She darted an anxious look at Sarah and then Sarah started laughing. Martha shouted, "Oh very funny, Oliver, very funny indeed."

"Mother says you two have to shape yourselves and stop messing about. She can hear you, you know."

"Right, Sur, get out of the bathroom and flush the lavvy before you go," commanded Martha. Sarah exited the bathroom as quickly as she had entered, leaving Martha to flush the lavatory.

After ten minutes had passed, Martha walked casually out of the bathroom. Sarah was ready and waiting on the landing just in case Oliver might steal in before her. Martha looked at her sister and said, "I'm sorry, Sur, for saying what I said in there," pointing at the bathroom.

"You're forgiven, Honey, let's not do any falling out today, it's a day for happiness."

"Thanks, Sarah. I hope we all have a wonderful day, obviously cousin Matilda and Jacob most of all. I hope Father gets his speech

CHAPTER 15

right as well."

Sarah heard footsteps on the stairs and immediately darted into the bathroom, waving to Martha as she went in. Martha met Oliver near the top of the stairs, "It's no good coming up to get in the bathroom, Oliver. Sarah will be half an hour at least." Oliver spun around and walked back down the stairs mumbling to himself.

"What's the situation upstairs with your sisters, Oliver?" asked his mother.

"They're hogging the bathroom between them as usual. All I want is to have a wash and shave, and then I can get down to the village to have breakfast with Scarlett at Mort's."

"Have a wash in the kitchen then. Where's your shaving stuff?"

"I'll get it from my bedroom."

"You know what your father's gone and done? He's only sneaked out! I know he'll have gone to finish that job off at Shripton Manor. Wait 'til I see him."

Fifteen minutes later, Ted waved to his son as he passed Oliver bolting down the lane to meet his sweetheart. Oliver drew his right index finger across his throat and pointed at his father. Ted instinctively knew what Oliver meant.

Walking into the house he said, "Well that's that job finished, Ruth. I don't have to go back there again, there was only had a bit of pointing to finish. It was in the shade so it shouldn't dry out."

Ruth thought for a moment and decided there was no point in saying anything argumentative to her husband, asking instead, "Do you want a brew, Ted?"

"I'll have a drink of water and then I'll have my pint mug of tea, love."

Ted was relieved that he wasn't on the end of a tongue-lashing from his wife just yet. He thought it might possibly come later but maybe not, since it was such a special day and they hadn't had one of those since their nephew Henry married Louise Cloister.

Ruth gave him his pot of tea. "What have you got there, Ted? Don't tell me you haven't rehearsed your speech yet!"

"Don't worry, love, I'll have it right for the wedding."

"I hope you're not going to take it out of your trouser pocket and read from it all crumpled up like that. Are you, Ted?"

Ted smiled at his wife and winked. "No dear, don't you worry about that, it will be crumpled up in my inside jacket pocket."

"Very funny, Ted Hunney! Do you want a bacon butty before you get ready? Then you won't be getting grease on your clothes."

"I'll have a fried egg on it and a slice of fried bread, thank you. Might as well go the whole hog."

"Well, as soon as I've made it, I'm going to have a soak in the bath and then do my hair. So just leave me to it, Ted, and don't forget to wash your hands before you eat. Those hands of yours look and smell like they've been down a drain."

"It's funny you should say that, Ruth love, because..."

Before Ted could relate his blocked drain cleaning story, Ruth intervened, "Don't bother, Ted, I don't want to hear another one of your grubby tales."

"I was only–"

Ruth raised her voice. "No, Ted. Don't bother, I said, I'm going for that soak, that's if Sarah has finished – you know how long she takes."

"Where's Martha, anyway? She's usually easy to hear, if you know what I mean."

"She's just nipped down to your mother's to make sure she's up and had her breakfast and starting to get ready. I hope your mother doesn't expect to see you picking her up, Ted. I hope she remembers we're calling for her in a taxi. You've got enough on your plate with getting Miranda to the chapel on time."

"Of course she'll remember. Anyway, Martha will probably remind her."

Ruth finished making Ted's food and then went for a soak in the bath. Ted sat at the table eating his bacon and egg with Shep sat by his side looking longingly up at him and dribbling from his muzzle.

"What's up, Shep, do you want some?" He gave his dog a small piece of bacon and half of his fried bread. Shep gobbled them down, then sauntered over to his water bowl, lapped some water,

CHAPTER 15

and flopped back down on the floor again. "It looks like you've had a gruelling run with Martha, lad." The dog lifted an eyebrow and then lowered it, panting momentarily as if to say, "You can say that again".

An hour later and the Hunney family were all ready for the wedding. Ted had been taken in the wedding car to meet Matilda at her home and Oliver had gone to meet Scarlett again after returning from seeing her at Mort's for breakfast.

The twins looked as pretty as pictures in their new frocks and with their nails painted a delicate shade of pink. Their mother had styled their hair. Martha's tousled black locks were swept back and hung down below her shoulder blades, held in place with a yellow ribbon. Sarah, who had worn curlers overnight, had long wavy tresses tied with a pink bow.

Ruth looked at her daughters, and smiling, she sighed, "You both look beautiful. Now mind you both behave yourselves today, like the becoming young ladies you are."

"Yes, Mother, we will," they replied together.

Chapter 16

The chapel was filled with Matilda and Jacob's relatives and friends from the village. Jacob was waiting outside near the side entrance, sat on a wooden bench, his friend Sam Kendal stood by his side. Martha, who had been chatting with Teddy Moore, noticed Jacob there and walked over to him. "Hello, Jacob, you look very smart in your wedding suit, and you too, Sam. You must be very nervous, Jacob, it's not every day you get married. Where's Noah anyway?"

Jacob looked at Martha and ignoring her comments said, "You look a bit different to what you did first thing this morning! I saw you going like the clappers through the field near the farm; are you training for something, Martha? You're not going into the army like Oliver, are you?"

"No, I'm not joining the army; I'm training for a hill race this autumn."

Sam looked surprised and said, "Well, Martha Hunney, I'll look forward to competing against you – that's if you're allowed to run!"

"Don't you worry, Sam. I'll be doing a run at one of the country shows in autumn."

"Oh, and how are you going to manage to do that then?" asked an inquisitive Jacob.

"I've got things in the pipeline to get me into one or even two events," said Martha optimistically.

"Here's Noah now," noted Sam, ignoring Martha.

"Come on, Noah, you've cut it a bit short, haven't you? Where have you been? I nearly asked Sam to stand in for you," said an

CHAPTER 16

irate Jacob.

"I was called into the station to sort a bit of paperwork out. Anyway, it's done now, so where's my best-man's flower?"

"It's here." Jacob pulled a white carnation from his jacket pocket and thrust it into Noah's hand.

"Steady on, Jacob, it's supposed to be one of the best days of your life." Noah started laughing. "Oh I get it; you're actually nervous. The man with nerves of steel is nervous."

Jacob looked at Noah and smiled, then he said politely, "Shut up, Noah, and let's get inside the chapel. Matilda will be on her way now and we don't want her stood at the front of the chapel with Martha's dad and the Reverend Boniface waiting for us two. That would be a desperate situation with those two glaring at us."

Martha chirped in, "You can say that about my father. He doesn't stand any messing. You had better get inside – isn't that the wedding car coming down the lane?"

"Yes, it is!" shrieked Jacob and set off running towards the chapel entrance shouting, "Come on, Noah, shape yourself."

Noah turned to Martha and Sam, winked at them and stated, "He's not Mr Cool now, is he?" and jogged into the chapel.

Turning around to join her mother and sister, Martha heard Ruth call urgently, "Come on, Martha, let's get inside the chapel." She walked quickly over to her mother and Ruth instructed her daughter, "You sit next to Sarah and me. Your grandma can sit at the end of the row; I don't want her struggling in and out of the pews. Your father will have to pass your grandma and sit between me and her once he's given Matilda away."

Jacob and Noah were standing at the front of the chapel facing Reverend Boniface who quietly asked, "Are you alright, Jacob?"

"I'm a bit nervous, Reverend Boniface."

"Just take some deep breaths, Jacob, and exhale each of them slowly. You'll be fine after that. Ten, in and out should do it; you as well, Noah."

Both men stood there staring in front of themselves, steadily breathing in and out. After the seventh intake of breath, the organ sounded out. Everyone in the chapel turned around as Matilda, her bridesmaid Miranda, and Ted made the short walk to the altar. Jacob was still concentrating on his breathing exercise until Noah nudged him sharply in the ribs. Coming out of his semi-trance he turned to see his bride in all her splendour. As Matilda stood next to Jacob, he looked at her and whispered simply, "Beautiful." Matilda rewarded him with a broad smile.

Ted nodded at Jacob, and as the organist stopped playing and choir's singing faded to a close, Reverend Boniface took two steps forward toward the betrothed and started to perform the marriage ceremony. He raised his voice until it resonated around the chapel.

"Dearly beloved, we are gathered here in the sight of God, and in the presence of family and friends to join together this man and this woman in Holy Matrimony, which is commended of Saint Paul to be an honourable estate instituted of God and therefore is not to be entered into unadvisedly or carelessly but reverently, joyfully and in the love of God. Into this Holy Estate these two persons present come now to be joined." He paused for a moment and then continued, "Who gives this woman to be wed?"

Ted replied confidently and clearly, "I do."

Reverend Boniface nodded at Ted and then with a slight forward movement of his hand motioned for Ted to go and sit next to Ruth.

The wedding ceremony went without a hitch. Jacob lifted Matilda's veil carefully away from her face and kissed her full on the lips. Seeing the tears in Miranda's eyes, Noah smiled at her and she smiled back. After the formality of signing the register in the vestry, the final hymn, 'Jerusalem', chosen by Jacob and Matilda, was sung joyfully by the chapel choir. Martha and Sarah had climbed the chapel stairs to join the singers while the register was being signed but as soon as the married couple walked down the aisle to the front entrance, they swiftly descended the stairs to join the wedding entourage.

Tripping over partway down the stairs, Sarah crashed into Martha who almost went sprawling down the last few steps, but fortunately for her, Teddy caught her in his arms and as he did so pulled her closer to him. Without hesitation, Martha seized the

CHAPTER 16

opportunity and kissed Teddy full on the lips – much to her sister's astonishment! Teddy was taken aback too but it didn't stop him pressing his lips onto Martha's for a full three seconds. Martha eventually stepped back, placed her hands on her hips, dropped her head in thought for a split second and then said to Teddy, "Hello, handsome!"

Teddy blushed but quickly replied, "Hello. How's the most beautiful girl in the world?"

Sarah grabbed hold of Martha and commanded, "Come on, Honey, you can carry on with Teddy later." Whispering sternly into Martha's ear, she admonished, "It's a good job Father didn't see you; he would have flayed you alive!"

Martha was half dragged by Sarah toward the front entrance but still managed to turn around and blow another kiss to Teddy who smiled and grabbing the invisible kiss placed it on his lips. As he did this, Martha replied to her sister, "I don't think Father would flay me alive, we've had a good conversation regarding Teddy and me. He likes Teddy and I've told Father I want Teddy to take me to the pictures. Did you hear what Teddy said about me, Sur?"

Sarah laughed, "Yes I did, Martha, and I'm just wondering where he's left his white stick and guide dog."

"Don't be so cheeky, Sarah Hunney."

"Come on you two," Ruth called to her daughters. "That's if you want to be on the wedding photographs with the rest of us. Isaiah Allbright has got a fancy camera and he's going to take some pictures outside the chapel and then on the village green near the oaks."

"Oh Mother, isn't it a lovely day?" sighed Martha.

"Well it certainly is a lovely day for the wedding, Martha love. And by the looks of you and Teddy, for you two as well." Martha's brown complexion turned red. "Don't think I didn't see you, because I did. It's a good job Sarah dragged you away from Teddy otherwise you would never have been on the wedding photographs. Anyway, you be careful, young lady; the sun, weddings and too much dancing can lead to romantic assignations. Think about your training, Martha."

"Don't worry about me, Mother. With Father and Oliver about, Teddy's not going to try anything on. Anyway, he's too much of a gentleman and a bit wooden as well. I just want him to take me to the pictures and do some steady courting. That's all."

After Isaiah Allbright had taken the photographs outside the chapel the wedding party walked slowly to the village green. It seemed that most of the population of the village was milling around when they arrived, and everyone took it in turns to congratulate the bride and groom.

Martha sat down on a bench in the shade of an oak tree and, to her sister's surprise, closed her eyes and to all intents and purposes fell fast asleep. Shaun McMullan, who had called in at the post office for some writing paper and envelopes, spotted them and sauntered across the green, weaving his way through the crowd. "Oh to be sure, yous two look as pretty as a blossom on a tree. Is Marta asleep there, Sarah? Why, she looks like the sleeping beauty, so she does."

Sarah, feeling slightly irate, quipped, "Okay, Shaun McMullan, don't overdo it, you sound to me as though you've kissed that Blarney Stone this morning. Where's Patrick, anyway?"

"He's repairing some stonework that the bull damaged the other day. It's a brute of a beast. It's only fit for two things: serving the cows and eating, and I don't mean eating grass, I mean as beef for us. It's as well that hedge – as well as the stone wall – was there otherwise it would have been out on the lane and running wild. Anyway, I have to be on my way so, good morning to you, Sarah and oh, by the way, I know Patrick is looking forward to seeing you this afternoon."

Before he had time to walk away, Sarah asked, "Anyway, Shaun, who have you got your eye on?"

"Well it's funny you should ask that, Sarah, because I have my eye on a pretty young lady from this village, not mentioning any names but she's a well-rounded filly not unlike yourself in certain places."

"Don't be so cheeky, Shaun McMullan, you're too forward, if

CHAPTER 16

you ask me."

"I didn't ask you anything, it was you who asked me. Top o' the morning to you, Sarah Hunney. I'll tell Murphy you were asking about him." Shaun walked away, smiling to himself.

Sarah nudged Martha awake, "Did you hear that, Martha? He's very cheeky that Shaun McMullan. He said he likes a well-rounded young lady who is not unlike me."

Martha rubbed her eyes then yawned and laughed. "Well then you should take it as a compliment, Sur."

"I'm not well-rounded, am I?"

"You are in certain places," commented Martha nodding towards her sister's chest.

"Very funny, Honey. I wonder who he means."

"It's got to be Beatrice Cloister, she's the only one in this village who can match you in that department. Yes it must be Beatty, alright."

"Do you have to be so coarse, Martha? I think you're probably right though. Here comes Teddy. Honey, I wouldn't start kissing him here if I was you, Father's stood just over there talking to Mr Allbright and he's been glancing over here while you were asleep."

"I wasn't asleep – just resting my eyes."

"You were asleep, Honey. Hello, Teddy, have you come for some lip service?"

"Who's being coarse now, Sarah Hunney? Take no notice of my coarse sister, Teddy."

Teddy, who was blushing, stuttered, "I've only come over to tell you that Mr Allbright is ready to take some more photographs. Your dad has just asked me to come and to tell you. That's all."

"That's a pity, Teddy; Honey was expecting some more kissy action."

Martha sprang up from the bench and in the same instance linked arms with Teddy saying, "Come on, Teddy. Take no notice of Sur." She turned to her sister, tossed her head back, then walked with Teddy over to the wedding party who were gathering together for the photo session.

After the photographs were taken, Sarah spotted Harry Smith

holding hands with Delwyn Williams and thought how fortunate it was that she and Harry were not going steady. Ruth saw her daughter watching Harry and Delwyn and informed her, "Harry Smith is going into the Royal Air Force, Sarah; did you know?"

"No, I didn't know, Mother, but there was never anything between us anyway. He's too flighty as far as I'm concerned," and then she laughed. "Do you get it, Mother? 'Flighty' as in 'fly' and 'air force'."

"Yes, alright, very funny, Sarah. So you never had any feelings for him then?"

"No, Mother, none at all. I've got my eye on someone else."

At that moment, Patrick and Shaun arrived on their motorbike. Most of the village knew this because the sound of the engine was deafening and if no one had heard it they would most certainly have seen the exhaust smoke billowing out of the ailing engine.

Sarah ran over to speak to Patrick who placed his hand gently around her waist. Ruth watched her and thought, 'I see, it's one of those Irish boys. I might have guessed.'

At one o'clock the band set up their equipment onstage in the village hall. Bryony and Bridget – who had arrived with their mother – Martha, Sarah, and Sofia Reynolds, all held an impromptu session with the band's accompaniment. Ava and Mort, who had closed his café after serving early breakfasts, were making sure everything was ready for the arrival of Jacob and Matilda along with all the guests invited to the wedding buffet. Scarlett and Delwyn Williams had placed the jugs of drinks on a table set to one side near to the kitchen; they both rushed out of the hall to be with their sweethearts as soon as they had finished.

Two o'clock arrived and the wedding party made their way to the village hall. Seeing the band, the decorations, and the sumptuous spread Matilda was overcome with emotion, not having realised the lengths that her family and friends had gone to, to make sure this day was as special as possible. She started to weep with joy. Jacob held her in his arms and kissed her on both cheeks. "It's a wonderful surprise, isn't it, Matilda"?

"More than I ever could have hoped for. Look at all the

CHAPTER 16

decorations, Jacob, and the spread of food!" She left Jacob for a moment and walked over to her Uncle Ted and Aunty Ruth. "Have you done all this for Jacob and me?" Not giving them time to answer Matilda grabbed hold of Ted and kissed him, tears rolling down her cheeks and then she hugged Ruth, who was also overcome with emotion, and couldn't hold her tears back.

"We all helped, Matilda. Ruth, the twins, Ava, Mort, Reverend Boniface and the others – we all mucked in. We're just so glad we could do this for you, and for Jacob. Anyway, let's all sit down and get on with the celebrations."

Ted climbed on to the stage and said, "Cyril, give us a loud blast on that trumpet of yours." Cyril did as Ted commanded and everyone turned toward the stage. Ted was standing with his hands raised in the air and shouted out, "Ladies and gentlemen, let me have your attention for a minute please, everyone." Then requested, "Mrs Benson, will you stop little Tommy from mauling the sandwiches, please."

Mrs Benson promptly grabbed hold of her son and clipped him round the ear. "Stop that, Tommy Benson, and behave yourself." Tommy rubbed his head and mumbled under his breath. "You can stop that mumbling as well or you'll get another."

"Yes, Mum, sorry, I won't do it again."

Ted continued, "Will you all take a seat please. Not on the top table – there's room for all, the top tables are for near family, with pride of place for the bride and groom. We'll have the speeches, toasts and that sort of thing, eat the food, and with the band playing we'll have a gradely old shindig. If you have any requests let Sofia know and, if they can, the band will play them. Before we start eating I don't have to remind you that we don't eat until Reverend Boniface says grace and thanks the Lord for our food and many blessings."

The formalities soon got underway. Ted gave his speech and there was a tinge of sadness as he recalled the grievous sadness felt by the family and community, but most of all by Matilda and her siblings at the death of their parents. Ted, not known for showing any emotion, held back the tears as he explained how honoured he felt to be giving his niece away in her father's stead. As he looked seriously at Jacob, he reminded him to look after Matilda, as a wife should be cared for, and Jacob nodded to Ted in acknowledgement of what he saw as a grave command from someone he looked up to and admired.

After all the speeches and the toasts to the bride and groom, as was customary at village weddings, flowers were handed out to those ladies who deserved special mention. Reverend Boniface gave thanks, blessed the food and drink, and then everyone tucked in. Scarlett, Delwyn, and Beatrice had started to hand the cold drinks out when Shaun nudged Patrick, pointed at Beatrice and jumped off the stage to help her. She smiled at him.

"Edward, I would prefer a cup of tea if you don't mind," said Ted's mother.

Shaun overheard her request and promptly said, "I'll be right on it if you tell me what strength and how many sugars you want, madam. And if someone can tell me where to make it."

"Thank you, young man, but I would prefer someone who knows what they are doing to make my tea," declared Mrs Hunney.

"Oh that's no problem to me; I used to be the All-Ireland Tea Making Champion back home."

"Yes, and I can see you kissed the Blarney Stone back home, as they say."

Ted laughed as his mother frowned at Shaun. Beatrice tried to reassure her, "It's all right, Mrs Hunney, I'll show the champion where the kitchen is and I'll supervise him on how to make a proper cup of tea!" She grabbed Shaun by the arm and pulled him towards the kitchen. "Come on, champ, I'll show you the way".

"Right you are, but go steady on the arm. You never know when I might need it for the tug-of-war or arm wrestling competitions at the country shows."

"Shaun, I'd beat you at arm wrestling, never mind any of the local farmers."

He replied, "I bet you would with the size of those biceps of yours, Beatrice."

CHAPTER 16

She laughed. "I might just wrestle you to the ground if you're not careful."

"I do believe you could, but I think it might be a pleasant experience for me."

"Come on, you silver tongued charmer. Let's make Mrs Hunney her tea."

When all the food and drink for the afternoon reception was consumed, Ava, Scarlett and Beatrice cleared away the crockery and cutlery. Mort was the chief washer-up and Mrs Benson dried. On the orders of their mother, little Tommy and his older brother Caleb played outside in the shade of the oak trees. "Keep out of the sun, keep your hats on, and don't go near the water, or you'll both be for it," she had told them. Ava kept a watchful eye on Mort. Mrs Benson was not known for high morality and although in her heart Ava knew Mort was as good as hers, she also knew the weakness some men suffered when faced with women of loose morals – and she was not going to leave anything to chance.

"It's a lovely day, Mort, don't you think?"

"Yes, it is, Iris," Mort replied tentatively.

"I think it's a day for couples today and I still miss James after all these years," she continued wistfully. Her husband had been killed some years before in a mining accident.

Ava overheard Iris and marched into the kitchen. "Mortimer, Ted wants a word with you outside, I'll take over the washing up," she snapped. Mort promptly went to look for Ted.

"Iris, I would like to say to you that, for your information, Mortimer and I are walking out together and I would appreciate if you did not try to get your claws into him."

"That's alright, Polski, I had my claws, as you call them, in him years before you came on the scene, and who's do you think those children are?" said Iris, brusquely.

Ava was mortified. She fled the kitchen in tears, brushing past Scarlett as she carried the last of the crockery into the kitchen. "What's up with Miss Fleischmann?" asked Scarlett.

"She said the wrong thing to me, that's what's wrong with her; Miss High and Mighty."

Scarlett was no shrinking violet and angrily laid into Iris. "What have you said to her, Iris? I hope you haven't been lashing her with that poisonous tongue of yours."

"She had it coming that one. Coming over here and taking over."

"Don't be ridiculous, she has come here to live a better life, not to be bullied by the likes of you. Don't you think she had enough of a rough time in that concentration camp? You should know better. If you can't say anything nice to the woman, don't say anything at all to her. I bet you've been trying it on with Mort again, haven't you? You're shameless!"

Scarlett took over washing the last of the crockery and Iris dried, glaring at each other from time to time. Presently Scarlett stated, "I hope you are going to apologise to Ava for upsetting her, and if you have said anything untoward I hope you put it right."

"You can hope all you want," sneered Iris.

"Don't you be spoiling her day. Just do it, Iris."

Iris thought for a moment and said, "Okay then, but I expect you to buy me a gin and tonic later."

"I'll do that, but first I want to hear you apologise." They finished the washing up and then went outside to look for Ava. They found her sitting on a bench outside by herself. A breeze had developed and was blowing her hair; she was busy replacing her hat which had blown off. Ava had tear-stained cheeks and the tell-tale signs of smudged mascara.

"Go on, Iris. Apologise," commanded Scarlett.

"I'm very sorry for everything I've said to you, Ava. It was all lies, and I'm sorry for calling you 'Polski'. And my children have nothing to do with Mort."

Scarlett was astonished at the thought of Mort being the boys' father and the fact that Iris had claimed such a thing out of nothing but malicious spite.

Ava thought for a moment and then looked at Iris. "Your apology is accepted. You should learn to curb that tongue of yours; it carries poison with it. Who is the boys' father, by the way?"

CHAPTER 16

"Why, what's it to you?" snapped Iris.

"Nothing to me, they are both handsome little fellows that is all I want to say. Now if you don't mind I want to fix my hat and make my face." She rose from the bench and walked slowly back to the village hall.

Out of curiosity, Scarlett asked, "Who is the father of your children, anyway?"

Iris turned and, looking Scarlett in the eye, shamelessly revealed, "George Garvan. And don't forget you owe me a drink." She walked over to where her boys were playing, took her shoes off and, smiling, joined in the game of tag they were playing with two of their cousins.

The day wore on. It was the hottest day of the year and apart from the children playing, most of the wedding party were sitting either on the grass or on the memorial benches spread about the village green. Courting couples walked slowly on the riverbank in the shade, holding hands or linking arms. Martha and Teddy sat on one of the benches. Martha's morning run seemed to have taken the edge off her energy levels and she declined Teddy's request to go for a walk.

"The band is having another practice session at about six o'clock, Teddy, and I need to have a talk to Patrick before they start. That's if I can prise him away from Sarah for five minutes. You don't mind, do you? I just want to ask him about training sessions this week, to see if we can fit one in together. I think I'll be going back to work on Monday and he works all hours on the farm, so we need to set a time for one evening." Martha held Teddy's hand, looked him full in the face and then kissed him on the lips. "Teddy, you don't mind me running with Patrick, do you? You're my man now, you know that, don't you?"

"Ever since that time on the bus, Honey, I knew you were going to be my girl and now you are. You go running with Patrick if you want. He and your Sarah are well suited to each other. At one stage I thought maybe it would be Harry and Sarah but he's courting with Delwyn, and besides, Harry is joining the Air Force. I'll wait for you here. Oh, by the way, Martha, there's a good film on at the pictures next Saturday – will you come with me?"

"Of course, I will – it's about time you asked me!"

Martha walked over to the riverbank where Sarah and Patrick were sitting in deep conversation. "I don't want to interrupt you two lovebirds, but could I have a word, Patrick?"

"It's got to do with running, I'll bet," commented Sarah.

Martha answered her sister, "You're right, Sarah. I'll only be five minutes, I promise."

Patrick laughed as he stood up. "What do you want, Marta?"

Before Martha had time to answer, Sarah said, "Give me a hand up, Patrick. I'll go and sit with Teddy over there while you discuss your running."

Patrick, with his strong left arm, lifted Sarah from the floor. She looked at him, smiled and said, "My, aren't you strong, Patrick Murphy?" making him blush.

Sarah walked slowly over to Teddy, and Martha beckoned Patrick to sit down again. "What's up with you, Marta? You're usually all action."

"I'm saving myself for this evening. Besides, I think I overdid the training this morning and I feel a bit tired. Which evening can we go running together this week? Apart from Thursday, that is, and definitely not Saturday."

"Wednesday at six," Patrick replied quickly. "McMullan will finish the cows off. I've already asked him." Patrick pointed at his head and then down at his feet. "You know the old saying, Marta, up there for thinking, down there for dancing. I knew you were going to ask me."

Martha was slightly bemused and said, "No, I didn't know that saying. Is it an Irish one or something?"

"It probably is, but I think it means use your brain for planning and that's just what I did."

"Alright, six it is then, Patrick. Will you come to my house? Otherwise, I can run to the farm."

"No, I'll come to your place."

They went back to join Sarah and Teddy, discussing the route they would run on Wednesday. They agreed on the same route as

CHAPTER 16

the last time they had run together but Patrick promised Martha she wouldn't be as successful at 'burning him' off as she was last time. As they approached the pair sat on the bench, Sarah asked, "Martha, do you know where Father is?"

"He's gone home with Mother to sort Shep out. I think they're taking him for a walk before the evening do."

"I don't know whether Father's working behind the bar tonight, and Bob Stokes wants to know if he's still needed, Father hasn't been to see him."

"I think Father will need him, I'll just nip across and tell him so that he'll be ready in time. He needs to get his leg and hand on, and that can take him a while sometimes."

Patrick asked, "Why, what's up with his hand and leg?"

"He had them blown off during the War, but he can still get about alright and he's a dab hand behind the bar. He's good in front of the bar as well!" Martha laughed mischievously at her own joke. "The last time a skirmish broke out between some lads from town and here in the village, he near enough sorted it out by himself. You were in on that one, Teddy, weren't you? He soon sorted it out, didn't he?"

"Oh yes, with some help from your dad. They are a formidable pair. That false hand of his packs a powerful punch, as I can testify," said Teddy rubbing his jaw.

Evening came and the wedding party made their way to the village hall. It was an open affair and villagers who were not at the afternoon wedding reception were welcome to the evening party. Ted, for once, was not working behind the bar but had organised three people from the village to serve the drinks. Bob Stokes was promoted to head barman for the evening and Maud Smith was his deputy. Marshall Broadbent was the third; he was a young farm labourer with designs on going to Cambridge University. He was what some in the village termed as a 'contradiction in terms', brilliant with figures but dim at everything else. He was a childhood protégé at science and had recently sat an exam to see if he could make the grade for Cambridge. Nowhere else would do for him; it was Cambridge or nothing as far as he was concerned.

Bob told Marshall to keep an eye on Maud; she was the opposite of Marshall when it came to adding up figures.

Matilda and Jacob took to the floor in the traditional manner and started the evening's proceedings dancing to 'The Tennessee Waltz'. Ted and Ruth followed suit and soon the floor was full of dancing couples. Presently, the band struck up their first individual tune; a rousing rendition of 'Boogie Woogie Bugle Boy' and Bryony, Bridget, Sarah, and Sofia sang the words with happy enthusiasm. Scarlett tugged on Oliver's arm and said, "Come on, army boy, show me what you've got." As quick as a flash they were on the dance floor boogying for all they were worth. Quickly following them, Martha, with renewed energy levels, dragged Teddy off his chair and proceeded to jive around the hall. Soon the floor was alive with gyrating couples, some excellent dancers, some novice beginners.

"Well, Mortimer, are you going to ask me?"

"Ask you what, Ava?"

Ava, in her deep Polish accent, rather sarcastically replied, "Let me see, do you think I would like to go outside, out of the way? Or what do you think, Mortimer?"

"If you want to, we can do," he numbly replied.

Ava raised her voice. "No, Mortimer," she shouted to make sure he got the message. She stood up and sashayed her hips. "I want to jive with you!"

Mort was astonished; he had never heard Ava raise her voice before and as for her hips swinging, he couldn't believe his eyes. He laughed. "I can't promise to dance like those young ones, but come on, Ava, let's have a go, we can only make fools of ourselves."

They smiled, laughed, and danced to the jive music along with the others, and although slower in their movements than the younger couples, they gelled together well. Ava fully enjoyed the dance and showed her affection for Mort with a passionate kiss on his lips. "I need to be like this, Mortimer, I know I am not in my youth anymore perhaps, but inside I feel like one of these young ladies and I have never felt like this before."

Mort smiled. "We'll enjoy ourselves tonight, Ava, and then I want to have a serious talk with you. Don't worry, it's about good things. We'll meet after chapel tomorrow. Come to my place for Sunday roast and we'll talk then."

The night seemed to rush by as a succession of speeches brought both laughter and tears, while the buffet magically disappeared. The music was enjoyed by everyone, and none more so than when Orla Rowley and her daughters joined the band to sing 'Only You'. Everyone agreed they were magnificent. Jack Snead, ogling the sensual Orla Rowley, commented, "Now that's what I call a woman. She makes Rita Hayworth and Sophia Loren look plain. Just look at her, Tom."

"Steady on, Jack. You'll be giving yourself one of your turns at your age; she's young enough to be your great granddaughter."

"Maybe so, but all the same, she's some woman. I think I'll ask her for a dance," was old Jack's retort.

"Come off it, she'll be holding you up and it'll be the end of you."

"I couldn't think of a better way to go, Tom."

"You're an old fool, Jack. Don't let Reverend Boniface hear you or you can bet he'll be preaching on the sins of the flesh in one of his sermons soon, and then your conscience will be pricking you."

Jack remarked, "Happen you're right at that, Tom." They both looked at Orla, sighed, and each had a sip of their beer.

Jacob and Matilda were seen off outside of the village hall, with tin cans tied to the back of their Ford Prefect clattering along the road as they departed for their honeymoon in Blackpool. An hour later and the band were playing the National Anthem and then everyone departed for home. Bob, Marshall and Maud had the dubious honour of clearing the bar and tidying the hall. Bob locked up and made sure Maud arrived home safely. Everyone agreed it had been a wonderful day.

Chapter 17

On Sunday morning, Ted announced to his daughters, "Mr Bradshaw has asked me to tell you two to be back at work at half past seven, sharp, Monday morning. You've to report to the office and Jack Simpson will have a word with you before you start on your normal work duties. There will be no repercussions for you both walking out. George Garvan will be back at the mill; that's if he's ever capable, but don't worry, he'll keep out of your way. You will see him but not as your works' manager."

Martha and Sarah rushed to their father and hugged him simultaneously, declaring with glee, "Thank you, Father, you are the best, I love you."

"Alright, but one more thing: you can thank God that Mr Bradshaw owed me a favour from before you two were born. When you see him, thank him for giving you another chance. Now, it's your works' sports day next Saturday and I expect both of you to come home with prizes and trophies." Ted smiled and hugged his daughters as they kissed him on his ruddy cheeks.

"Is your mother ready for chapel yet? She's been upstairs for ages. Go and see if she's ready, Martha, and don't shout – your Mother had a headache when she got up this morning, and don't go bounding upstairs either making your racket."

"I won't, Father."

Martha tiptoed up the stairs and knocked gently on her mother's bedroom door. She whispered, "Are you ready, Mother? Father's been asking."

"Will you ask your Father to come up, Martha dear?"

Martha said nothing and bounded downstairs. Ted gave his

CHAPTER 17

daughter a stone-faced look. She got the message.

"Well, how long?"

"She never said. She wants you to go up."

Ted bowed his head, mumbled incoherently, and trudged up the stairs to his wife.

"Something's going on, Sur. Mother was very quiet and her voice was shaky, I think she was on the verge of crying, something's definitely wrong."

"But Mother was on top form yesterday. She looked as though her and Father really enjoyed the wedding. Did you see them dancing cheek-to-cheek last night? There's nothing wrong with them, Honey, it must be something else."

"Maybe it's Oliver going back tomorrow that's upset her. She worries about him over there in Cyprus with the trouble and everything. Although Scarlett will be devastated as well when Oliver goes, I've never seen a couple so close." Then Martha laughed impishly. "Well apart from Matilda and Jacob, and look what's happened to them."

Ted appeared at the kitchen door. "We'll be coming to chapel a bit later, so you can go as soon as you're ready, you'll have plenty of time to walk. Is that all right, girls?"

"Yes, we could do with some fresh air, couldn't we, Sarah?" Martha replied.

"Definitely. We'll take a leisurely stroll and see you and Mother when you get there. Should I tell Reverend Boniface you might be a little late?"

"No, you don't need to do that, Sarah, we should be on time. Your Mother and me just need to spend a little time together, that's all." Martha asked. "Is Mother bothered about Oliver, Father?" He nodded and then went back upstairs.

"Like I said, Sarah, something's not right."

Sarah changed the subject. "Honey, I think I'll start wearing my wedding dress for chapel next week. That's if it's warm. It's a pity we can't wear them today."

"I definitely can't wear mine today anyway, Sur. Teddy, the oaf, knocked Mr Proctor's drink over onto me and my dress is stained with beer. Mr Proctor told Teddy that if he was eighty years younger he would have taken him outside! Anyway, Teddy apologised and bought Mr Proctor another drink, and one for Mr Snead too, although he'd fallen asleep. Mr Proctor was satisfied with that. At least, it saved Teddy from a beating."

Martha started laughing at the thought of ninety-six year old Tom Proctor laying into Teddy. Sarah started giggling, and soon they were both laughing uncontrollably.

A little while later the Reverend Boniface's voice resonated around the chapel; his tone was serious for the moment. "There has been evil afoot in this village during the past week. You might well think to yourselves, what does he mean? What I mean is that one of our parishioners is critically injured in hospital. And it seems that it might not have been an accident. But the good Lord sees all and he shall put right what has been put asunder. Let us all pray for George Garvan's full recovery."

A disgruntled murmur ran through the congregation – not many in the congregation were friends of George Garvan – he wasn't well liked in the community.

Reverend Boniface was quick to react. He raised his voice and authoritatively reminded those present, "'Let he who is without sin cast the first stone. Think well before you pass judgement, less ye be judged'. Is any one of you not guilty of some sin or another? Some greater than others?" A number of the older congregation were visibly squirming in their seats. Silence fell once more in the chapel.

On a happier note, Reverend Boniface continued, "It was a glorious day yesterday for the marriage of Jacob and Matilda and also, from a personal point of view, a most enjoyable day. And I can safely say I witnessed a great deal of enjoyment and happiness from those at the wedding service and the celebrations afterwards.

"The delivery of the music and songs in the evening was excellent. However, a word of caution to you: beware of the lyrics in some of these modern songs. Don't let them lead you astray and take hold of your inner thoughts, mind."

Although the Minster smiled as he spoke, his gaze, as well

CHAPTER 17

as his words, seemed to penetrate directly into the hearts and minds of the younger congregation. As the sermon came to an end the Reverend Boniface requested, "Let us now sing our final hymn. That wonderful hymn penned by Charles Wesley: 'Soldiers of Christ, Arise'. Let us hear those nightingales, who sang so majestically last evening, sing their praises to the Lord our God with sincerity and reverence."

Following Reverend Boniface's formidable directives, the choir and congregation sang with gusto.

Although it was apparent to Reverend Boniface that his sermon, at face value, had had an effect on most of his parishioners, how long it would last was of great concern to him. As was his custom he stood outside the great oak door of the chapel, to commune with his flock. "So, you are going back to your army duties tomorrow, Oliver. May God protect you in your work and grant you a safe journey."

"Thank you, Reverend Boniface." Oliver motioned the Reverend to one side and whispered to him, "You'll have another job on your hands in the not too distant future, if you know what I mean. Please don't broadcast it, though. Nothing is definite yet."

"Not a word shall pass my lips, Oliver; you can be assured of that. Where is Scarlett by the way? I haven't seen her this morning."

"She's nursing her mother who had one of her turns yesterday evening and isn't well at all." Oliver pointed towards a group of people. "Her sister Delwyn is over there talking with Harry Smith and one of those Irish lads; she'll be able to tell you how Mrs Williams is."

"Yes, thank you, I'll go and have a word with Delwyn. The Irish lad's name is Shaun, by the way. As I said before, have a safe journey back to your duties, Oliver."

Chapter 18

The next morning, Martha and Sarah returned to work. Martha seemed anxious about her brother.

"I hope Oliver has a safe trip back. Mum and Scarlett were very upset when Major Coulthurst picked him up. I managed to mention to the Major about his contact and he says he is going to write to me with any news he gets about whether he can get me running in a fell race."

Sarah replied sharply, "You know, sometimes you can be quite cold-hearted, Martha. Is running all you think about?"

Martha interrupted, "No it isn't, Sarah Hunney. I'll miss Oliver as well you know, but I'm not his mother and I'm not marrying him either. Come on, let's get to the bus stop quick, we don't want to be late on our first day back, do we? Father wouldn't be too pleased if we were late after he's sorted everything out with Mr Donald."

"I suppose not. Honey, I'm sorry for calling you cold-hearted and I do hope you can run in one of those fell races, even if it's only to stop you going on about them."

They laughed and walked to the bus stop, linking arms, discussing the wedding, the fun they had had, and especially, Teddy and Patrick.

The sisters were welcomed back to work and soon took up their daily routine. The week seemed to fly by for Martha and then Wednesday – training session day – finally arrived. It was raining when she got home from work.

"I'll have to put my waterproof on, it's started to throw it down outside and it doesn't look like it's going to stop. Patrick should

CHAPTER 18

be here soon so don't go collaring him, Sur; we need to get our training done. You want him to do well in the fell races, don't you?"

"Of course I do, but there's no harm in saying hello."

"Yes, but there's a difference between saying hello to him, and snogging his face off."

"Why are you so coarse, Martha Hunney? It's kissing, not snogging, and we won't be doing that sort of thing in public. I'm not Scarlett, you know. And by the way, I know you've kissed Teddy but has Teddy kissed you yet?"

Martha blushed. "You know he has, not that it's anything to do with you; and I'm not Scarlett either." Martha lowered her voice to a whisper. "But I'll tell you something, if you keep it a secret: Teddy's got a luscious pair of lips!"

"Oh, you strumpet!" her sister retorted. They both giggled, and at that moment there was a loud knock on the back door.

"That'll be Patrick. Two minutes with him and that's your lot." Martha opened the door and called out, "Sarah, it's a dripping wet Patrick if you want to see him. Have you no waterproof, Patrick?"

"No, I've nothing like that, Marta. Don't you worry, I'll dodge the raindrops."

"Well, you haven't made a very good job of it on your way over here. It's as well it's warm rain, otherwise you'd be frozen."

Martha whispered, "Two minutes, Sarah, don't forget," and then louder, "I'll go and ask Father if you can borrow his waterproof, Patrick."

"No need, I'm okay."

Martha had already barged her way into the living room. "I left it at work," was her father's reply. So she hurried back to the kitchen, keen to be off.

"Right, time to go, Patrick, Father's left his waterproof at work so you'll just have to dodge the raindrops."

Patrick held Sarah lightly round the waist. "See you, Sarah," and he kissed her on her cheek.

Martha smiled at her sister. "You're nearly as wet as Patrick now, Sur," and then set off through the back gate with Patrick close on her heels.

Martha pushed the pace for two hundred yards until they reached the field and then slowed slightly. "I still keep forgetting to warm up properly and now my calf muscle is hurting." She bent down and rubbed her left calf muscle vigorously then set off again at a very easy pace.

"You're like a bull in a china shop, Marta. You should always warm up properly. When I raced back in Ireland I always did some limbering up exercises and a mile run before I raced and I was never injured."

"I'll bear that in mind; if I can help myself."

"Well if you don't, you'll not be doing any races this autumn and even if you do, you won't do yourself justice because you'll end up injured most of the time you should be training."

Martha wasn't the best at taking advice and was vexed at Patrick for voicing his opinion. "Alright, Patrick, thanks for the coaching tips; if I need your advice I'll be sure to consult you."

"No problem," Patrick replied. "I'll keep it zipped then; my lips are sealed on the matter, to be sure."

They carried on silently for a few hundred yards and then Martha pulled up abruptly and started rubbing her calf muscle again. "I'll have to go back, it hurts too much. You carry on, Patrick."

"No Marta, I'll walk back with you and then carry on again."

Martha snapped, "You don't need to. I can manage on my own."

Patrick was unperturbed by Martha's attitude. "I'll see you back to your home and that's that," he insisted.

She was taken aback by his forcefulness and conceded, "Alright, come on then, but no stopping with our Sarah. You've got to get your training done."

"Now who's advising who what to do, Marta?"

Martha laughed and then winced as she put her weight on the injured calf muscle. As they walked back through the wet fields, Martha commented, "It's the well for me when I get back and that will cure it."

CHAPTER 18

Patrick looked perplexed. "What are you on about, Marta?"

"Have you forgotten already? I've told you before, it's the well at the back of our house, it's got special water with curing abilities." Pointing to her leg, she said, "I'll give it a couple of treatments with the water and it will be right for the works' sports day on Saturday. I can't miss that, I've a score to settle with Bonny Parker and Sarah."

"Why's that then?" Patrick asked inquisitively at the mention of Sarah's name.

Martha mumbled, "They both beat me last year in the sprint."

"What's that, Marta? I can't hear what you are saying."

Martha raised her voice. "They beat me last year."

"Well, you won't be beating them this year, not with a leg like that."

"I've told you, Patrick, my leg will be right by Saturday. If you don't believe me, ask our Sarah. She'll tell you how good that water from the well is."

"You'll be telling me it's as good as the water from Lourdes next."

"It is; ask Sarah."

The rain stopped as they jogged in the backyard entrance. Patrick said goodbye and set off across the field again, intent on a very hard and fast training session.

Martha limped into the yard, picked up an empty bucket and hobbled down the steps to the well where she promptly scooped it three-quarters full of cool, clear water. She sat on the bench up against the house wall and gingerly removed the plimsoll from her injured leg. There was an old cloth hanging from the washing line; Martha reached over to take it down, soaked it in the water and tied it around her sore calf muscle. Securing it firmly – not too tight but enough to keep it in-situ on the place intended – she said to herself, "That should do it. A couple of treatments should be enough," and nodded her head, full of confidence that the water treatment would fully heal her injury.

The back door opened and Ted stuck his head out. "Who are you talking to, Martha?"

"To myself, Father, just me, no one else."

"What's that you have tied round your leg? And why are you back so soon?"

"I've injured my leg, but it's nothing to be bothered about, I'll still be doing the sports day on Saturday."

Ted smiled at his daughter and teasingly asked, "Will you be fit enough to go to the pictures with Edward Moore in the evening, though?"

"Of course, I will. I think Sarah's going with Patrick Murphy as well. Has she told you, Father?" Martha asked impishly.

"I know, Martha, so don't try to get your sister into any trouble."

Martha laughed and then winced as she stood up and put her weight on her calf muscle. "As if I would do anything like that, Father."

"Are you sure that leg of yours is alright? Because it doesn't look all that good to me."

"Stop fussing, it's stiffened up that's all, but it will be right for Saturday with some more treatment."

"If you say so, Martha. Oh, by the way, Mort's been here, said he wanted to see you. He asked me to tell to you he's seen the cobbler today and he wants to arrange for you to go and meet him. He said to call in at the café on Saturday morning sometime, if you have no other plans, and tell him when you'll be available to see the cobbler."

Martha started hopping about on her good leg shouting, "Whoopee!"

"I thought that would make you happy," Ted said quietly and vanished back into the kitchen as Martha continued her war dance.

The following Saturday soon arrived – the works' sports day at last – and Martha and Sarah walked into the village to meet their friends.

"I've just got to nip in and see Mort before we catch the bus into town, Sur. We have ten minutes to wait anyway, so we can have a brew while I talk to him."

"Is this about the shoes, Honey? Your running shoes I mean."

CHAPTER 18

"Racing shoes, actually. Yes, I won't be long so we won't miss the bus leading to my victory and your vanquishment."

"Have you been dreaming again, Martha? That one where you finish just in front of Bonny and me and then wake up to realise it was just a fantasy? Well, that's all it will remain: a dream and you'll be going home sulking yet again."

Martha had opened the café door and was half in, half out when she turned to her sister and countered, "It will be you and Bonny sulking at precisely three thirty p.m., Sarah Hunney, just you wait and see. Anyway, come on we haven't time to mess about."

"I won't – you will," Sarah said as she pushed past her sister into the café.

As soon as Mort saw Martha he beckoned her over to the table where he was seated studying the horse racing form in his daily paper. "Which horse do you fancy in the three thirty at Doncaster, Martha?"

Martha looked over Mort's shoulder and after scanning the names of the twelve horses she reached over, stabbed her finger on the name Swift Operator and said, "That one definitely. It's number ten – my favourite number and it's got Scobie Breasley on top. He's Australian and he's won some top races over there including the Caulfield Cup a few times. It'll win, Mr Johnson."

"Right then, ten bob on the nose it is, at about five to one that should make me two or three quid. Anyway, sit down, you and your sister can have a tea on the house in lieu of my big win." He called over to Scarlett who was chatting with Sarah, "Two teas for these girls and a top up for me, Scarlett, love. You've come at the right time, Martha; it's the calm before the Saturday morning storm, especially on a beautiful morning like this. Those cyclists, motorbike riders and sports car people will be rolling up in the next half hour or so. Anyway to the point: Walter Walsh, the cobbler I know, has said he needs to have a talk to you and measure your feet to make sure the shoes fit exactly. He'll take plaster casts of each foot if that's okay."

Martha was so excited at the thought of having her racing shoes custom made she couldn't help her overenthusiastic reaction to

Mort's comments – she whooped with joy and leaned over to kiss Mort on the cheek. "Thank you, Mr Johnson, you're the best!"

"Steady on, Martha, you'll have people talking."

"It's alright, Mr Johnson, Sarah and Scarlett will say nothing and there's no one else about. I think we'll be okay." She gave him a cheeky wink into the bargain.

Mort laughed and asked, "How about next Monday evening after you finish work? You can come to the shop and I'll take you straight there to his shop in Farrington."

"Will it be alright for Sarah to come for the ride?"

"Of course she can."

Martha shouted across the café, "Do you fancy coming with Mr Johnson and me on Monday, to Farrington, after work?"

"If I don't get a better offer, I suppose so."

Scarlett nudged Sarah and laughed as she teased, "'Better offer'. Who do you mean by that? Tony Curtis?"

Sarah blushed. "No, Scarlett, I've only got eyes for Patrick, and never mind any film stars." She noticed the bus arriving and called to her sister, "We need to get going, Martha, the bus has just arrived."

"Coming, Sur. See you on Monday, Mr Johnson. Thanks for organising for me to see Mr Walsh." Martha gulped her tea down and then, rushing past Scarlett, called, "See you," and leapt through the doorway before it shut behind her.

"Look who's at the bus stop waiting for you, Martha. So that's definitely, at best, third place for you."

"Hi, Bonny, looking forward to the races?"

Bonny was not known for her modesty or tact. "Of course I am – and looking forward to picking up two trophies! Are you two looking forward to the minor places in the eighty yards?"

Martha was instantly riled. "Modest as usual, Bonny Parker; well we'll see about that. You could be in for a shock, and it might be you relegated to a minor place as you call it. Come on, Sur, get on the bus."

There was a great deal of light-hearted banter and leg pulling between the mill workers on the bus and in the midst of it all was

CHAPTER *18*

Jonny Jones – the mill joker and general dogsbody for the male workers and older women. He turned to the twins and asked, "Are you doing the wheelbarrow race again, you two?"

"Only if I'm the barrow and Sarah's wheeling me. If Sarah wants it the other way round she can forget it."

Sarah retorted, "Well it's only because you're a weakling, Honey, you couldn't even hold me up last year."

"Maybe it's because of something else, Sarah. Maybe something was weighing you down."

Sarah blushed and poked her sister on the arm.

"Did you see that, Jonny, she's trying to nobble me before we've even got there? That's because she knows I'm going to beat her in the eighty yards."

Sarah exclaimed, "Martha, you couldn't beat an egg, never mind me."

Jonny and those listening laughed. Martha mumbled to herself, "We'll just see about that, won't we?"

"Stop talking to yourself, Honey, it's only a bit of fun we're having." Sarah placed her arm round her sister but Martha ignored her reconciliatory advance and shrugged it off.

"Be like that then. I'll see you on the field of battle." Sulking, Sarah moved to the front of the bus and sat with Bonny Parker.

"Are you alright, Martha?" asked Jonny.

"Of course I am, Jonny, but I'm not letting our Sur know." She laughed quietly and put a finger to her lips, saying, "Don't say anything though, let her stew. Anyway, what are you doing this afternoon – are you going to beat Arthur Murray in the eight eighty?"

"I'll try, and I've actually done some training as well. I've taken a leaf out of your book on that one, Martha." Jonny paused for a moment and then announced quietly but excitedly, "And I'm having a go at the fell race on Josiah Leveridge's land when he has his country show. It's the first one round here, isn't it? Anyway, I think I'll beat Arthur this time. I think David Sanderson will be hard to beat, though. He was the best in our year at school and used to win the cross-country races as well. He didn't run last year though because of that accident he had in the mill. Can you remember that, Martha?"

Martha spoke in a whisper, "Yes I can, it was Mr Garvan's fault, but he got off with that as well." She raised her voice again and said enthusiastically, "So you're going to do the fell race; wow, you're a dark horse, Jonny."

"I'm going to train hard for it as well. Are you still hell bent on doing one, Martha?"

"I guarantee it, Jonny, as sure as Mort's horse will win the three thirty."

"Well Martha, Mr Johnson is not noted for his success with the horses."

"Oh it'll win, Jonny, just you wait and see," replied a confident Martha.

"Come on, Martha, you can't be that sure."

"I'm even more confident that that horse will win than I am about me beating Sur and Bonny in the eighty yards!"

Chapter 19

"Well done, Jonny. I knew you could do it. You put in a fast finish there, I thought David had you but you came past him like a whippet in the last fifty yards."

"Oh, let me catch my breath, Martha. I've had it!"

Martha stood with hands on hips for a moment, "Ok, I'll see you later. Well done anyway."

Jonny gasped out, "Good luck in your race, Martha."

"There'll be no luck about it if I win."

Jonny managed a short laugh as he lay on the grass gasping for air and thought, 'That's Martha Hunney, alright, not a negative thought in her body.'

A message came over the loudspeaker. "Will all those ladies competing in the eighty yards straight race come to the start please. You have precisely five minutes before you are called to your mark."

Martha had been doing her warm-up regime, stretching, jogging, and striding out in short bursts. She rubbed both her calf muscles and felt confident that the one she had injured three days earlier had healed perfectly – she felt no pain from it. Concentrating intensely, she maintained complete tunnel vision. Her sister looked towards her as they made their way to the start. Martha was oblivious.

The starter called the girls to their marks, "Ladies, take your marks." The girls all crouched into the start position, apart from Sarah; she bent over slightly, one foot in front of the other. The starter then rapidly shouted, "Set. Go."

Bonny Parker set off like a rocket and was two yards in front after the first ten. Shirley Philips was second and Martha third. Sarah was about two yards behind Martha. Thirty yards into the race and there was no difference in the positions or the distance between each of the girls. The crowd lining the eighty yards grass-track were shouting and cheering wildly for their favourites. Martha, pumping her arms, and knees nearly touching her chest was making good inroads on Bonny's lead; she passed Shirley Philips, and within another fifteen yards was level with Bonny.

Sarah was now only two yards behind and was picking up speed after her slow start. Meanwhile, Martha was totally unaware of her sister's looming presence. She passed Bonny with fifteen yards to go and with five yards left was a yard in front. Sarah came thundering up to level with her sister, the twins lunged for the finishing tape and Sarah touched it first. They both decelerated over the next few yards and as soon as they stopped, Martha threw her arms around her sister and gasped, "Well done, Sur," and kissed her on her left cheek. Sarah looked down at her chest and said, "They come in handy sometimes – I think I beat you by a bra size, Honey!" They both laughed and hugged each other tightly.

Bonny Parker and Shirley Philips congratulated the twins. "Who got it?" asked Bonny.

"Sarah – by a chest!" said Martha, laughing. Bonny and Shirley took it in turns to hug Sarah and both patted Martha on the back.

"Are you going to the pictures tonight, you two?" asked Shirley.

"You bet. With our fellas!" the twins said simultaneously.

"Oh, that reminds me, talking about betting, I'm just going to ask over at the marquee if anyone knows who's won the three-thirty at Doncaster." Martha jogged over to the marquee and asked Charlie Finnick, a retired bookmaker, which horse had won the three thirty.

"Swift Operator," he replied. "Why? Have you had a few bob on it, Miss Hunney?"

Martha whooped with joy. "No, Mr Finnick, but I know someone who has won a few pounds." She jogged back over to where her sister was waiting for her.

CHAPTER 19

"Hurry," urged Sarah, "the wheelbarrow race is starting now. Get down on the starting line and let me lift your legs up."

"OK, bossy."

Martha lay face down on the ground and, standing behind her, Sarah gripped both of her legs at the ankle. Martha pushed up on her arms and as they struggled to get their balance the starter shouted, "On your marks. Set. Go." The seven couples charged off. Martha managed only three yards of the fifty yard course then fell over laughing.

"Stop it, Martha. Get back up."

Still laughing, Martha said, "Who's the competitive one now, Sur?"

Sarah shouted, "Shut up, Honey, and get going."

"Yes, sir!" she spluttered, laughing even more. The sisters managed to reach thirty yards and were in second place with nearly all the competitors falling over apart from Bonny and Shirley who were leading by three yards. Martha fell again after her arms gave way.

"Get up, Martha. We don't want to be beaten by Bonny Parker," hissed Sarah.

Martha summoned all her strength and set off like a shot with Sarah gripping her ankles tightly. They passed the faltering Bonny and Shirley, who were just recovering from a fall, and crossed the finishing line four yards in front of Gwendolyn Pritchard and Delwyn Williams. They had passed Bonny as she stood with hands on hips swearing at Shirley who had fallen over again and was rolling about on the floor laughing uncontrollably.

At the end of the day the bus trip back to the village was a fun one filled with light-hearted banter.

On the top deck Jonny claimed his success as the 'top athlete' of the works' sports day, with Sarah coming a close second.

The mill workers all sang 'For he's a jolly good fellow' to him and the young women each took their turn at smothering him in kisses. Four of them had purposely spread lipstick very thickly on their lips and he emerged covered in various shades of red and pink lip shapes.

Pinning him to the back seat, Shirley kissed him full on the lips, and said, "Take me to the pictures tonight, handsome."

"Only if you pay, I'm skint," was his reply.

"You're on, Jonny! Meet me for the seven o'clock bus. I hope you've got enough for the bus fare."

"Just about, and for a couple of ice creams as well."

Walking slowly home in the warm early evening sun, Martha declared, "In, tea, washed, changed, and out again, Sarah."

"You've forgotten the full report we'll have to give Father before tea. You know how he likes to know how we get on at sports days. We can show him our trophies and tell him how you nearly won the eighty yards and nearly lost us the wheelbarrow race with laughing."

"Yes, very funny, Sur. But I do have to admit you did excellently well today, Sarah." She gave her sister a big hug and said, "You're the best sister ever."

"So are you, Martha," and Sarah returned her sister's hug.

"Well, I see you won then, by the looks of the trophies you're both waving about. Who won what?" asked Ted as they strolled in the door.

"If you notice, Father, Martha's holding two trophies but I've only got one."

"I can see that, Sarah, and so can your mother. But who has won what?"

"Tell them, Martha. I'm too modest!"

Martha held a small silver-plated cup with a wheelbarrow adorning the top. "We won this one for the wheelbarrow race. We were first."

"Well done, girls," both parents said proudly.

Martha held a bronze coloured cup. "This one is for runner-up in the sprint. I beat Bonny Parker who won it last year."

"Well, who won the sprint then?" asked her father.

"Go on, Martha, tell them."

Martha pointed at her sister and smiled. "Sarah won by a half of an inch."

"Oh, well done, love. Well done to you, Martha, as well," Ted

CHAPTER 19

said.

"Yes, well done both of you. I suppose you both want your tea now and then you'll be getting ready for your dates?" Ruth asked with a broad smile on her face.

"What's on at the pictures, girls?"

"Around the World in Eighty Days, Mother, starring David Niven and Shirley MacLaine. It's the best film out, and it's won the Academy Award in America."

"Oh well, Martha, it must be if it was made in America," said Ted sarcastically.

"That's what Teddy told me anyway, and he should know – he near enough lives at the cinema at weekends watching all sorts of films."

"Yes, well, you and Edward keep off the back row. And you and Patrick, Sarah. I know what goes on the back seats."

"Yes you do, Ted, you sat there with me often enough 'watching films'!"

Martha and Sarah laughed, and said together, "Oh please, Mother, no more. We don't want to know!"

Their father looked sheepish and uncomfortable.

"Don't you worry, Father, we'll all be on our best behaviour."

Ted and Ruth had already eaten so after their mother had served the girls their tea she joined her husband in the front room and left her daughters to eat. Martha and Sarah sat down at the kitchen table and wasted no time in demolishing their potato pie and beetroot. Martha made a pot of tea and placed a kettle full of water on the stove so it would be ready to wash the crockery and cutlery. They both drank two cups each and as soon as they had finished, Sarah washed up and Martha dried.

"What's that there, Sur?" asked Martha.

"What?"

Martha pointed in the general direction of the back door of the kitchen and said, "That, on the wall, over there!"

Sarah went over to investigate, and as soon as she did, Martha threw the tea towel on the table and bolted out of the kitchen and upstairs as quick as a flash. Her sister sprinted after her but it was too late, Martha was locked in the bathroom and water was running into the bath. Sarah banged on the bathroom door and shouted, "You're a cheater, you are, Martha Hunney."

Martha laughed. "You might be a faster sprinter than me, Sur, but you certainly aren't as clever. Anyway, I'll only be five minutes, honest, and I won't use all the warm water, promise."

"You'd better not either, you... you..."

A gruff voice called from the bottom of the stairs, "Don't say it, Sarah. No calling your sister names. What's going on anyway, what's all the racket about? You sounded like a herd of elephants charging up the stairs."

"Martha tricked me into her getting in the bathroom first, Father."

"Well, one of you had to be first. You'll have to be a bit smarter next time, Sarah. You should know what your sister is like by now, you've known her long enough."

"Yes, Father."

Ted had made his way to the bathroom door. "Martha, don't be too long in there. I want a wash after Sarah and I'm going out in half an hour so shape yourself."

"Yes, Father, four more minutes, and I'll be out. Father will you ask Sarah to get me a bath towel from the cistern cupboard and leave it outside the door? I forgot to get one."

"You heard what your sister said, Sarah. Just get her the towel, and then go into your bedroom or somewhere else so you're not falling out with each other."

Half an hour passed. Ted and his two daughters, after saying goodbye to Ruth, walked down the lane together into the village. It was still warm and the twins were wearing their summer frocks, each carrying a cardigan. Ted was going to the village pub for a drink with Mort and Bob Stokes. As usual the topics of conversation would be: work, war, and horseracing.

"Father, if you see Mr Johnson will you ask him how his horse went on in the three thirty at Doncaster?"

"Is there a reason I should ask him, Martha?"

"None in particular; it's just that he was studying the horses

CHAPTER 19

when Sarah and me popped into the café this morning and he asked me which horse I fancied in the three thirty."

"Ok I'll ask him, but I think you already know, Martha."

Martha laughed, Sarah shrugged her shoulders, and Ted reminded them both that it was chapel tomorrow and not to stay out too late.

Leaving their father at the pub, the sisters walked across the road to the bus stop. Teddy was waiting for Martha and Beatrice was expecting Shaun and Patrick to arrive in the next five minutes. Jonny Jones was standing with Shirley Philips and Bonny Parker.

"Well, Martha, you did well today: a first and a second. You must be pleased."

"Best I've done in the works' sports, Teddy. Sarah did even better, though."

"Wait 'til you run in a fell race, Martha, no woman will be able to beat you in one of them, will they?"

"That's because there are no more female fell runners, only me."

Teddy grabbed hold of Martha round her waist and kissed her. "Anyway, well done, Martha, I'm proud of you."

"Oh, thank you, Teddy, that's lovely," and she kissed him back.

A low roaring noise got louder and louder as Patrick and Shaun arrived accompanied by a plume of two-stroke engine smoke. Shaun shouted in his high-pitched voice, "Hello everybody it's a gradely fine evening, to be sure."

"Where are you going to park your motorbike, Shaun?" asked Beatrice.

"Over there at the garage. It'll be okay just there; I've a chain to fasten it to that iron pole."

"You don't actually think anyone will pinch it, Shaun, do you?" laughed Martha mockingly.

Patrick intervened. "McMullan thinks it's a collector's item and an antique, Marta."

Martha had another look at the motorbike and commented, "Possible. Maybe in another fifty years. You'd better look after it until you're seventy, Shaun, and then it'll be worth a small fortune."

"Leave off with that sharp tongue of yours, Martha," snapped Beatrice.

Shaun quickly set about calming a possible storm. "Just bit of fun, to be sure, eh, Marta?"

"That's all it is, Beatty," replied Martha, smiling at Beatrice.

The bus arrived in town and the party of cinema-goers made their way to the Palace picture theatre, on the corner of the Sunken Gardens Esplanade. Everyone was spellbound by the content of the film and they all enjoyed it immensely. At the end of the film and after the National Anthem, which everyone stood for, the couples set off back to the bus stop. Martha with Teddy, and Sarah with Patrick, each couple walking slowly along, arm in arm, through the fading summer twilight.

Suddenly a bellowing voice shouted, "Hey, Paddy, what do you think you're doing over here, courting our English girls?"

"Oh no, it's that loud mouth bully, Colin Bellshaw, and he's with Billy Briggs. Ignore them, Patrick, please," pleaded Sarah.

"Don't worry, Sarah; I'm not afraid of bullies."

"Just ignore them, Patrick," repeated a nervous Teddy.

Bellshaw ran over to the group and rowdily repeated his question. Shaun, who was walking with Beatrice thirty yards behind the other couples, heard the loud aggressive voice and sensed danger.

"Stay here, Beatrice," he commanded and jogged the thirty yards to listen to what was happening.

"I'll ask you again, you Irish Paddy. What do you think you're doing with our English women?"

The sisters were very nervous and said nothing. Sarah was holding onto Patrick and pulling him back away from Bellshaw. Beatrice also made her way to the group.

Shaun commented boldly, "It doesn't look like they are your English girls to me."

"Shut up, you. You sound like an Irish bitch girl anyway." He took a swing at Shaun but with nifty footwork, Shaun dodged the punch and head-butted Bellshaw on the bridge of his nose which started pouring blood.

CHAPTER 19

"I might sound like a girl but I fight like a man. Be off with you before you get some more." He turned to Beatrice and said, "Did I ever tell you I was the All Ireland Head-Butting Champion? Even the bulls on the farm back home wouldn't take me on."

Patrick raised his eyebrows at Billy Briggs and said, "Do you want some too?"

Billy shook his head, grabbed hold of Colin Bellshaw, pulled him away and dragged him slowly towards the bus stop.

The three couples soon overtook them and sat in the bus terminus waiting for the nine-thirty bus back to the village. When Billy Briggs and Colin Bellshaw also reached the terminus, Shaun walked over to them and said, "No hard feeling, fellas, we don't want any more falling out among us, do we?"

He held out his hand, and Bellshaw mumbled, "I suppose not," and shook Shaun's hand self-consciously. Shaun then offered his hand to Billy and they too shook hands.

"No hard feelings then, fellas, and no more trouble?"

They both answered, "No," in unison.

As Shaun was negotiating his peace-making, Patrick said to the others, "He's a handy fellow to have around sometimes is McMullan, to be sure. That is when he's not filling his face. How many ice creams did he have, Beatty?"

"Oh, only two and an ice lolly. Oh, and a bag of Butterkist. That's all I think."

Martha and Sarah started giggling, and Martha said, "The greedy great lump."

Beatrice replied, "Yes but he's my lovely greedy great lump, Martha Hunney."

All five started laughing just as Shaun made his way back to them. "What are you all laughing about?"

"Nothing at all that would interest you, McMullan, nothing at all," answered Patrick.

"That's all okay then. I'll tell you what though; I've got an awful headache now."

"Oh come here, my hero and I'll kiss it better." And before Shaun knew what was happening, Beatrice wrapped her ample frame around him and smothered him in kisses. He didn't offer any resistance.

Each of the young men walked their girls safely home. Teddy walked back into the village with Patrick where they met up with Shaun. "I'll see you at chapel tomorrow then. Take it easy on that motorbike of yours. Like Martha said, it could be worth a small fortune in fifty years."

"Oh be off with you, Teddy. We'll see you in the morning," laughed Shaun.

Patrick winked at Teddy. "See you tomorrow for another riveting sermon by the very Reverend Boniface."

Chapter 20

Martha had arrived at the café with Sarah where she was meeting Teddy while Sarah went on a bike ride with some of her friends. A concerned Scarlett, who was working in the café, observed, "You're looking tired, Martha – have you been overdoing it?"

"No, I haven't been overdoing it. Our Sarah's decided to start snoring in bed. She's been at it the last three weeks. If she carries on she'll have to sleep with the dog in the kitchen. It's the first local fell race next weekend and I intend doing it."

"Why don't you get her to sleep in Oliver's room then, Martha?"

"I can't do that, Scarlett, it's Oliver's room."

"Well, what has that got to do with anything? Oliver's away."

"Scarlett, it's Oliver's room and Mother won't allow anyone in her boy's room," Martha commented sarcastically.

Mort had been listening to their conversation and interrupted. "How's your new shoes doing, Martha?"

"Fantastic, Mr Johnson. They're the most comfortable trainers I've ever had. Excellent when I'm running downhill. They've loads of grip on the rough stuff, and on slippy stones and rocks."

Mort looked at Martha and smiled. "Don't get your hopes up for racing on old Leveridge's land next Saturday. No disrespect to you or any female, but he's a woman-hater. Never married and he hates those feminist types. He thinks all women should be housed in the kitchen and tied to the sink."

"I'll still turn up and try, Mr Johnson. Has he anything against the Irish, because Patrick Murphy is thinking of racing?"

"It wouldn't surprise me in the least, he's biased against most things is Josiah Leveridge."

"He must like sheep and dogs or there wouldn't be any show at all," chipped in Scarlett.

"He usually picks up a trophy or two. Either through his terriers or ferrets, or whippet racing and he usually wins a few quid." Mort thought for a moment and then continued, "Come to think of it, your dad and I usually pick up a pound or two ourselves. Is young Murphy worth a pound bet, Martha? You should know, you've trained with him a few times; I know that because your dad tells me how your training's going."

"Put it this way, Mr Johnson, he could be a dark horse and shock one or two of the more fancied runners." Martha laughed impishly. "Then again, if I race, you could bet on me being the first female."

Scarlett pushed Martha. "Oh, you are modest, Martha Hunney. Anyway, I bet you wouldn't beat Lydia Burton if she took up fell running. She's the best cyclist round here bar none."

Martha glared at Scarlett. "Maybe she would beat me. But the point is, Scarlett, she doesn't run, does she? Anyway, she'd probably not be able to get those giant thighs of hers uphill. There's a big difference between biking uphill on a tarmac road and running up and down a steep, rough fell, you know."

"Customers arriving, Scarlett, see what they want," ordered a relieved Mort, knowing the girls were heading for an argument.

"Mr Johnson, is your clock right?"

"On the dot. They could put Big Ben right with that clock now; I put it right last week," said Mort jokingly.

"Teddy's late. You know, Mr Johnson, I've run six miles this morning, done my chores, had a wash, done my hair and come down here in plenty of time and that Teddy, who only lives round the corner, can't get here on time. We're only going for a walk. I've a good mind to stand him up and go home."

The café door swung open and Teddy strolled in looking as though he hadn't a care in the world. Mort was standing out of Martha's sight and motioned to Teddy, pulling two fingers across his throat and mouthing silently, "You're for it."

Teddy smiled at Martha as she glared at him. "Cat had a

CHAPTER 20

puncture, that's why I'm late."

Martha shouted, "What?"

"I mean my tyre had a puncture – the cat's okay. It's just got a sore tail."

"Well, that's the best excuse I've ever heard from anyone being late, Teddy. What's happened?"

"I ran over the cat, swerved, ran over some glass and fell off my bike then took the cat to the vet."

"How's the cat?"

"It's got a bandaged tail but he's alright, the scruffy article. I've bashed my knee, though."

"Let's have a look, Teddy."

Teddy rolled up his trouser leg and showed Martha his grazed knee. Martha leapt from her chair and kissed Teddy, "My poor boy, that's a nasty graze." She slapped him on his broad, muscular chest, laughed, and ordered, "Watch it doesn't get infected, you big oaf."

"Yes, nurse," Teddy replied.

"You wish, Teddy Moore."

He had no idea what Martha was implying and she giggled impishly, asking, "Are we having a drink here, Teddy, or going for a walk along the river bank?"

"Definitely a brew here, the walk can wait for a few minutes. Anyway, Honey, you look tired, so we're not going to spend hours on our feet."

"And I suppose you could walk for miles and miles on your poorly knee, my idi bidi Teddy."

"No, I couldn't, but stop avoiding what I've just said, you do look tired and you've got dark rings under your eyes to prove it. What's wrong?"

Feeling harassed Martha instinctively replied, "Yes, I'm tired but you can't badger me, you're not my husband. There's no ring on this finger, is there, Teddy Moore?" as she pointed to her ring finger – implying it was about time there was.

Teddy blushed, ignored Martha's comment, and then composed himself even though Martha stared at him po-faced.

"Why do you look tired, Martha, for the last time of asking?" he demanded.

"It's Sarah's fault, Teddy. She's keeping me awake with her snoring."

"So you're not running too much then?"

"No, I'm not; I'm just not getting enough sleep."

Making her way across the café, Scarlett interrupted them, asking haughtily, "What do you two want, since you're stood there neither coming nor going."

"We are customers here I'll have you know, Scarlett Williams, and expect to be valued as such," Martha replied with her nose in the air.

"Well, sit down again, stop making the place look untidy and order something like customers do!"

Martha laughed, "I'll tell you what Scarlett, our Oliver will have his work cut out with you, if you get hitched."

"Not if, Martha – when. And I could say the same thing about poor Teddy here."

"Oh, Martha's not that bad really, Scarlett. She just gets a bit carried away sometimes."

"So that means you will be getting hitched sometime then does it, Teddy?"

There was a brief silence. Martha was smiling and tapping her right foot rhythmically under the table.

"Err I'll have a glass of cold lemonade and a slice of Mort's best almond cake, please, Scarlett. What do you want, Honey?"

Martha pointed at her finger again, and nodded at it, "Apart from a ring on this finger, Teddy? A pot of tea and a raspberry slice."

Walking away, Scarlett turned to Teddy, pointed to her ring finger and blew him a kiss.

Teddy turned to Martha, and smiled nervously. "Martha, you know that entrance exam I took for Cambridge. Well, I've got an interview."

Martha sat with mouth agape, eyes staring. Eventually, she whispered, dry-mouthed, "Why that's absolutely wonderful news

CHAPTER 20

for you, Teddy." She rose out of her chair, took two steps forward, bent down, and kissed him full on the lips for what seemed like an eternity to Teddy who was in utter bliss.

Returning with their order, Scarlett banged the table with her foot but to no avail. She coughed loudly and said, "Shall I get a bucket of water, Martha, or are you going to let Teddy draw breath before he passes out?"

Martha pulled away from Teddy and caressed his face as she did so.

"What's the occasion then? Have you proposed, Edward Moore?"

"No," Teddy replied catching his breath.

"Teddy and I have no announcements to make concerning marriage or any other matter."

"Well, something's going on. I've never seen you kiss someone like that before, Martha Hunney. Even Mort started to blush and that's a first. It's a good job your dad didn't see you," Scarlett said, giggling.

"Will you put the tray on the table, Scarlett, and stop gabbing. It was a moment of passion on my part, that's all."

"Well I must admit: Teddy is easy on the eye."

"And you can stop that off as well or our Oliver will find out you've been flirting with the handsomest man in the village."

Scarlett laughed, Teddy blushed and then said irately, "Give over, you two, and Scarlett, put that tray on the table like Martha asked you."

Mort was looking on and noticed the other three customers watching Martha and Teddy. "Take no notice of those two," he said. "They're in love," and then sighed theatrically.

One of the customers, a sweet little elderly lady looked up at Mort and declared, "It is a lovely day to be in love, though."

Mort nodded, threw his tea towel over his shoulder and walked back to the counter saying to himself, "Oh, what am I going to do about you, Ava?" and sighed again.

Outside the café, the cyclists, including Sarah, Lydia Burton, the mill owner's niece, and Shaun McMullan, were congregating in a small group.

"Have you seen who's with Lydia and our Sarah out there, Teddy? I don't believe it! Look at those shorts he's got on; they leave little to the imagination. That is a sight to behold! Come on, Teddy, let's go." Martha leapt out of her chair and bolted for the door.

Mort shouted after her, "Martha dear, aren't you forgetting something?"

"Teddy, will you pay Mr Johnson, please?"

"How much, Mr Johnson?" Teddy sighed.

"Three shillings and tuppence."

Teddy paid and two minutes later joined Martha outside. The group of cyclists had swollen to six with Beatrice, Jonny, and Shirley joining the others.

"Where are you all off to then?" asked an inquisitive Teddy.

"We've just been telling Martha, we're off to Amblers Caves over Treedown Moor; it's about fifteen miles away."

"Well, I hope you've plenty of water and a hat apiece otherwise you'll be collapsing in this heat. Do you think you'll manage it, Shaun?" asked Martha, showing a slight concern.

"Don't worry about me, Marta. I am to cycling what Murphy is to running. I could have been the All-Ireland Cycling Champion if I'd have taken it seriously. You ask Murphy."

"I'll give you your due, Shaun; you're not low on confidence, are you?"

"Those words are not in my vocabulary, Marta. I'm fairly good at swimming as well you know."

"So am I," interrupted Lydia.

"And I'm good at cycling and swimming and very good at running, so maybe we could have a competition sometime down near the lake," suggested Martha.

"Well I'd give it a go," volunteered Shaun. "Even though I can't run for nuts. If we had the swimming first, the cycling second and the run last, I'd probably give you all a good walloping, apart from Murphy that is, and I'd give him a real good walloping."

There was a crescendo of laughter from those standing around.

CHAPTER **20**

"What's so funny?" Shaun asked, genuinely puzzled.

Beatrice replied, "You are, Shaun McMullan, and that's why I like you so much."

"Who's for it then? A competition to see who the best all-rounder is. Swimming, biking and running; all down by the lake. It'll be a bit of fun," challenged Martha.

Her sister asked, "Are you sure about that? You know what you're like, Martha when it comes to competing. Anyway, I'll do it just depending on how far we have to run, I think I can finish it anyway."

"It won't have to be too far, the running I mean. I'll be okay with the swimming and cycling but I don't know about the running," Lydia remarked.

"The best thing to do is to have a bit of a meeting if we intend doing it properly. And nobody else to be involved apart from us here. Everyone agreed?"

"No," said Shaun firmly. "I want Patrick to do it too, if he wants. It's a good chance for me to put one over on him. I'm a better swimmer and rider, but I'm a bit like Lydia here on the running side of things. What does everyone else think?"

"It's alright by me," said Jonny. "It's only a bit of fun anyway and I think it's a good idea of yours, Martha."

"I'm easy," Beatrice commented.

All the girls burst out laughing. With a smile on her face, Martha enquired, "Would you like to rephrase that, Beatrice?"

Beatrice blushed. "Trust you, Martha Hunney! I think Patrick should do it and I'll do it as well, depending how long the running is. I'd say two miles, absolutely maximum."

Martha quickly demanded, "Three miles."

"No, Martha, two miles," insisted Beatrice, and Sarah and Lydia nodded their heads in agreement.

Teddy quickly intervened before an argument ensued. "I won't be doing it because I've punctured my bike. Anyway, come on, Martha, before this sun starts cracking the flags, let's go for that walk."

"You can fix your puncture in time, Teddy."

"Yes, but I'm no good at swimming. You'll all have finished before I swim the lake, and you'll have to have a lifeguard on hand just in case. Come on now, Martha. You lot get going before the tarmac on the road melts and your tyres get stuck in it."

"Don't be silly, Teddy," Lydia stated in her upper-class accent. "It's not that hot really."

Teddy walked away, half-dragging Martha with him. She turned to the group and said, "Have a good ride and have a think about what we've been talking about. And Sarah, you need to pull your skirt out of your knickers, it's tucked in at the back."

Sarah nearly cricked her neck as she spun her head around and realised Martha for once wasn't having her on. She dismounted her bike and as discreetly as she could, pulled her skirt from her knickers and brushed it down with both hands.

"I told you you should have worn shorts, Sarah, but oh no, always the lady, aren't you?" Beatrice intoned.

"Oh shut up, Beatty. Come on, let's get going before it gets dark," snapped Sarah.

"Tally ho," enthused Lydia. "Off we go then, no stops before Amblers Caves, and we can call at The Crag Café on the way back."

Martha and Teddy had reached the village green, where the local children were playing football in the shade of the trees. "Are you having a good game, Freddie?" Teddy asked his little nephew.

"Yes but their goals aren't as wide as ours, so it's harder to score. We've only scored one, they've scored three, and they've got one more player than us," complained Freddie.

"That's not fair is it, Teddy?" remarked Martha.

"Not really."

"Well, what are you going to do about it?"

Teddy stopped the game and called the five boys and two girls together. "What's going on, you lot? Why are those goals over there at least a yard wider than these over here? If you're going to play, play fairly."

"Well, he'd better give me back that dinky car I gave him then," said Bobby Smith pointing at William Jones.

CHAPTER 20

"Oh, and why's that then, Bobby?" asked Martha.

"If we are going to make the goals the same size, he'll have to give it me back because I gave it to him so that he would make their goals wider than ours."

Martha and Teddy were dumbfounded. "Why, you little twister, Bobby Smith! And I suppose you put more players on your team as well," observed an irate Martha.

"Yes," Bobby replied, brazen and unrepentant.

"Well, you can jolly well make the goals the same size and give them one of your players to even things up a bit. Or do you want Teddy to play for their team?"

Little Sadie Thompson said meekly, "That won't be fair because he's a grown-up and will score loads of goals."

Martha replied, "You know what to do then, Sadie, play fairly. No wonder they need referees in games. Are you listening, you lot? Stop cheating each other and play fairly. And as for you, Bobby Smith, stop bribing other players, you're corrupting the game."

"I would do if I knew what you were on about," replied Bobby. "I only want my team to win."

"Well, win fairly then, you little twister. Come on, Teddy, let's leave them to it."

"Have a good game and don't forget to have a rest when you're getting hot, and don't forget to have a drink of your Spanish water," said Teddy pointing to two bottles of black liquid leaning against the bow of an oak tree.

As they walked towards the riverbank, Martha remarked, "I don't like cheats and cheating, I prefer a level playing field."

Teddy, not one for missing an opportunity to play the comedian, asked, "Don't you mean a level hill, Honey?"

Martha laughed, "Oh, you're so funny, Teddy Moore, as funny as toothache even." Suddenly Martha's mood changed. "When are you going for your interview, Teddy?"

"I have to go in two weeks. I only got my letter yesterday. For some reason, it's been stuck in the post office in town for five weeks and someone found it behind a rack. The postmaster has apologised but said it happens from time to time. As soon as I opened it I was shocked."

"I thought it would have been a pleasant surprise," Martha answered.

"Yes, I was surprised. But anyway, I phoned the College in Cambridge where the interview is to take place; I explained the situation and the Professor told me to come on the day stipulated in the letter."

"I suppose you'll be studying mathematics then, since you were brilliant at that in school."

"I will."

"If you get in, Teddy, you won't forget me, will you?"

"If I get in and assuming I get my degree, I'll be coming home to marry you, Martha Hunney."

Martha was speechless. Eventually she stopped staring at Teddy, lifted her ring finger to his eye-line, and said, "Does that mean I'll have a ring on this finger soon, Teddy?"

"As soon as I've spoken to your father, Martha – that soon." A cold shiver ran down Martha's spine at the thought of what her father might say. Teddy noticed the colour drain from Martha's face as she became ashen.

"Don't worry, Martha, your father can only say no or not yet, and we'll get married anyway in a few years, and don't worry about me not coming home during holiday time – I'll be home as quick as a flash to see my sweetheart. The girl I love." He turned to Martha, held her gently and kissed her lovingly. Looking into his eyes, Martha returned his kiss and smiled at him contentedly.

As they continued their stroll Martha noticed that Teddy was walking awkwardly and said in a sympathetic voice, "You're limping, Teddy. Is your leg sore?"

"It is sore, Honey, it's started to sting as well. I think we'll have to cut the walk short, say just three miles instead of the usual ten."

"Teddy, you couldn't walk ten miles to save your life."

"That's only because I've never tried!" he replied airily.

Martha pushed Teddy gently and said, "I think not, Teddy."

Grabbing Martha around the waist he pulled her to him as she started giggling, and before they both realised it they were laid

CHAPTER 20

on the ground entwined together in the shade of a giant oak tree kissing tenderly as sweethearts do.

Chapter 21

"He's come round."

"Who has?"

"Well, who do you think? Who's been laid in a hospital bed for the last few weeks unconscious?"

"Oh, you mean George Garvan. Is he compos mentis, sir?"

"I don't know, Constable Abrahams, go over to the hospital, and see what you can find out."

"Yes, sir. Do you mean now, sir?"

"Well not next week, Abrahams, of course now," growled Superintendent Ramsden. "Tell no one what Garvan says to you; especially Inspector Loncton. And don't forget your helmet, laddy."

"Yes, sir, I'll set off now."

Superintendent Ramsden gave Noah Abrahams a glaring stare with a slight smile on his lips and motioned him toward the door.

Ramsden looked at Sergeant Fredrick and said, "On second thoughts, you had better go with him, Sergeant. You know Garvan, I believe. You may be able to get more sense out of him than Abrahams; that's if Garvan can speak. Away, go now and catch him before he drives off."

Sergeant Fredricks ambled out of the door and waved Constable Abrahams down just as he was about to set off. He climbed into the police car and said laconically, "I've had my orders off the Superintendent to come with you. You can still drive, Noah, but no speeding, it's not an emergency you know. It's not as though George Garvan is going anywhere."

"Right oh, Sarge, I'll take it easy then."

CHAPTER 21

They arrived at the hospital and after a brief conversation with Dr Richardson, entered the side room where George Garvan was lying on his bed with his eyes staring into space. The ward matron followed them into the room whispering, "Not too long, Sergeant, Mr Garvan is very tired, he only came round three hours ago. He's been asking for his father, so that's a good sign."

"Not really, Matron, his father's been dead over twenty years. His mother is still alive."

"Don't we know it! She visits nearly every day. Mrs Garvan would make an excellent nurse, she has really kept the staff on their toes making sure her son has had the best care. It's probably due to her that he is still alive." Matron Skinner looked at George Garvan and gently laid her right hand on his shoulder. "Mr Garvan, you have two visitors."

He turned his head towards the matron and said in a frail voice, "Who are they?"

"Two policemen, they've come to see how you are."

"Policemen? Why? I've done nowt wrong," he said dismissively.

Jim Fredrick intervened. "Hello, George; it's good to see you are back in the land of the living – how are you?"

"Who are you then, and him for that matter," Garvan said faintly. "I don't know either of you. Can I have a drink, nurse? I've a throat like a lime burner's clog."

"Just a sip for the time being," Matron replied. She poured some water from the large glass jug into a glass beaker and placed it to his lips. Garvan struggled to swallow the water and coughed as he tried. He managed a few sips, and after placing two fingers into the bottom of the glass and wetting them, rubbed the drops on his lips.

"Can you tell me what has happened to you, George, why you are in hospital?" asked Sergeant Fredrick.

Garvan barely muttered, "I was hoping someone might tell me; no one seems to know, that woman who says she's my mother doesn't know."

Matron Skinner looked at both policemen and whispered, "That's enough for now if you don't mind. As you can see, Mr

Garvan is very weak and tired."

"Fair enough, Matron, but we will be back in a day or two to see how Mr Garvan is. We need to get to the bottom of what has happened to him; it's a mystery at the moment. Has he had any other visitors apart from his mother by the way?"

"Not that I can remember, Sergeant?"

"My name is Sergeant Fredrick, Matron." He pointed to his colleague and said, "This is Constable Abrahams."

She nodded to them and introduced herself as Matron Skinner. "Pleased to meet you both, but if you don't mind…" She motioned them towards the door.

Jim Fredrick turned toward George Garvan and said, "We'll be back another time, George, hope you improve." Garvan said nothing. The two policemen walked out of the side room and down the corridor towards the exit.

"What do you think, Noah?"

"I'm not sure, Sarge. If he's bluffing, and knows something, he's doing a good job of it."

"I know what you mean. He didn't exactly give us a warm reception. Then again, George Garvan has never been the most affable of people. We'll just have to bide our time. If he knows who has attacked him and is saying nothing, then it's for a reason only he knows."

"Allegedly, Sarge. We don't know whether he has actually been assaulted. For all we know that ferocious bull of Lord Letherby's might have tossed him over the hedge. It has been known to be in that field near where Ted found him."

Jim Fredrick laughed. "That's a bit fanciful, Noah, but nevertheless, a very slight possibility. He'd have a very sore backside if the bull has done it!" He laughed again and shook his head. "Just think – a bull! Come on, let's report back to Ramsden."

Noah took a sideways glance at Sergeant Fredrick and started laughing himself. They drove back to the police station and reported to Superintendent Ramsden. Constable Abrahams offered his hypothesis to the Superintendent, who roared with laughter.

CHAPTER 21

"Well laddy, you need to do two things then. Check Mr Garvan's backside for injury and go to Lord Letherby's Estate and find out when that bull of his when Mr Garvan was found." He turned to Sergeant Fredrick and asked caustically, "By the way when is his Lordship due back from Ireland?"

"In four weeks, sir. In time for the country show on his land."

"Is that so?"

"Yes, sir, he always opens the show, it's the best one for miles around."

"It might well be, Sergeant, but those miles around don't stretch as far as my bonnie land, do they?"

"I suppose not, sir, but it's the best in these parts; I don't know what they are like in Scotland, sir."

"Do you have caber tossing?"

"No, sir, but we have wellie throwing and tug of war."

Ramsden roared with laughter, and sputtered out, "If nothing else this job brings some humour round these parts. Go on, both of you and see what you can find out. Phone the hospital back to see if Mr Garvan has any horn marks on his posterior, and then go up to Lord Letherby's place and find out what you can."

The colleagues walked out of the room leaving Superintendent Ramsden still chuckling to himself.

After Sergeant Fredrick had phoned the hospital and managed to speak to Matron Skinner, they left the police station and drove to Lord Letherby's Estate.

"Well, Noah, perhaps your theory is not all that foolish after all. The matron has confirmed that there was extensive bruising to George Garvan's backside. However it still doesn't mean that the bull did the damage!"

"Well, all I can say is there's been more comical causes of injuries to the general public. And the authorities have found innocent people guilty of heinous crimes. Can you remember when Jack Thorbury drove over Bob Jefferson's foot with his tractor and he was convicted of causing grievous bodily harm? It turned out that it was the circus elephant that crushed it. It was proven later by that photograph Charles Smythe had taken when the circus paraded through town. He was taking a picture of his allotment at the time."

"Okay, Noah, I get the message; Bob blamed Jack because of the feud they had been having and because Jack just happened to have been hired by the circus to move some stuff during the parade and was quite near the elephant, Bob said Jack had driven over his foot. So much for forensic evidence eh, Noah?"

"The photograph didn't tell a lie though, did it? It's a pity it took Charles nine months to develop the photographs on that roll of film though. He was quite upset about it; he thought he had taken a bad picture getting an elephant on it instead of his beloved allotment." Noah laughed and Jim shook his head.

Sergeant Fredrick pointed to a lay-by near the farmyard gates. "Pull up here, Noah; don't drive into the farmyard – it looks as though they've just brought the cows in for milking. There's cow muck all over the place and we don't want it on the tyres. Those two Irish lads are over there and that looks like Martha Hunney as well. She's in her running kit and so is one of the lads."

"That'll be Patrick Murphy, Sarge. They're training for one of the country show fell races, except Martha won't be able to race for obvious reasons."

"Oh, and what would they be then?"

Constable Abrahams looked at Sergeant Fredrick nonplussed. "Well for one, she's a female."

"Get away with you, Noah, she never is, is she?" said Sergeant Fredrick sarcastically. "You wouldn't like a small wager on it by any chance, would you? I reckon that young woman has more about her than the village and this area give her credit for; how about a quid?"

"You're on. She's no more chance of running in one of those races than that carthorse over there running in the Derby."

The two police officers shook hands and then climbed out of the car and walked over to where the threesome was standing.

"Hello there, how can we help?" shouted Shaun in his high-pitched voice before they had entered the farmyard through the gate. Neither answered until they reached him. "Evening all, it's

CHAPTER 21

just a routine enquiry," commented Sergeant Fredrick, looking down at his left boot which now had a smearing of cow muck on it. He looked at each of the three in turn.

"Do you want a drink of something, officers, perhaps a cool drink on this fine evening?"

Constable Abrahams answered, "No thank you, sir, I'll get straight to the point. Can either of you two men recall the day that George Garvan was found by Mr Hunney at the side of the lane over there?" He turned to Martha and continued, "That's Miss Hunney's father, by the way."

Martha interjected, "It was my sister, Noah."

"Sorry, to be more precise, Sarah Hunney found him."

Patrick answered, "Oh that would be the day that the bull tossed that fella over the hedge."

"And how would you know that?" asked Sergeant Fredrick."

"He was strolling through the field before the one where the bull was, and he must have wandered through that one as well."

"That doesn't mean the bull tossed him over the hedge, does it, Mr Murphy?"

"No sir, but if Mr Garvan's rear end was checked, you could either rule the bull out or blame it, if he has marks on his back or posterior."

"A regular detective, aren't we, sir?" commented a slightly irate Constable Abrahams.

"We didn't see anyone else about, sir. Did we, McMullan? So it doesn't take a genius to work out that it must have been the bull."

"The point is, Mr Murphy, you and Mr McMullan were about, weren't you?"

"And so was I," exclaimed Martha.

Noah Abrahams' tone moderated. "Is that correct, Martha?"

Martha's eyes slitted and her nose wrinkled. "Of course it is, Noah Abrahams. Why should I tell you a lie?"

Sergeant Fredrick intervened. "On second thoughts, Mr McMullan, we will have a drink. I'll have a cool lemonade. What about you, Noah, what do you want?"

"I'm okay, thanks," answered Noah rather irately.

"Right, I'm on it now; do you want a drink, Martha?"

"I thought you'd never ask, Shaun. I'll have the same as Sergeant Fredrick, then I'll run home." Martha turned to the police officers and continued, "If that's alright with you."

"Don't forget me, McMullan or am I invisible? I'll have the same."

Martha laughed at Patrick's comment and said, "You look like you need one after that thrashing I've just given you."

"It's alright, Marta; I'm saving some for the race on Saturday. It's no good leaving your best in the training, you know."

"Well I was only going at half pace anyway, Murphy," Martha joked, "and the race is four days off, ample time to recover from a hard training run."

"I think not, Marta. You were trying," insisted Patrick.

While Martha and Patrick were discussing their training run, Sergeant Fredrick pulled Constable Abrahams to one side.

"Go easy on Martha, will you, Noah; she's not the lying type. We've absolutely no evidence to suggest those two had anything to do with Garvan's injuries. I'm more inclined to believe it was the bull, as bizarre as it seems."

"Okay, Sarge, fair enough. I'll apologise to Martha. I had to sound her out, though."

"How long have you known her, Noah? You're only about four years older than her, and you've been to her home often enough when you used to mate round with Oliver."

Noah felt slightly guilty at the thought of his questioning Martha's integrity. He called to her, "Can I have a word, Martha?"

She walked towards him and Sergeant Fredrick ambled away from the couple, taking a drink from Shaun who had just come from the farmhouse with six drinks of cool lemonade on a large, silver tray.

"McMullan, you're an idiot. Is that one of Lady Letherby's pieces of silverware?"

"Well, Murphy, I thought under the circumstances, with the visit of the constabulary, it was only fitting that we should use the posh stuff."

CHAPTER 21

"Yes, it's confirmed, you are an idiot."

"Have a cool drink, Patrick old son, obviously, the hard run and the sun has taken its toll on you, so I'll forgive you for calling me an idiot twice."

Patrick took a drink and said, "You'd better get that silver tray back where it's supposed to be, Shaun, before Lady Letherby finds it missing."

Sergeant Fredrick stood totally bemused at the Irishmen's conversation.

Constable Abrahams had apologised to Martha, and after she had finished the dregs of her lemonade she set off jogging across the field to her home. Quite unconsciously, Noah had also taken a drink from the tray and swigged it back in one gulp.

"I shouldn't think we will be troubling you two again regarding George Garvan. We bid you good evening then. Don't forget, lads, keep your noses clean," commented Sergeant Fredrick.

"Yes, sir, right you are, sir," Patrick and Shaun said in unison.

The Sergeant nodded to both of them and thanked Shaun for the lemonade. The two policemen walked back to the car. Jim Fredrick bent down and tugged at a clump of parched grass, pulled a fistful from it and wiped the cow muck off his shoe. He looked at Noah and nodded. "It's no good stinking the car out is it, Noah? Come on, let's report back to the Superintendent."

Martha arrived home, and sat on the bench in the back yard, untied her new shoes and said to herself, "Just the job, you'll do just dandy." Shep ran through the gate, came up to Martha and licked her salt-stained legs. She stroked the dog, tickling his ears at the same time.

A voice came from the outside the backyard gate. "Talking to yourself again, Martha?"

"Hello, Father, where have you just come from? Only talking to my new training shoes."

"I've had a stroll over the moor with the dog. I saw you at the farm, from up there. What did the police want?"

"Oh they were asking questions about George Garvan. I think they've come to the conclusion that Lord Letherby's bull tossed him over the hedge onto the roadside." Martha started laughing. "That's ironic, Father, isn't it? Most people think he's been beaten up by someone because of his filthy antics and really it's a bull that's sorted him out."

"They must know something more, Martha. I wonder if Garvan's come to. I'll nip down to see Sergeant Fredrick later this evening and ask him what he knows. Don't say anything to your mother or sister, Martha, until I come back from The Lamb, that's where he'll be after work for an hour anyway."

Martha changed the subject. "Do you think there's any chance of me running in the fell race at the show on Saturday, Father?"

"If I could swing it for you, you know I would Martha, but I've no clout with Josiah Leveridge; in fact, I've a score to settle with that feller and he knows it. So, no love, I don't think you have a cat-in-hell's chance of running the race on his land, but don't forget, Martha there's two more races locally."

A still positive Martha looked at her father and smiled. "I'll still go with my kit, all the same, Father, you never know."

Later that same evening Ted called in to see Jim Fredricks at The Lamb. Fredricks explained, "Don't worry, Ted, you're out of the frame. Superintendent Ramsden is happy to close the case after reading Garvan's medical report. The injuries are consistent with 'uninvited contact with a heavy beast' rather than any harm a human is capable of causing. So that's the end of the matter."

"That's a weight off my mind, Jim. Thanks for letting me know."

Chapter 22

The day of the first country show dawned warm and sunny, and Mort was busy challenging Josiah Leveridge to allow Martha to run the fell race.

"There's no girl ever going to run in a race on my land, and that's the end of it."

"What, are you afraid of Leveridge? Frightened that a wee stripling of a girl will beat some big macho males?"

"You'll be off my land if you carry on like that, Johnson."

"And you'll be barred from my café," retorted Mort.

"It's my land and that's that."

Mort shook his head and walked over to where Martha, Teddy, Sarah and Patrick were shouting enthusiastically at the tug-of-war competition between the young farmers and the mill team.

"There's no chance of you running, Martha," Mort shouted over the din. He pointed over to where Josiah Leveridge was standing and continued, "That old skinflint won't allow you to race on his land and what he says goes, and that's the fact of the matter."

"Well if you can't race, Marta, I'll not race either," said an angry Patrick.

"Don't be silly. You must do the race; you've trained for it. Don't let my situation stop you running."

"Our Martha's right, Patrick," said Sarah. "Don't let Mr Leveridge spoil your ambition."

"I'm not running and that's it," insisted Patrick. "We'll go for a training run after the show, if that's alright with you both."

Sarah was taken aback by Patrick's forceful attitude. She

couldn't help herself and kissed him in full view of all those standing watching the tug-of-war, whispering in his ear, "I love you, Patrick Murphy."

Instantly, Martha piped up, "Steady on, Sarah, don't swallow Patrick, we're going running after the show, and I don't want him weak at the knees!"

"Oh give over, Marta, I'll be fit enough to give you a good beating – like I would have done in the race," joked Patrick.

"We'll see about that at the Incleton show a week next Saturday."

Teddy, who had been quiet most of the afternoon, gently held Martha around the waist. "That's if you get to run, Honey. I hope you can, but there's a lot of opposition to you running any of the races, not least from the show organisers and landowners." He paused for a second and before anyone could comment he mused, "Though Lord Letherby might allow you to run, Martha. The entire fell race will be on his land, so no one can interfere with his decision."

"Lord Letherby isn't known for being a supporter of the feminist movement by any stretch of the imagination," interrupted Mort. "He's very old-fashioned in his views and not keen on change. Still, Patrick works for him, so he might be able to approach him."

"I might, but I know someone who he might listen to more than me," Patrick revealed.

"Who's that?" asked Sarah.

"Orla Rowley. Lord Letherby might listen to her, even though she is a woman."

"And what do you mean by that then, Patrick?" Martha demanded.

"He's not one to get into conversation much with females, that's all, but I've noticed him and Mrs Rowley talking together a few times so you never know, he might listen to her."

"Who's going to talk to Orla then?"

"Leave that to me, Martha. Ava knows Orla quite well; I'll ask Ava to have a word with her. She will do, I'm sure of it," bragged a confident Mort. "Anyway, I'll leave you young ones to it." He looked at his watch. "I promised Ava I'd meet her in the beer tent

CHAPTER 22

at three and it's five to now. I'll have a word with her, Martha, don't you worry."

In one accord, the twins said, "See you later, Mr Johnson." Teddy and Patrick both nodded at him. He lifted his left hand to shoulder height and nodded back.

"Well, won't you look at that fella McMullan? He has the rope wrapped round his chest, and holding it with one hand while eating a sarnie with the other. He's one greedy fella, that's all I can say."

Beatrice, who had been walking around the show with Delwyn, overheard Patrick and walked over to where the group were watching the tug-of-war. She remarked, "Yes, but the young farmers won the first tug and now Shaun's getting his strength back for the second round, Patrick."

He looked at her in disbelief and laughed. "He's as strong as a horse, Beatrice; he doesn't need to get his strength back. He just likes eating!"

"Well there's nothing wrong with that, Patrick Murphy," she retorted.

"Anyway, blow you, Patrick, we want the mill to win, don't we, girls?" Martha didn't give anyone the time to answer and shouted raucously, "Come on, Bradshaw's, put your backs into it!" Turning to the girls she said, "It's a pity Roger Thompson has lost all that weight, we haven't the fire power in our team now. But he might not finish last in the fell race this time after losing weight. We might have runners from the mill in the first three this year, especially with Jonny and David both running."

Martha looked at Patrick. "Are you sure you don't want to run, Patrick? You've still got time to enter, you know."

"No, I'm not doing it, Marta, and that's the end of it."

The young farmers won the tug of war three nil. Jonny Jones approached Shaun and asked, "Do you fancy a run in the fell race, Shaun?"

"I don't think so, I'm built for comfort not for pain; I'm quite good at dishing it out though!" He laughed and added, "Although I am going to have a do at the little competition next Saturday down by the lake." He pointed to Patrick. "I reckon I'll beat yon Murphy."

"Well, why don't you do the fell race as a bit of training then?"

"I think I will then. I've got me shorts and me boots so I think I'll get round it. How much is it to enter, Jonny?"

"A shilling. Come on, let's go and enter, there's only fifteen minutes to the start."

"I'll be right on it with you. I'll go and tell Beatrice, and then she won't miss me. You know how it is with girls!"

At that moment, Shirley Philips tapped Jonny on the right shoulder and dodged to the right, as he turned around. "Hello, handsome."

Jonny blushed. Shaun winked at him. "See you at the race-entry tent," and then lumbered over toward Beatrice.

"You make sure you don't overdo it, lover boy, but make sure you beat David Sanderson if no one else," Shirley ordered Jonny.

"Shirley, David's next to favourite. I know I beat him in the works' sports, but this race is a different kettle of fish altogether!"

"Just do your best, lover boy."

Jonny kissed Shirley and then ran over to the race-entry tent where Shaun was waiting to pay his entry fee.

"Are you sure you're fit to run, lad?" asked a wizened old farmer taking the entries. "You look a lot on the bulky side to me."

"Sir, I can assure you I'm in prime fitness and raring to go."

"Aye, and I do believe you've given that Blarney Stone a right good kiss as well, lad. That'll be a shilling. Still, you'll probably roll well down the hill. Next."

David Sanderson placed his shilling on the table, signed his name and then turned to Shaun. "He means no harm, Shaun, it's just the way he is."

"No need to apologise on his behalf, David, there's no offence taken."

Patrick had strolled over to the tent where Shaun was entering the race. "This is too much, Sarah; I'm not having that big lump McMullan being the first man from Ireland running in a fell race over here – I'll have to do it now."

CHAPTER 22

Sarah, delighted that Patrick had changed his mind, said, "Good on you, Patrick, show them what you can do."

Martha echoed, "Yes, you get stuck in, and then I'll know where I might have finished."

The race was about to start.

The starter called out over the loudspeaker, "To your marks. Set. Go." Jonny set off like a scared rabbit on the hard rutted ground with David Sanderson close behind.

"Too fast," Patrick thought and settled in at about fifteenth place in the field of twenty-five, with Shaun lumbering on at the back.

After six hundred yards and approaching the first short craggy climb, the favourite, Sam Kendal, and Bob Rand the sheep farmer from Westmorland in his first Lancastrian race, were closing in on the two leaders; twenty yards off the pace, to be precise, and running comfortably. Arthur Beardsworth was a few yards further back and he too was moving easily. Patrick moved gradually up to tenth place. The scramble up the crag saw the field of runners spread out quickly, with Sam Kendal now at the head of the field. Apart from Arthur Beardsworth, no one had challenged Sam during the past two years in any of the trio of races, and once in the lead, it was almost inevitable he would win.

"He's leading again, Ted," commented Mort, looking through his field glasses.

"Not worth a bet at that price though, Mort. Three to one on. You'd get next to nowt in return and he could fall at that."

"It's not the National, Ted."

"You know what I mean, Mort. It's supposed to be a right rough course underfoot, you can guarantee someone will come a cropper and it might be him."

"No, not Sam, he's more sure footed than a mountain goat. In fact, he looks a bit like one with that tuft of hair shooting out his vest." Mort raised his field glasses up to his eyes and said, "Eh up, you're right, Ted, someone has come a cropper, they're limping back, I think they've blood on their face. I'd better tell the first aid woman to get ready."

"Can you see who it is, Mr Johnson?" asked Sarah anxiously.

"Don't fret, Sarah, it's not Patrick Murphy. It looks like little David Sanderson."

"I'll run and tell Floella to expect a casualty then. Does he look badly hurt?"

"He's upright and limping on, so he mustn't be too badly injured." Before Mort could finished answering, Sarah had sprinted off to the first aid tent. "It looks like your Martha has gone to help him. She's moving faster than a gazelle towards him," Mort carried on with his commentary. "Yes, she's reached him and she's got his arm around her shoulders. Good girl, Martha"

"That's my girl," Ted boasted proudly. "She'll help anyone."

Teddy was standing by Ted's side, he smiled and thought, 'That's right, and best of all – she's mine, I've got her now.'

"What have you done, David? Lean on me."

"I got my foot wedged between two rocks, Martha, and then I fell and banged my nut."

"Did you damage the rock with your head?" Martha joked and gave David her handkerchief. "Here, put my hanky on that gash and push it tight, that'll stop it bleeding."

David winced and then managed to laugh. "I split the rock in two! I was going well too. Jonny looks good, although Sam Kendal has just passed him and gone into the lead. That boyfriend of your Sarah's seems easy as well. He was only about sixty yards down."

"Yes, but that's about two hundred when the course flattens out. You will need to see Floella when you get back, she'll know what's wrong with your foot. It might be a trip to the hospital for you, David."

"Don't say that, Martha, I've got a date tonight."

"You're a dark horse, David Sanderson, who's it with?"

"You won't tell anyone, will you, Martha, if I tell you?"

"Of course I will, I can't keep anything like that a secret!"

"Oh alright then, it's Lydia."

Martha couldn't believe her ears. "Lydia," she bawled out. "How did that come about, David?"

CHAPTER 22

"I don't know; we seem to get on well together, so I decided to ask her to the pictures and she said yes."

"Flippin' heck, David. It's a bit of a mis-match, isn't it? Mill boy and mill owner's niece! You're brave, aren't you?"

"You know as well as I do, Martha Hunney, if you don't try you don't succeed! I expect to be racing against you in one of these fell races one day."

They reached the first aid tent. Martha in her boisterous manner shouted, "Here's the first casualty of the day, Floella. David needs your best attention, he has a date tonight, so can you put him together again?"

"Thank you, Martha. I hope to see you at work on Monday."

"Or maybe the pictures tonight." She laughed and ran over to Teddy who was standing close to the finish line.

"We should be able to see them coming off Rivestone Pike in about three minutes, Teddy, if my timing is correct by my Timex. It'll be six minutes to the finish then," commented Martha and went to join her father and Mort.

"Can I have a look through your glasses, Mr Johnson? Sarah's biting her nails down to the bone over there, Father, worrying about Patrick; she thinks he's going to come a cropper. She's nowt to worry about, though; he's like a mountain goat. I should know, I've trained with him enough."

"Here, Martha, your eyes are better than mine, give us a commentary."

Martha placed Mort's field glasses to her eyes and reverted to her secret Raymond Glendenning running commentary.

"Here we are at Josiah Leveridge's stadium, eagerly anticipating the imminent arrival of the leaders in the annual Rivestone Pike fell race. There has been one casualty already – I hasten to add – not fatal. Oh, wait a second, yes; yes I can see two figures silhouetted against the moorland backdrop speeding toward the five hundred yards mark where a steep grassy descent leads to the long undulating run to the finish."

"Who are they, Martha?" her father asked anxiously, more concerned about the each-way bet he had placed on Jonny Jones at six to one, rather than who was going to win, or for that matter what place Patrick would finish in.

Martha continued her commentary, "It's last year's two leading runners, Arthur Beardsworth and Sam Kendal, going shoulder to shoulder. Wait a moment; two more athletes have appeared on the horizon, with a third a few yards behind. I will let you know as soon as I have identified them. This is unbelievable; I can't believe what I'm seeing. Roger Thompson, and Bob Rand going neck and neck, and Jonny Jones chasing those two."

"You're having us on, Martha. Roger Thompson? Never."

"Well it is. Here have a look for yourself, Father."

Ted took the field glasses from his daughter. "Blimey, it is Roger. Well I hope young Jonny catches them both; I've got a pound each way riding on him." Ted passed the field glasses back to Martha. "Here, carry on with your commentary, Martha."

"Sam Kendal is pulling away from Arthur. He looks to be about thirty yards in front, near the bottom of the descent. Bob Rand has pulled clear of Roger, Jonny has passed him as well and he looks like he's gaining on Bob now."

Ted shouted, "Come on, Jonny; make me a bit for tonight in The Lamb! I'll buy you a drink, Mort, if he finishes third."

"It's your round anyway, Ted," Mort replied laconically.

"Well, I'll buy you two. Is he still catching him, Martha?"

"Catching him, Father? He's passed him and now he's chasing Arthur."

"You're not getting away from me this year," Arthur Beardsworth gasped, and started to chase Sam Kendal down. They were both now on the last rutted and undulating six hundred yards run-in to the finish. Jonny Jones was a further thirty-five yards behind them and had a few yards of tricky descent to negotiate. Sam glanced back and Arthur could see he looked distressed. Arthur, his eyes burning into Sam's back, realised that this was it – his big chance. He ratcheted his pace up and gradually pulled to within touching distance of his adversary. A moment later, Arthur fell to the ground, only for a split second, but to him, it seemed like an eternity. He had tripped over a small rock. He rolled over, pushed

CHAPTER 22

himself up off the ground and was on his feet again but lagged twenty-five yards behind Sam Kendal.

Jonny, meanwhile, had closed down swiftly on the leading pair and leapt over Arthur as he set off after the leader. Sam Kendal had found something extra and started pulling away from his pursuers.

"Arthur's fallen and Jonny's passed him and Sam Kendal's pulling away again. Arthur's up again. He seems okay and he's chasing them both."

"Come on, Jonny," Ted shouted again. "Where's Roger Thompson, Martha?"

"He's been passed by two others, and I think one of them is Patrick."

Sarah squealed with delight. "Come on, Patrick. Isn't he doing well, Father?"

"Not bad for his first run. As long as he doesn't catch Jonny and knock him back to fourth."

"There's not much chance of that, Father, Patrick's about two hundred yards behind and Jonny has nearly caught Sam, but Arthur is only about fifteen yards behind Jonny."

Jonny passed a flagging Sam and started pulling away. With three hundred yards to go, he was looking the likely winner. Seizing his chance, Arthur sprinted past Sam Kendal, his stride lengthening, his knees nearly touching his chest, and his arms pumping like pistons. In Arthur's sights, Jonny was now in overdrive and finishing like a half-miler but ten seconds later he was swimming in a sea of lactic acid. Arthur swept past him and with arms aloft broke through the finishing tape to rousing applause from the sizable crowd that had gathered to see the grand finale. Moments later, Jonny finished with a wrecked Sam Kendal coming in third.

"Come on, Patrick," shouted Martha and Sarah simultaneously. A moment later Sarah ran over to a prostrate Patrick, fell on her knees, and smothered him in kisses. He gasped and then laughed.

"Remind me not to bother doing another race ever again. Oh, that was painful. Who won, Sarah?"

"That big head, Arthur Beardsworth."

Martha walked slowly over to where Patrick and Sarah were kneeling on the ground. "Well done, Patrick," she laughed and then joked, "I take it you won't be training with me later?"

"No, afraid not, Marta. It's the pictures tonight with your lovely sister and then a good night's sleep."

Arthur Beardsworth came swaggering past.

"Well done, Arthur, it's about time you won a race, you've been threatening to for long enough," Martha remarked.

"There's one thing for certain, Martha Hunney, you'll never win one, or finish one for that matter, will you?" He smirked, laughed and strutted away.

Sarah, irate at Arthur's comments to her twin, insisted, "But you will do another race, Patrick, and put that big head in his place."

"Well, I'd better get some more training done then. We'll have to run together twice a week, Marta, and then I'll do a couple on my own." He happened to glance across toward the finishing line. "Well will ya look at that fella, he's actually going to finish."

Shaun approached the finishing line, hands held aloft, and as he finished, took a bow. Patrick scrambled up off the ground and jogged over to him.

"Well done, big fella. I didn't know you had it in you."

"Oh, it was just a light training session for next Saturday, Murphy."

"So we're definitely going to do the competition then? Are you sure the others are keen to do it, Shaun?"

Jonny had dragged himself off the ground with Shirley's aid and was chatting to David Sanderson and Martha. Shaun shouted over to the group, "Are you all okay for next Saturday then?"

Jonny assumed an Irish accent, "To be sure we are, aren't we, lads and lasses?"

"Eight o'clock at the lake – all of us – for an eight fifteen start," Martha quickly insisted.

Shaun, who was now being held up by Beatrice because his legs had started to wobble, walked gingerly over to the others. Patrick had already joined them and was holding hands with Sarah.

CHAPTER 22

"I'll be timekeeper, and start official starter and finish official finisher with Beatrice. If that's alright with you, Beatrice?" asked Teddy.

"Oh no, I'm having a go. I'm a good swimmer and cyclist. No good at running though, but I'll manage two miles."

"I thought you were joking when you said you would do it." Martha looked surprised.

"Incorrect, Martha. I said I would do it and I will. Shaun and I will win as a team as well. Best overall time for pairs, that is."

"Oh, and who will be in my team? Teddy's not doing it and Sarah will be Patrick's partner." Martha shouted over to David, "Will you be in my team next Saturday, David?"

"Thanks for asking me, Martha, but I'm with Lydia."

There was a look of disbelief on Martha's face, while Sarah, Jonny and Beatrice started laughing. Patrick and Shaun looked on blankly and wondered why they were laughing.

"What's the crack, Marta? How's it they're laughing and you aren't?" Patrick asked.

"Because they are a bunch of ignoramuses and I've no partner," Martha replied, deflated. "I'll just have to do it by myself and win it too."

"Come off it, Martha. Do you honestly think you can beat Patrick and me?" her sister asked.

"You might be in front of me after the bike ride, but you'll still be running on Sunday! It's not a hundred yards, you know, it's an undulating two miles!"

"Very funny, Martha, we'll see won't we?"

"Yes, we will. Come on, it's time for the prize giving. What a good run by Jonny and you did really well for your first fell race, Patrick."

"What about me, Marta, how did I do?"

Martha looked at Shaun and smiled. "You finished, Shaun. Well done," and then said sulkily, "At least you got to start in the first place."

Walking to the presentation tent, Teddy linked arms with Martha. "Honey, don't be too downhearted. Next Saturday is just a bit of fun, you need to keep focused on the two remaining fell races.

"But what if I don't get to a race, Teddy?"

"Listen, Honey. I'm certain you will be able to race at least one of them. I was talking to Shaun and he says that for some reason or another Orla Rowley has a lot of influence with Lord Letherby, and after Ava has had a word or two with her, I'm sure Mrs Rowley could sway it for you to run on his Lordship's land. So stop bothering yourself about Saturday's competition, go and enjoy it, it's just a bit of fun. Anyway, it'll be a good training session for you."

Leaving the country show behind they wandered toward Martha's house in the early evening light. They arrived at the front door and Teddy kissed Martha but before leaving her, said, "See you later, Honey. It's a very good picture tonight, 'Seven Year Hitch'."

"Is James Dean in it by any chance, Teddy?"

"As a matter of fact, he's not, Marilyn Monroe is, though." Teddy kissed his sweetheart again and walked back toward the village.

Martha watched him disappear and then rushed through the door, bounded upstairs, threw herself on her bed and wept. Her mother was in Oliver's bedroom dusting, and hearing Martha she promptly tapped on the bedroom door. "Are you all right, Martha love, what-in-ever's to do?"

Martha sniffled and replied, "No, Mother, I'm not alright really."

"Can I come in, Honey?"

"Not yet, Mother, give me a few minutes."

"OK love. Will you be wanting some tea before you go to the pictures?"

"I'm going for a run in a few minutes, Mother. I'll have some when I come back." But Martha couldn't hold back any longer; she blurted out, "It's Teddy, Mother, he'll be going away for at least three years and I don't think I can cope without him."

Ruth opened the bedroom door and sat on the bed next to her

CHAPTER 22

daughter. "Why on earth is Teddy going away?"

Martha wiped her eyes. "He's got an interview at Cambridge, for mathematics. If he passes the interview – and he will – then I'll only see him at Christmas, and a few weeks in summer. I'll miss him so much, Mother."

Martha hesitated for a moment and then looked her mother full in the face. "Teddy says he wants to marry me when he has finished his studies. He said he's going to ask Father if we can get engaged."

Her mother gently put her arms around Martha and said, "Oh Martha love, that's a lovely thing for Teddy to want, but is he being realistic?"

"We love each other, Mother. Teddy wants to be honourable and do the right thing. He's thinking of our future together. The education he's bound to get at a place like Cambridge University will set him up for a very good career after he finishes there. I know that but I don't want to be like Miranda though, hanging on for years and years."

"Miranda's different, Honey. Jack's always away at sea and shows no intention of giving up that life yet. You've already told me Teddy wants to marry you as soon as he finishes his studies. If he's a man of his word he will do just that."

"He will, Mother, I'm sure, and I'm sure I want to marry him."

"Dry your eyes, Honey love, and go for your run; you'll feel a lot better for it. I'll have a word with your father then when Teddy does ask him he won't collapse with shock." Martha managed a short giggle; her mother smiled, gave her daughter a hug and left the bedroom, going downstairs into the kitchen. Martha swiftly changed into her shorts and tee shirt, walked round the back of the cottage, pulled her running shoes on, and set off across the field to Wickelton Pike.

Not usually part of Martha's thinking, she decided to have an easy run. She took the run comfortably, not pushing on any part of the route, and walking most of the climb up to Wickelton Pike. Even Shep seemed to run and chase the customary stick that Martha threw for him at a leisurely pace. She arrived home, her head clear of worries and all the anxieties caused by the events of the last few weeks, and looked forward to spending an evening at the pictures with Teddy. Martha sat on the bench in the backyard and took her shoes off, opening the laces for once instead of dragging them off still fastened. Shep had slumped down at her feet and Martha was tickling his ears as the back door opened and her father walked out, sitting beside her without saying a word. He had a serious look on his face as he regarded his daughter. Martha's heart sank but his face brightened into a smile and he said quietly, "Your mother has had a word with me regarding Edward's intentions toward you. I've nothing at all against him; he's a fine, decent, bright young man. I will have to have a serious talk with you both though, once he decides to talk to me about his intentions. That's all I have to say on the matter, apart from I hope Teddy does get the chance to further his education. There's nothing wrong with him working at Gaskells but, with a brain like he's got, he needs the opportunity to use it to its full potential and hopefully he'll get a professional career out of it."

Martha gave her father a kiss on the cheek and then went to get ready for her night out with Teddy. After the family had had their evening meal, which for Martha was a swift affair, she walked into the village with Sarah.

"Guess what? Teddy is going to ask Father if we can get engaged."

Sarah was shocked and so overcome with emotion and excitement that she screamed out loud as she held tightly onto her sister's arm. "Martha Hunney, are you having me on? Is it true? No, it's one of your jokes; you're playing one of your pranks on me! Oh Honey, when is Teddy going to ask Father about you getting engaged? Father will keel over with shock. Oh, I hope he doesn't give Teddy the cold shoulder and tell him where to go."

"There's no need to worry, Sur. Mother has had a word with Father, and Father has had a word with me, and everything is okay. Father won't be in shock and keel over." Martha laughed at the thought of her father fainting with shock and Sarah who had had the same thought laughed along with her.

CHAPTER 22

"We won't be getting married for a few years though, Sur."

Sarah looked perplexed and questioned, "Why ever not? I hope you two aren't going to be like Miranda and Jack Seymour, or you'll never get hitched."

"No Sarah, I've told you, Teddy's going to go to Cambridge for an interview. You know how brainy he is at mathematics, well he got a golden opportunity to study there. He'll get sponsorship you know."

"But how long will he be there?"

"Three years, maybe more, but he'll be coming home regularly, summer and Christmas and Easter probably."

"Teddy and Marshall Broadbent were both brain boxes at school. It looks like they'll be going at the same time, just different courses. How do you think you will manage without Teddy, Honey? I know you've only been courting a couple of months but you must mean so much to each other to be getting engaged."

"We love each other and that's the bond that will see us through. That's enough – it will have to be. I'll carry on working and running, and we'll write to each other on a regular basis, and talk to each other on the telephone. And I'll save up like mad."

Sarah hugged her sister again. "I hope everything turns out well for you, Martha." She paused for a moment, laughed and then said, "I wonder when Patrick will ask to marry me?"

"Who knows?" Martha answered.

Sarah sighed, "Well I, for one, don't. I think it will be Oliver and Scarlett next."

Martha changed the subject. "I don't really fancy the pictures tonight, Sur, I'm going to ask Teddy if he wants to stay in the village instead. We might even go into The Lamb, not in the same room as Father though. I'll have a glass of lemonade, and Teddy can have a pint of bitter, that's what he drinks when he's out with Harry Smith."

"I don't fancy the pictures tonight myself, Martha. Have I to ask Patrick if he wants to have a drink in The Lamb as well? He drinks stout and so does Shaun; it's an Irish thing I think."

"Yes, you ask Patrick and maybe Shaun and Beatty as well.

He's funny, Shaun, isn't he, Sarah?" They both laughed.

"You can say that again. I've never met anyone like him, he's tough as well. He sorted that bully Colin Bellshaw out and no messing. Patrick's got good friends in him and Beatty. Shaun's a decent bloke."

The sisters reached the bus stop and as they were a few minutes early they sat on a bench across the road on the village green. Beatrice was next to arrive.

"Do you fancy going into The Lamb tonight instead of the pictures, Beatty?

"Not really, Martha, I fancy watching the film. It's a romantic comedy; it might bring out Shaun's romantic side with a bit of luck." Beatrice gave the twins a smile and then said, "If you know what I mean!"

"Yes, Beatty and it might bring out his even funnier side. Funnier than what he already is."

"I hope not. Do you know he's only kissed me twice and both times it was on the cheek." Beatrice sighed. "He's been closer to Colin Bellshaw than me."

"Yes, but that's because he was protecting us from that bully."

"I suppose so."

The familiar sound of the motorcycle could be heard approaching fast.

"Here come the Irish," stated Martha. "I hope Teddy isn't too long. Sarah's going to ask Patrick if he wants to go to The Lamb. Beatty, are you sure about the pictures?"

"I'm sure."

"Hello, ladies," Shaun shouted before he dismounted the motorcycle. "It's good to see you two lovely Colleens, and you my loveliest rose."

All three girls blushed. "You're a right flanneller you are, Shaun McMullan; everyone says you kissed the Blarney Stone."

"I'd rather kiss you, my Rose of Sharon."

Beatty leapt off the bench and before Shaun had time to climb off the motorcycle, threw her arms round Shaun's neck and said, "Now's your chance, big boy." She pressed her lips hard onto his

CHAPTER 22

and Shaun responded with gusto.

Patrick had already climbed off the motorcycle and stood smiling down at Sarah. The sisters stared boggle-eyed with their mouths wide open at Beatrice's brash and forward manner. Patrick laughed, "Well, won't you look at that? McMullan's truly stuck for words for the first time in his life. He'll have to come up for oxygen shortly or he'll smother."

Teddy strolled across the road to where Martha was sitting, as she noticed him he leapt off the bench and grabbed him; thrusting both hands round his neck she kissed him on the lips and told him she loved him. "What's brought this on, Honey?" he asked.

"You, Teddy Moore! You're my man, and my Father knows all about your intentions toward me. Mother told him so that he wouldn't keel over with shock."

"Oh, and who told your mum, Martha? As if I didn't know."

"I had to. I was so upset when you left me this afternoon, my mother heard me crying. I had to tell her about you going to university."

"I haven't gone yet, Martha."

"Yes, but you will, I'm certain of that, Teddy."

Sarah intervened, "The bus is coming. Are you coming to the pictures? Patrick wants to and so does Shaun and Beatty so I'm going with Patrick."

"I don't want to go, Teddy. Do you want to go to The Lamb with me?"

"Of course I do if that's what you want, Honey. I didn't fancy that picture after all when I thought about it."

Chapter 23

The following weekend, the friends had gathered together at the lakeside and readied themselves for action. They laid clothes out ready to put on over their swimming costumes as they emerged from the water after their swim which was the first part of their competition. Each of them had a pair of plimsolls except for Shaun who had brought his boots for, as he said, 'traction on the rolling surface'.

Their bicycles where leant against trees nearby ready to use as they ran from the lake. They doused themselves and each other in the cool water for a couple of minutes and then were ready to go.

The event began with Teddy shouting, "On your marks. Set. Go!"

They all darted from the side of the lake and splashed into the cool water. Shaun set off as if he were taking part in a hundred yards freestyle final across the three hundred yards stretch of water. No one headed him across the lake or all the way back. He climbed out of the water a minute in front of the next finisher, donned his baggy shorts and tee-shirt, dragged his boots onto wet feet, and set off on the bicycle he had borrowed from Scarlett.

Lydia Burton was next out and a few seconds later Sarah dragged herself from the water; both wasted no time pulling on shorts, tee-shirts and plimsolls. Last out of the water was Martha. She was a poor swimmer but had managed to keep her time deficit down to only four minutes behind Shaun. She had calculated before the competition started that she could possibly catch up to him somewhere near the end of the first lap of the run.

The bike ride was about five miles over three laps around the

CHAPTER 23

lake; taking into account three detours through the hamlet at the far side of the lake and through the wooded area located two hundred yards after the last cottage on the east side of the hamlet. Although Lydia was by far the quickest cyclist on the road, she struggled along the rugged rise and fall of the course. There were only three hundred yards of road on each lap and Lydia only gained a maximum of ten seconds on each one. After the first lap of the bike ride, Martha had moved up to sixth place, she had passed Beatrice and was gaining on both Jonny Jones and Patrick. She knew that she had to gain as much time as possible on those two or she would have a right royal battle to finish in front of them. She thought Jonny would be faster on the two mile run but she didn't know how she would fair against Patrick.

"Come on, Shaun, you were two minutes in front of Lydia after the first lap; keep it going."

"No problem to be sure, Teddy. I'm just warming up; I'll soon be in overdrive. How far is Murphy behind me? Am I going to lap him?"

Teddy shouted, "About four minutes," before Shaun went out of earshot. He took his left hand off the handlebars, raised his arm in acknowledgment and fell off his bike. No sooner was he on the ground than he clambered back up and was on his way again.

Martha had gained on, and passed, Jonny half way round the third lap. Patrick was a minute in front of her but she was still three minutes behind Sarah and was losing time to her. Three hundred yards later, Martha caught up with Patrick who was running with his bike thrown across his shoulder. Martha rode straight past him.

"Thanks for asking, Marta. I've got a puncture in my tyre," Patrick gasped.

Martha shouted back, "I gathered that. You wouldn't have one anywhere else."

"Very funny, Marta. I'll see you on the run."

Speeding off, Martha said to herself, 'I think not, Patrick Murphy.'

"Hard luck, Patrick, you've only about two hundred and fifty yards and then you're on the run," Jonny said as he too passed him.

Patrick called out, "I'll see you there then."

Jonny laughed to himself and thought, 'If you can't beat me in a fell race you're not going to beat me over two miles, mate.'

Surprisingly, Sarah had closed the gap on Lydia and the two were only a few yards behind Shaun at the changeover point.

"Come on, Lydia, you can beat these two over two miles easy," shouted David Sanderson.

"Don't be so sure of that, David. I can manage two miles you know. I did four in the fell race," yelled Shaun.

"That's true, Shaun, but you were timed with a calendar, not with a stopwatch."

"Hey – less of the funnies, David, that's Shaun's department!"

Shaun shouted back, "I heard that! Very funny, Sarah. I'm off. I'll see you at the finish, take a good look at my back because that's all you're going to see until I cross the line."

Within half a mile both Sarah and Lydia had passed Shaun as he slowed to a snail's pace. "It's all right, girls," he gasped, "I'm gathering myself for a final push."

Lydia turned and cried, "Yes, we believe you, McMullan," and promptly tripped over a tree root and plummeted to the ground dragging Sarah with her.

Shaun immediately quipped, "It's a good job I slowed down for you ladies, so it is. Here let me help you up like the gentleman I am."

They both clambered to their feet with Shaun entangled amongst them. Speeding up alongside, Jonny asked mischievously, "Aye aye, what's going on here then?" Seeing that they were all okay he looked behind, saw Martha looming up behind him, and sped off.

Martha quickly caught up with the trio who had started running again. She swerved around her sister, slapping her backside as she passed. "See you at the finish, Sur. Don't be last!" Sarah ignored Martha; she had set her sights on beating Lydia and Shaun, and wasn't concerned with her sister's performance. After the first

CHAPTER 23

mile of the course, Jonny was leading and pulling clear of Martha again.

Patrick had passed the threesome, who were in close proximity to each other with Lydia just ahead. Another four hundred yards further on and he had reached and swiftly passed Martha who had started to labour.

Further up, Jonny turned around in the clearing of a wooded area expecting to see Martha but was shocked to see Patrick instead. He started to accelerate but his legs were feeling leaden and he couldn't maintain his pace. He began to fade visibly but managed to hold Patrick off until three-hundred yards before the end of the race.

Patrick swept past the flagging Jonny and then a rejuvenated Martha also passed him a few seconds later. She tried to catch Patrick but he was far too fast for her and he pulled away to win comfortably by fifty yards.

"That was great fun, so it was," laughed a happy, smiling Patrick.

"Oh, I enjoyed that. What happened to you, Jonny? I thought you had it in the bag."

"I ran out of steam, Martha. I thought I would have been the fastest on the run, but my legs packed up on me. It's strange what the swimming and the cycling can do to you, don't you think?"

"Well, I've never done anything like this before. You never know it might catch on in time. What do you think, Patrick?"

"Could do. What's up with Beatrice? It looks like she's hurt herself."

They walked over to where Beatrice sat at the water's edge with her left leg dangling in up to her shin. Martha asked, "What's happened, Beatty?"

"I climbed onto my bike, my foot slipped off the pedal, and that was the end of my race. I think I've twisted my ankle. It's swollen up anyway. I thought that if the water in your well can make things better then so can this water."

"Come up to our house when Shaun's finished and stick your foot in the well water. That'll definitely heal it, no problem. Do you think Shaun will take Beatty on the motorbike if you walk up with Sarah, Patrick?"

"Of course he will, Marta, they're sweethearts after all, aren't they?" Patrick turned to see Sarah approaching the finish. "Come on, Sarah that's my girl, well done."

He ran to her and she grabbed hold of him gasping, "Never again. Shoot me if I ever agree to do something like this again. I'll stick to cycling and sewing in future."

"You've done marvellous just managing to complete it. And we've won the couples between us!"

"Oh, that's good, Patrick, we beat Martha, and Lydia! Great, Martha won't be able to brag too much. How did you do?"

"First past the post. Only just though. Your Marta wasn't so far behind me and Jonny just behind her."

Sarah kissed Patrick and said, "Well done," then slumped to the ground and lay flat out. "Will you get me some water please, Patrick, and splash it over me. I'm boiling."

Patrick took a water bottle from his bicycle and said to her, "Here, have a drink, and then I'll fill it up from the lake and pour it on you."

She took the bottle, had a long drink and then said, "Don't you dare pour it on me, just sprinkle it over me."

"McMullan's here with Lydia. Look at the state of him! He's all but hanging on to her." He shouted, "Come on, Shaun what kept you?"

"I think we must have done three laps of the running, haven't we, Lydia?"

Lydia laughed. "Which school did you go to, Shaun? I only counted two."

"It must have been that bang on the head when I fell off Scarlett's bike. Anyway, how did you go on, Murphy?"

"First. And Sarah and I were the first couple. Your team didn't finish. Beatrice has her foot in the water over there. She's hurt herself."

Shaun left Lydia talking to David and Patrick, and staggered over to Beatrice.

CHAPTER 23

"How are you, Beatty? What's the problem with your leg?"

"It's my ankle, Shaun, it's all swollen."

"I'll take you to the hospital on the motorbike, Beatty. Straightaway."

"No, take me to Martha's well and that water will make it better. She swears by it."

"That's blarney; it's just a coincidence. I don't believe in those things at all." He paused for a moment and continued, "Although my Nan can set a bone without any hospital treatment. She mended my arm when I fell off a rope swing and broke it. Isn't that right, Murphy?"

Patrick raised his dark eyebrows. "Just take Beatty to the well, Shaun, if that's what she wants. I'll run and get the motorbike."

"Right you are, Patrick. I'll help Beatty up." Shaun bent over her, saying, "Let me take your weight, Beatty, you rest on me."

"No, I'll stay down here until Patrick gets back. You sit here right next to me, handsome, and keep me company. It's getting hot now and the others will want to be getting off. By the way, how did you go on, Shaun, did you finish alright?"

"I could have won it if I hadn't fallen off my bike."

Martha laughed, "In your wildest dreams, Shaun McMullan. You were nearly four minutes in front at one point and still managed to finish last."

"Joint last with Lydia, if you don't mind, and that's only because I fell off the bicycle."

The others laughed at his assurances and set off on their way.

Martha and Sarah rode steadily home chatting about the morning's events. Meanwhile, Patrick arrived back with the motorbike.

"Come on, Beatty, I'll help you up. Rest your arm round my neck and I'll take your weight." Shaun literally picked Beatrice off her feet and sat her on the pillion of the motorbike. Ten minutes later she was sitting on the second bottom step of the well with her foot immersed in the water up to her calf.

Patrick had made his way there to see Sarah, and while he was waiting for her to get cleaned up and change into a summer frock,

Martha made arrangements to train with him during the following week. They arranged to run on Monday and Wednesday evenings.

Martha was hopeful she could race up to Tockton Beacon at the Incleton show on Saturday but if the weather stayed fine, Patrick would be haymaking and wouldn't be able to race at all.

Chapter 24

"Hello David, has your leg recovered? Are you racing?"

"I'm going to set off slower and finish this time, Martha. I've managed a couple of runs this week so I should be alright. So, yes I am having a go. What about you?"

"My father has just gone to the competition tent to see what the job is. He knows one of the organising committee and he's going to see if they'll let me race."

"I don't see why you shouldn't; you've definitely got the stamina. You proved that last Saturday. Jonny's still smarting about you beating him."

Martha stood with hands on hips, long lean legs astride, chin jutted out. "Well, he ran out of steam. He did that at Josiah Leveridge's a couple of weeks ago and missed a chance of winning as well as beating Arthur Beardsworth. He should have had more porridge for his breakfast."

She spread her hands apart and made a huge circle with them as she continued, "Arthur Beardsworth – the big head! Anyway, I've told Jonny to have more to eat for breakfast on the morning of a race. He works hard all week and needs something extra in him when's he's racing, for extra energy. It's not a half mile flat race; it's a three and a half mile gruelling hill race."

"You might make a good coach one day, Martha."

"I'd rather get the chance to be a good fell runner, David. That's what I really want a chance at, that's all." Martha pointed across the show field. "Look, here's Jonny now with Shirley. Hiya, Shirley. Hiya, Jonny. Are you raring to go?"

"Hiya, Martha. I've taken your advice and had more porridge

for breakfast. Only trouble is I feel a bit bloated."

David laughed. "You've an hour and a half before the race, Jonny, you should be okay by then. Just beat Arthur is all we ask. I won't, but I'm still running."

"I don't know; it's a rougher course this one and goes a bit further than the last one."

Martha interjected, "And you're two weeks fitter, Jonny, with no injuries. Just get out there and give it a good go. Hopefully, I'll be chasing you."

Shirley smiled and poked Martha in her side. "Oi, steady on, Martha, he's my man, don't you go chasing after him."

Martha giggled and replied, "Don't worry, Shirley, I've got Teddy. He's my man."

"Well, where is Teddy? I haven't seen him for a couple of days."

"He hasn't come back from Cambridge yet. He was due this morning but the train broke down and he's not likely to be back until later this evening."

"Oh, and what's he been doing in Cambridge?"

"Nothing to do with you," Martha replied curtly with her nose in the air. She walked away from the group and made her way towards the competition tent. Ted walked out of the entrance, cap in one hand and scratching his head with the other.

"They're having a meeting, Martha, and a vote to see if you can run."

Martha interrupted, "Race, Father, race."

"I know you're nervous, Martha, but be civil."

"Yes, Father, sorry."

"They're taking it seriously, you know. They'll have a vote when the meeting's finished."

Ten minutes passed then Jack Shearsmith, the chief steward, called Ted back into the tent. "Sit down, Ted, here have a drink, it's hot out there. It'll prove very difficult conditions for those runners. Most likely too warm – even for those who are just sauntering about."

Ted took a mouthful of beer, swallowed it and then asked, "Well, what's your decision?"

CHAPTER 24

"Three to two, Ted, she can't run. Committee's decision is final. Maybe next year if the weather's cooler and when Martha's a year stronger, but not today."

Ted rose from his seat. "Race. Martha wanted to race not run. Thank you for considering it though. It's more than Josiah Leveridge did for us," said Ted as he left the tent.

Martha knew as soon as she saw her father's face what the decision was. "You'd never make a good poker player, Father."

"Sorry, Martha. I did the best I could. I think they might have let you race if it wasn't so hot. The vote was only three to two. Next year they reckon, if it's not so hot and with you being a year stronger, they'll let you run; well, that's what Jack Shearsmith said. Maybe if there was a woman on the committee things might have been different for you."

Martha linked her father's arm. "Well, there isn't, Father." She continued in an authoritative and slightly agitated tone, "But I am strong enough now, Father, and I've been training in the heat as well, all summer."

"You have, Martha, but either in the morning or evening when it was a bit cooler than now. It must be eighty degrees out here, and getting hotter. Anyway, you have one more chance this year – hopefully you can race on home turf on Lord Letherby's land."

"I hope so, Father."

"You go back to your friends, Martha; I'm going to meet Mort for a drink. See you later."

On her way to re-join her friends, Martha bumped into Arthur Beardsworth. "Not running again, Martha? I don't blame them for not letting you run; it's not for girls this sport, it's for men."

"Well, if that's the case, why do they let you run, Arthur Beardsworth?"

"Oh very witty, Martha. But I'm still running – you're not!"

"Oh shut up, Arthur. I'm going to beat you before this summer's out."

"You couldn't beat an egg, Martha Hunney, never mind me."

Not far away, Jonny could see Martha was getting irate and walked over to the pair. "What's going on, Martha?"

"Oh, nothing really, Jonny. It's just Mr Big Head here. He thinks he's wonderful. I'm fed up with his snide remarks."

Arthur stood smirking.

"Leave her alone, Arthur, it's bad enough Martha not being able to race without you having a go at her. Why would you be bothered whether she runs or not?"

"What's it to you, Jonny?"

"Sport is for everyone. If Martha's good enough to race then she should be allowed to."

Martha could see they were both getting irritated; she grabbed Jonny's arm. "Come on, Jonny, leave it. I can fight my own battles." She whispered to him, "Just beat Mr Big Head in the race, Jonny. You can do that, you're more than capable. After all, you've had extra porridge." She giggled. "What time does the tug-of-war start, anyway? The young farmers don't have Shaun on their team, he's haymaking with Patrick, and so the mill team could stand a chance."

"Well, we could have had, only we have no team. If Roger Thompson hadn't lost four stone in weight and all his power at the back of the rope, we might have stood a chance. Anyway, Shaun's girlfriend Beatrice is pulling for the young farmers instead of Shaun and she's nearly as powerful as him."

Martha broke into near hysterical laughter. "You're joking, aren't you, Jonny? She never is!"

"I tell you she is. Look, she's over there with her boots on and a big back-belt. She certainly looks the part, doesn't she, Martha?"

"She certainly does! Come on, let's go and cheer her on since we haven't a team. And then you had better get warmed up."

"Yes, Coach, but I think 'warm up' in this weather is a bit of a joke. I'm sweating cobs now! I'd be better go sit in the shade."

"Half a mile jog, some stretches, and a couple of sprints, and you'll be raring to go, Jonny. Mark my words. In fact, if you want, I'll warm up with you. I'm going for a run whether the committee like it or not. I'll sneak on to the course and run round it. I'll cheer you and David on. It's a pity Patrick's not racing, he really hammered me in training on Wednesday and he seems to be

CHAPTER 24

getting fitter all the time."

"I'll warm up on my own, Martha, if you don't mind. I like to do some mental preparation and need to concentrate to get my 'tunnel-vision'."

"That's all right by me, Jonny. It's something I'd do if I was racing. I wouldn't look at or talk to anyone at all for half an hour before the race."

They arrived at the tug-of-war arena where Lydia was at the rear of the young farmers' end of the rope, her heels dug into the hard turf, belt tight around her waist and ready to pull. One mighty tug by the young farmers and the local cycling club team were all picking themselves off the ground; it was a complete mismatch, even with Lydia anchoring their team. David, concerned about Lydia, shouted, "Are you okay, Lydia?"

Lydia picked herself up off the ground and strode towards David. She laughed. "Yes, I'm okay, thank you, David. I only have to pick myself up off the grass twice more, and then I will come and cheer you on in the race." And with a wry smile on her face she cried, "I won't be too long!"

Ten minutes before the start of the race, Martha discreetly set off at a jog toward the climb of the steep hill. She loped gracefully across the first newly mown fields and on to the rutted stubbly field before the climb. She carried a container of water with her and had tucked her long hair under a moistened hat to keep her head cool and to stop the sun from beating directly down on to it. Although she wore shorts, Martha had a long sleeved baggy top covering her torso and concealing her bust line. From a distance, she could easily be mistaken for a gangly youth, even with her long shapely legs showing.

She reached the first ascent of the race just as the runners came into view. The sun was shining directly from the direction in which Martha was looking. She shielded her eyes with the flat of her hand resting on top of her nose and raised her head slightly to see the runners coming toward her. Squinting, Martha could make out four runners almost together with only a few yards separating them. As they rapidly approached the spot where she was standing she recognised all four of them.

She was surprised to see David leading the small bunch; at the rear was Jonny; Arthur Beardsworth and Sam Kendal were sandwiched between them. Trying to disguise her voice she shouted in a deep guttural tone, "Come on, David. Come on, Jonny. Well done."

Arthur Beardsworth instantly recognised Martha and shouted, "Pathetic," in her direction. A few seconds later Roger Thompson ran past Martha.

"Come on, Roger, you're looking good. See off that big headed Arthur, if you can."

He gasped in reply, "I'll try, Martha. Do you have a sore throat?"

Martha laughed and watched the rest of the runners pass her then followed the tail-enders up the climb. If Martha had been doing a training session, she would have had little difficulty in jogging this section of the climb. But the tail-enders were going so slowly she had difficulty staying behind them. Eventually, she jogged horizontally wide and passed by them while ascending once more.

As she gave the field a wide berth and jogged to the left of the course markers, Martha started passing more runners with little effort. She reached the top and then rapidly descended to reach the bottom of the last climb, passing three more runners along the way. To her surprise, she could see the leaders ascending only about sixty yards in front of her, and David tailing off from them only thirty yards in front of her. Roger had gained on the three leaders and was only a few yards behind him. Martha ran wide of the markers again as she started the next ascent and soon caught up with David.

"Are you okay, David?"

"No, I've had it. Not enough training and it's too hot. Jonny's going well, though. I'll finish in my own time. What you doing here anyway, Martha?"

"I'm just watching the race, David."

"They should let you do one if you can run on a hot day like this. Carry on, Martha and leave me be."

CHAPTER 24

"Alright. Keep going, David. You'll run better next time."

Martha carried on and up toward the top of the climb. She could see a small crowd assembled at the tower. She decided to take a shortcut which took her back to the course after the final descent and within about half a mile of the finish. She reached this point just in time to see Jonny flying past with Sam Kendal in hot pursuit ten yards behind. Roger and Arthur Beardsworth were both twenty-five yards behind him. Martha took another shortcut to the finish line and arrived there as Jonny came sprinting towards the finishing tape.

Sam Kendal was another thirty yards behind, and Roger and Arthur Beardsworth were locked in a sprint to the finish. Jonny breasted the tape and punched his right fist into the air in triumph. Shirley was standing a few yards from the finish, Jonny caught sight of her from the corner of his eye and ran over to kiss her on the cheek. She swivelled around and she kissed him full on the lips.

"Well done, lover boy," she whispered in his ear. He smiled broadly. Sam Kendal finished in second place and to Martha's sheer, ecstatic delight, Roger Thompson out-sprinted Arthur Beardsworth for third place.

The crowd cheered in appreciation of a race well run and many of the runners sat on the ground hot, sweaty, and glad to be finished.

Chapter 25

"Honey, there's a letter on the mantelpiece addressed to you." Martha walked to the mantelpiece, picked up the letter and looked at the envelope for a moment wondering what might be inside. Her Mother stood close to her with eyebrows raised, one hand in her pinafore pocket and the other on her hip. "Are you going to open it or just look at the envelope, Honey?"

"I don't know who would send me a letter in such a posh envelope, Mother. Do you?"

"Of course, I do, but I'm not spoiling your surprise."

Martha opened the envelope and to her delight, it was a letter from Major Coulthurst. She read it and then read it again.

"Well, who's it from then?"

"It's from Major Coulthurst, and he says Oliver is well and coming home on leave in two weeks. He says I don't need to worry about the authorities in London. His friend has informed him that: 'Open or professional fellrunning does not come under Amateur Athletic Association rules. However, if you choose to compete in one of those fell races you will be barred from ever taking part in any future Amateur Athletic event'. Does that mean I can run in one, Mother?"

"No, what it means, Martha, is that if you run in a fell race and there are monetary prizes, you will never be able to run in any amateur sports again. You're right though, they can't stop you running as a female entrant."

"Well that's ridiculous, Mother; I think the winner only gets a few pounds. It's not as though we don't work for a living. Who'd ever make a living out of fell running?"

CHAPTER 25

"It's your choice, Martha, that's if you ever get to compete in a race."

"There are no amateur fell races around here that I know of, and I'm certainly not going to scour the entire North of England for one when there's other local fell races here. I'll write back to Major Coulthurst and thank him for his letter and the information he sent me."

"You do that, Honey. I knew Oliver was going to come home on leave; I received a letter from him today. You never know, he might be home for Lord Letherby's show a week on Saturday, and maybe, just maybe, he might see you run in the race."

Martha's heart started thumping with excitement at the thought of not being rejected and being able to stand on the starting line with all the male competitors.

"Has Father said anything about Miss Fleischmann having a word with Orla Rowley, do you know? Mort was going to ask her to have a chat about me racing at the show."

"Yes dear, he has, and Mrs Rowley is going to have a word with Lord Letherby. According to Patrick she has magical powers of persuasion when it comes to the male of the species. Mind you with those stunning looks, is it any wonder?"

Martha giggled. "Yes, Mother, I have noticed men's heads turning and tongues hanging out as she walks by. I heard Mr Snead say she made Rita Hayworth and Sophia Loren look plain – honestly, that dirty old man, he must be nearly a hundred."

"Martha Hunney, that's enough of that sort of talk from you." Ruth paused for a moment. "Mind you, it wouldn't surprise me though. He's been married three times and has ten children all told. God rest his three wives, and the five sons he lost in the war."

"I hope Teddy doesn't carry on like that when I'm not with him."

Her mother raised her eyebrows, both hands on her hips and with her head tilted slightly backwards said, "Honey, don't be naïve, he's a young man – that's all I'm saying, other than he'll get older!"

But Martha said confidently, "No, Mother, not Teddy, he's not like that. I mean he'll get older but he won't be like Mr Snead."

Sarah walked into the kitchen. "I thought you were going running with Patrick tonight, Martha."

"I am but not till seven. He's doing some extra work because Shaun's gone somewhere with Beatty. I thought you'd know anyway."

Sarah looked at her sister, slightly puzzled. "I don't know everything about what Patrick's doing, you know, Martha. I'm not seeing him this week. He's training hard three evenings and we have choir practice on Thursday. I'll be seeing him on Saturday at the next village dance. He's playing in the band again, I know that."

Martha ignored her sister and homed in on Patrick's training schedule. "He's training three nights? He must be serious about the race."

"Oh, that's not all, Honey. He's been running in the morning as well, at least three times a week over the last three weeks."

Martha's jaw dropped and her eyes nearly popped out of her head. She shouted, "Three times in the morning! Does he think it's the Olympics? He never told me!"

"Oh, oh, that's got you, Honey. It's no good panicking now. Anyway, why should he tell you everything? He's my boyfriend and he doesn't tell me everything. By the way, you might not even get to run in the race."

"You mean race in the race, Sarah. There's no point in just running. I'm a racer; a competitor."

Ruth interjected, "And don't we know it, Honey. Your works' sports competition bears testimony to that!"

"There's no point in just going through the motions, Mother. No point at all."

Sarah changed the subject. "When does Teddy go to Cambridge, Honey?"

"Third week in September, he's even sorted his accommodation out."

"He's done well to get in and get sponsored. Two young men from this village going away to university – it's unheard of."

CHAPTER 25

"There must have been something in the water when they were conceived, Mother."

"They might have had a drink out of the well, Honey. It worked on Beatty's foot, didn't it?"

"Well, Sur, you saw how she pulled in the tug-of-war last week. There was nothing wrong with her foot even with the strain she put on it." Martha laughed. "She could have beaten the cyclists on her own."

"Honey, what's healing an injured foot and someone having a special gift got to do with our well water?"

"It must have special properties, Mother, to give people special talents, and healing properties to heal bodies. That's all I can think." Martha abruptly left the kitchen and bounded upstairs to change into her training clothes. As she did she muttered to herself, "Three mornings a week indeed."

Her mother and Sarah overheard her and started to laugh. "Mother, I sometimes think there's something wrong with my twin. She's completely obsessed with running."

"Sarah dear, it's racing she's obsessed with. Once Honey has achieved her ambition of competing in a fell race, she might not be so bothered about it again."

Sarah smiled at her Mother. "I wouldn't bank on it."

Patrick arrived at the back door and tapped on the window alongside it.

"Sarah, why does he do that instead of using the door?"

Sarah shouted, "Come in, Patrick. It must be something he used to do in Ireland, Mother. I must say he has a few strange habits. I've noticed he always rubs his left ear between his finger and thumb when he answers a question, and when he's going up some steps he puts his right foot on the first step, takes it off, and then goes up using his left foot first. He's always doing it, aren't you, Patrick?"

"Doing what, Sarah?"

"Touching your ear, and shuffling up and down on the first step."

Patrick looked puzzled. "Not that I've ever noticed. It would be peculiar to be touching my ear and shuffling up and down on the first step. Why would I want to do that?"

"Never mind, Patrick." Sarah kissed him on the cheek and said, "How are you this wet evening? I see you got yourself a waterproof top."

"I'm sweating like mad underneath it. It's clammy outside and if we weren't going up to the Pike I wouldn't have put it on."

Martha walked through the kitchen and out into the backyard without saying a word and started dragging her damp training shoes on.

"Before you ask, Patrick – don't. I've told her that you've been running in the mornings and I think it's unhinged her."

"I'll say nothing. It looks like I'll be in for a silent run then, which will make a change." He turned to Ruth. "Your daughter can't half witter on sometimes, Mrs Hunney."

"Somehow, I don't think it will be a quiet run, Patrick. Martha will be giving you the third degree." Ruth pointed at Sarah. "She only hasn't said anything because she knows this one here will start pulling her leg and then she will get mad and retaliate."

"Oh well, I'd better get outside then. See you later, Sarah, Mrs Hunney." Patrick went out into the backyard, closing the door behind him. "Hello, Marta, how are you?"

Martha grunted and set off running. Patrick set off behind her and then quickly ran up alongside her. They ran silently through the fields before reaching the footpath leading to the beck. Martha gradually increased the pace and Patrick dropped behind a few yards.

"Just as I thought, Patrick Murphy. You're training too hard, you can't keep up with me after three-quarters of a mile and we haven't even reached the climb."

Patrick was astonished at Martha's remarks. "Marta, it's a single file track; I'm not dropping behind you. I can't run at the side of you or I'd be on the rocks. And I'm not training too hard."

"Well, what about three mornings a week as well as the evening runs then? Is that not too much?"

"No, it's not, Marta. Anyway, I'll only be doing it for another

CHAPTER 25

week and then I'll start tapering down for the race."

"How many weeks have you been doing it for then?"

"Two. One more and I'll be as fit as a fiddle. Why are you so bothered anyway? You have your own training schedule and I have mine."

"Oh, I suppose so, sorry for being so abrupt."

The rain poured down incessantly throughout the training session and caused the conditions underfoot to become treacherous on the rock and moss strewn descent. Patrick nearly fell twice but regained his footing and his balance after slipping precariously. Martha was as sure-footed as a mountain goat and reached the bottom of the descent a full sixty yards ahead of him.

Patrick caught her up and shouted, "I'll tell you what, Marta; I don't think there will be anyone to touch you going downhill in these conditions if you get to race at the show. I wasn't going to speak to him about you, but I'll have a word with Lord Letherby myself when he gets home from Ireland, and I'll tell him how sure-footed you are."

"It's my trainers, Patrick, they've brilliant grips on the bottom."

"Marta, it's you. My shoes have good grips too; you just flow naturally on the downhills."

After they had finished the training session Patrick ran home. Martha had a bath, dressed and ate her evening meal. The sisters set off for choir practice as the rain stopped and they walked leisurely along the country lanes to the chapel.

After choir practice Martha approached Reverend Boniface. "Can I see you, Reverend Boniface? Just for a few minutes, I need to ask you something and I'd like some advice."

"Of course, Martha. Give me five minutes and then I'll be with you."

Sarah asked, "What's all this about, Martha? You don't usually hang about after choir practice. You always say you're too tired and need to get to bed early."

"I'll only be ten minutes, Sur. Are you going home or waiting for me?"

"I'll wait, the nights are drawing in a bit now and I don't want you walking home on your own."

"Oh thanks, Sur, you're my best sister."

"Only sister, as well, Honey, by the way. Are you going to tell me what it's about or are you going to keep it to yourself."

"It's private, Sarah, between Reverend Boniface and me."

All the choristers had left the chapel apart from Lydia. As Reverend Boniface came back to listen to Martha, Sarah took the hint and walked over to talk to Lydia.

"Now, Martha, are you all right to talk here or do you want somewhere more private?"

"No, I'm quite okay here, Reverend Boniface. I wanted to ask you if you think it's all right for me to do a fell race. Whether God thinks it will be all right. I mean, I don't want to offend him, or you. Do you think it's all right for me to race? It's just that each time I try to race in an event I'm stopped. It's because I'm a female and it's a male sport."

Reverend Boniface clasped his hands and furrowed his brow. "Well, Martha, I know you are very keen to compete in one of those fell races because your father has told me, and I say compete because he says you are highly competitive. As far as I'm concerned I can see no reason why you shouldn't race. The only thing in scripture that I know of, which you should definitely consider, is the matter of dressing modestly. But I believe that revolves around not wearing excessive jewellery and plastering on make-up to the extreme. If you do get to compete in a fell race make sure you give those males nothing to ogle at."

Martha blushed at the reverend's comment. "Yes, Reverend, I'll be sure to dress modestly."

"As for what God thinks, well, you need to pray about that. A simple prayer straight from your heart, laying a fleece before the Lord like Gideon did. If it is right for you to compete, ask God to remove the obstacles and he will, and if he does not, you will know that it's not right. Is there anything else you need to ask?"

"No, thank you very much, Reverend Boniface. I'll do as you say and hope that God will remove those obstacles."

"I'll see you on Sunday then, Martha. Will you do me a favour?

CHAPTER 25

If you are going to the village dance on Saturday, will you remind all those who are singing there not to overdo it and save their fine voices for service in chapel on Sunday?"

"I will."

Martha had a smile on her face as she approached her sister and Lydia. "Are you on your bicycle, Lydia or walking home?"

"I've a sore leg after that last tug-of-war and I can't get rid of it, so I can't ride at the moment. I'll walk with you to the village and then Father will drive down for me after I call him from the phone box."

"Maybe you should come to our house and soak your leg in our well. It works, you know, it healed Beatty, Sarah and me, so it could do for you as well."

"Thank you for offering, I shall rest it for another four days, Martha, and if it doesn't heal in that time I will come and soak it in your well."

The twins arrived home. After having two slices of toast and a pot of tea, Martha said good night to her family and, going to her room, she knelt down at the side of her bed and began to pray.

"Dear God, I thank you for my family and all the blessings you give to us. I ask that you will give our Oliver a safe journey home from Cyprus and he will have a good rest when he does come home on leave. Now, I need to ask you about racing in the fell race a week on Saturday at the country show at Letherby Hall, and if it's right for me to do it, racing against the men. I promise to wear modest clothing and behave appropriately. If it's not right for me to race I ask that you prevent me from doing it. If it is right, Lord, I ask that you will remove any barriers and obstacles that are in my way. Please help me get on better with Arthur Beardsworth so we aren't saying nasty things to one another. I thank you once more for all the blessings and for getting a place for Teddy at Cambridge. Amen."

Sarah had walked upstairs and joked, "Are you talking to yourself again, Honey, or is it one of your little invisible friends?"

"Actually neither, I was praying, if you must know."

"What about?"

"Sarah, you should know better than to ask that. You know that it's private between God and me, just the same as if you were praying. Anyway you definitely wouldn't tell me if I asked you, would you?"

"No I wouldn't, Honey, I'm sorry I asked."

"Don't stand on ceremony at the door, Sur. You can come in, you know, it's your room as well as mine."

"No I'm going back down to do some sewing; I'm not as tired as you." Sarah laughed. "Besides, you need more beauty sleep than me, don't you?"

"Very funny, Sarah, my sides are splitting with laughter, can't you hear me?"

"Yes, I am rather witty, aren't I?"

"Sarah."

"What, Honey?"

"You're about as funny as toothache. Goodnight, and don't tramp down the stairs like a herd of elephants."

The sisters' conversation ended with their father's booming voice ordering Sarah down the stairs. "Sarah, down here now before you and Martha start scrapping. She was nice and quiet before you disturbed her. I'm fed up with you two arguing. It's about time you both grew up."

Sarah rushed downstairs. "Yes, Father, sorry."

Ruth was baking in the kitchen when Martha sneaked back downstairs. "Mother, what's up with Father, he's not usually that grumpy?"

"He's had a bad day at work, that's all."

Martha had a small cup of water and on the way out of the kitchen said, "Sorry, Sur." The sisters hugged each other and then Martha opened the living room door, saying, "Sorry for the noise, Father."

Ted lowered the newspaper he was reading, turned to his daughter, nodded and said, "Okay." He raised the paper and carried on reading. From then on the evening was a peaceful affair.

That Saturday evening at the village hall dance, Martha held on to Teddy's arm and holding back the tears she looked straight

CHAPTER 25

into his eyes.

"There's only one more dance after this, Teddy, and then no more for you and me until you come home at Christmas. You will be coming home, won't you, Teddy? I couldn't bear to be without you at Christmas, you know."

"Honey, wild horses wouldn't keep me from coming home to be with you. I promise, as soon as I've finished the term, I'll be on the next train home."

He kissed her gently on the lips and caressed her cheek, then reiterated, "I promise, Honey, I'll be home, and don't you worry."

"When we go into the dance I want a word with Miss Fleischmann and maybe, Orla Rowley if she is here tonight."

"Why's that, Martha?"

"It's to do with the fell race at the Letherby Show. Miss Fleischmann was going to have a word with Orla Rowley about persuading Lord Letherby to let me race. Evidently she has some magical power over men and could perhaps talk him into allowing me to race."

"I think it could be more to do with her looks, Martha."

She turned quickly to Teddy and dragged on his right arm.

"Hey, that hurt, Martha."

"Never mind that, what do mean by 'her looks'?"

Teddy knew he had said the wrong thing but thought to himself, 'In for a penny in for a pound, I'm in trouble anyway'. He pulled away from her and carried on walking into the village hall. "Well, she is a stunner despite her age."

Martha was crestfallen. She started to cry and blubbered, "Why did you have to say that, Teddy? Mother's right, all men are the same when it comes to women. I thought you might be different."

"I was merely looking at her from an aesthetic point of view, Honey, and not a sexual one. There are some men who can do that, you know – what about artists who paint nude women?"

"Yes, well, I bet they get a kick out of it or they wouldn't do it. You don't get women painting nude men, not that I know of anyway."

"Please, Martha, don't let this spoil our night, we've only got a couple of Saturdays out and then I'll be gone for nearly three months."

At that, Martha started crying even more and ran to the toilets. Sarah was already in the hall talking to Patrick and when she saw Martha, she followed her. She tapped on the door and asked quietly, "Are you okay, Martha, what are you crying for?"

Martha sniffled. "Give me a couple of minutes, Sur, and then I'll come out. I need to speak to you but not in the hall: outside."

"I'll wait here for you then. I won't go outside until you come out and we can walk out together."

Martha came out of the toilet and they made their way outside. Teddy noticed the sisters and walked towards them but Martha held the palm of her hand out as if to say 'stop'. He stopped in his tracks. Sarah looked at him and shook her head and then beckoned to Patrick to go over to Teddy.

Patrick nodded in the direction of the sisters who were leaving the hall and asked in his deep Irish drone, "What's going on with those two, Teddy?"

"I think it might be something I've said to Martha. I only mentioned in conversation that Orla Rowley was stunning and I think it's upset her."

Patrick laughed. "Not very tactful if you ask me, Teddy; although you're quite right about Orla Rowley it's not something you should mention in front of your beloved. I'll give you a tip, Teddy old son, never mention anything positive about another woman's appearance in front of your betrothed. It will only make life difficult for you in the short and the long run. I remember my old stepdad falling into the same trap back home, my mammy still brings it up from time to time, much to his displeasure."

"I'll take your advice, but it looks like I've blotted my copybook with this one. I don't think Martha will forget!"

Patrick draped his arm around Teddy's shoulder and waxed lyrical. "Take it as a learning curve in the rich tapestry of life, and take this one on the chin, old son; apologise until you are blue in the face."

Martha and Sarah had walked across the road and were sitting

CHAPTER 25

on a bench on the village green.

"It's a lovely evening, Sarah, we've been blessed with sunshine all summer and it looks as though it's going into autumn as well. I hope it's not boiling hot next Saturday for the race."

"Never mind all that, Honey – what's the problem? You don't often run to the toilets crying, in fact, it's the first time ever that I can remember."

Martha wiped the moisture from her eyes and attempted to separate her long dark eyelashes. She sniffled, "It's Teddy. I thought he would be different but he's not. Not at all."

"What on earth are you on about, Honey?"

"He made a comment about Orla Rowley being a stunner."

"Well, Honey, let's face facts: she is, isn't she? You can see men's heads turning as she walks by. But Teddy shouldn't have said anything – the fool. Martha, he's only saying what most men think from time to time about us females. You don't want to be so upset, it's natural for a man to admire a good-looking woman. It's not as though he's going off with her, is it? Just make him suffer for a while, and he'll not make the same mistake again. I'm sure of that."

"I suppose not."

"I'll sit with you tonight and we'll dance together; just give Teddy the cold shoulder for a while – he'll get the message." Sarah placed her hand on her sister's shoulder and said, "Come on, let's get inside, the music's started."

At that moment, Orla Rowley and her two daughters came walking toward the village hall. Bryony spotted the sisters and waved at them. Bridget copied her sister. Orla looked across and, seeing Martha, walked over to her. In her husky Irish accent she said, "Hello Marta," and nodded in acknowledgment towards Sarah. "Can I have a word with you?"

Martha was taken aback by Orla's forthrightness but she composed herself and said, "Of course."

"Ava Fleischmann has been to see me and asked on your behalf if I will have a word with his Lordship regarding you competing in the hill race. Well, I am quite willing to ask for you – I think you are trying to do a brave thing by running in one of those kinds of races."

"Racing, Mrs Rowley, not just running."

"Well, whatever you wish to call it, you are still very brave. I must tell you though that Lord Letherby is no feminist, in fact he's far from it. He is a traditionalist and if you think my feminine charm will affect him positively in your favour, I'm afraid it might not. I will speak to him though."

She abruptly turned from Martha and strode across the road with her daughters following like two little ducklings. Two men seemed to be gawking at her from a short distance away. Martha and Sarah stared at Orla, and Martha had to admit, "Orla Rowley is stunning looking, there's no point in denying it. Look at those two over there." She recognised Terry Sutcliffe from her school days and shouted across the road, "Put your eyes back in, Terry, before you lose them, and tell your friend to pull his tongue in."

"Give up, Martha, Orla must have heard you. It is Terry Sutcliffe, isn't it? My, he's turned into a bit of alright, hasn't he? He was a right skinny, spotty article at school, a bit like you actually."

"Oh, thank you very much, Sarah. Anyway, you haven't changed much either, you were a roly-poly then and you are now."

The sisters had reverted to one of their usual verbal exchanges – this one a volley of insults about their looks.

"Well, all I can say, Martha Hunney, is that Patrick likes me just the way that I am, and for that matter, I do as well."

"Yes, and I like the way I look, and so does Teddy, and I don't care what you think anyway."

The twins looked at each other, started laughing and walked back across the road.

"Are you going to ask her for a dance, Terry?"

"Hello, Martha, who do you mean?"

"Come off it, Terry, you know, that woman you were both gawping at, that's who."

"Martha, that woman is old enough to be my mother. No, it was that young woman at the back who I was looking at, and Oscar here, remember him?" Oscar nodded at the sisters and they

CHAPTER 25

returned the nod. "He fancies the one who was in front of her, don't you?"

"Too true, we've talked to them before on the bus into town."

"Do you want me to put a good word in for you both then?"

"No Martha, we've already made contact and we're singing with them tonight; their mother doesn't know yet though. We're singing 'Mambo Italiano'."

"Oh, I like that one, Terry," Martha enthused, "How have you managed to practise that?"

"It was with the two Irish fellows, Shaun and Patrick, at the farm. We practised a couple of times in the barn with them playing the trumpet and sax. Those girls sing like nightingales and don't sound at all Irish."

"I don't think there's anything wrong with sounding Irish. Bryony and Bridget have a wonderful accent you know, Terry."

"I know that, Martha, but all I'm saying is you can't detect it when they are singing the song. After all, it is supposed to be Italian."

"That's okay then, Terry, as long as you're not being mean to them."

The sisters walked back into the village hall, followed by Terry and Oscar, who promptly made their way over to Bridget and Bryony where they sat with their mother, Harry Smith and Delwyn Williams. Martha didn't acknowledge Teddy as he looked toward her and Sarah snubbed him as well.

The band had warmed up and started their first session with Cyril Squire singing 'Hernando's Hideaway'. Harry was first to his feet pulling Delwyn up off her chair but she didn't move and he fell on top of her and they both rolled onto the floor. Teddy tried to help them both up but he stumbled over as well making both Martha and Sarah laugh. The band stopped playing, Sofia Reynolds thinking a fight had started, and Ted and Mort rushed over to see what was happening. Teddy held his hand up, "It's alright, Mr Hunney, we just fell over, that's all. No harm done unless Delwyn has squashed Harry."

As Harry tried to lift her off the floor, Delwyn bellowed out,

"Don't you be so cheeky, Teddy Moore, or I'll squash you if you're not careful!"

Martha and Sarah laughed even more at all the palaver.

"And you two can shut up as well."

Martha retorted, still laughing, "Oh give over, Del, it looks funny from where we're standing. You'd be laughing your socks off if you were sat here and it was our Sarah on the floor."

"Oh be quiet, beanpole," Delwyn shouted.

Sarah nudged her sister and feigning a shocked high pitched voice asked, "Yes, Martha, what do you mean by that?"

"Well if I'm a beanpole and Harry was pulling me out of the chair, I would have flown out and landed on the floor like you, Delwyn."

Ted, realising what was happening, said firmly, "Martha, help Teddy up. Harry, do what you were going to do, start the dance off as usual; we don't want a rumble, do we?"

"No, sir. Come on, Del, let's get the ball rolling." Delwyn looked at Martha and Ted, tossed her head back and then followed Harry onto the dance floor.

Sofia called, "One, two three," and the band started up again with Cyril singing. Soon the dance floor was filling up. Martha and Sarah danced together, and Teddy sat on his own, feeling dejected, his chin resting on both hands, his elbows on the table.

Ava Fleischmann walked into the hall wearing a pair of elegant but rather curious elbow-length white lace gloves. Mort caught up with her and they walked half the perimeter of the dance floor and sat at the same table as Orla, who greeted them both and then commented, "My, those are classy gloves, Ava; they're fit for a wedding."

Ava couldn't contain herself. At the word 'wedding' she pulled her left glove off to reveal a sparkling new engagement ring. After giving Orla a secret glimpse, she kept her hand partly covered with her glove and placing a finger to her lips whispered, "Shush, Orla, not a word, I'll let you see it properly when Mort and I have announced our engagement later."

Eyes wide, Orla whispered, "Ava, that's a beautiful ring," and

CHAPTER 25

then said, "Let me be the first here to congratulate you!"

Ava and Mort smiled at Orla, and Ava placed her finger to her lips again whispering, "Not a word."

The night drew on. The barn dance, the Gay Gordon, and the military two-step had most of the revellers on their feet; even Jack Snead managed a circuit around the dance floor. Admittedly he was being held up by Scarlett, but he enjoyed himself before sitting down and falling asleep. Tom Procter nudged Jack awake and told him not to be so ignorant when there were fine young fillies to look at.

Martha, sitting close by with Sarah, elbowed her and nodding towards the two old men said, "Did you hear what old Tom Procter said to Mr Snead? They're both ninety odd years old if they're a day, and still eyeing us girls up."

"Well, Martha, you might as well get it into that thick skull of yours that those two are what Patrick and Teddy are likely to be like when they're not in our company. So get used to it."

Martha tutted, "Oh I hope not, or else Teddy is going to be in for a hard time if I catch him making comments like he did about Orla Rowley."

"You can rest assured that you won't hear anything like that from Teddy's mouth again. I know that because Patrick has had a stern word with him – he told me when the buffet was on. Mind you, that's not to say it won't happen when he's in male company."

"Oh you know, Sur, sometimes I can't stand men. In fact next Saturday I'm going to beat as many as I can – it will give me the greatest of pleasure!"

It was time for the Rowley sisters to sing. Bryony was the lead vocal with Sofia, Bridget, Terry and Oscar backing her. Shaun and Cyril both played trumpet, Patrick played the piano and Joe Preston plucked bass. After the initial quiet start to the song, they swung into action. Orla was flabbergasted, she couldn't believe what she was hearing, or seeing, with her two daughters gyrating on the stage, and Shaun strutting up and down it like a peacock, playing his saxophone. Instantly the dance floor filled to capacity.

Ava dragged Mort to his feet and, the most unlikely of men,

Charles Smythe asked Orla to dance, and she accepted. Charles was an excellent ballroom dancer and he adapted admirably to the swing music. Orla Rowley moved so gracefully on the dance floor that she had grown men drooling. If ever there was an instance in which more men in one dance hall where nudged and pummelled it would have been very difficult to find.

The hall was in a frenzied state. Martha couldn't contain herself and leapt to her feet, ran over to Teddy and literally lifted him off his feet and onto the dance floor. They bumped into Mort and Ava and as Martha turned to say sorry she noticed the engagement ring on Ava's finger. When the music had finished, Orla turned to kiss Charles on his cheek and walked off the dance floor, beckoning Charles to sit down with her.

Ted climbed the steps onto the stage and grabbing hold of the microphone held his hand up and shouted, "Can we have a bit of hush for a few minutes, please." After everyone was settled, Ted smiled at the crowd. "That was some number, wasn't it? I've never seen the dance floor so alive in all the times I've been at the village dance, and that's even before the twins were born."

He looked at Bryony and said, "Bryony, who would have known that you could sing like Rosemary Clooney? Well done! In fact, thank you to all the band and the singers – excellent performance."

Bryony blushed, lowered her face and managed to say, "Thank you, Mr Hunney."

Ted nodded at Bryony and continued, "Our Martha asked me earlier to mention for you singers not to overdo it and save some of your voice for chapel tomorrow. That's at Reverend Boniface's request by the way. Now, if Mort and Ava would like to come up on the stage, I think they have something to say."

Mort climbed the steps to the stage and as he reached the top step, turned and placed his left hand into Ava's right hand and they walked to the centre of the stage. Ted handed the microphone to Mort and without a moment's hesitation, as he looked into Ava's beaming face, he announced, "It is my great pleasure to tell you all that Ava and I are engaged and will be married on the

CHAPTER 25

twenty-seventh of October. Everyone present is welcome to the evening do, which will be here in the village hall."

Ava took hold of the microphone and in her husky Polish accent declared, "At this moment I am the happiest woman in the whole wide world," and in front of everyone, she kissed Mort full on the lips. There was rapturous applause and as they walked off the stage a number of women ran over to congratulate them. Martha was first there, she couldn't contain herself and flung her arms round Ava and kissed her on the cheek. She grabbed her hand and examined the ring.

"Oh, Ava, it's exquisitely beautiful." She kissed Mort on the cheek and said, "Congratulations, Mr Johnson; you will look after her, won't you?"

"Of course I will, Martha, you needn't worry on that score and, by the way, it's about time you called me Mort, you're old enough now. Tell your Sarah as well." Martha smiled and walked back to where Teddy was waiting for her.

"You should look at Ava's engagement ring, it's beautiful."

"I would have walked over with you, Honey, but you were off like a rocket."

She smiled and then laughed. "I won't be setting off that fast but I will be finishing like that when I race. Teddy, when are we getting engaged?"

"Before I go to Cambridge, like I told you last week, your mum and dad are happy with it now that we've convinced them we are intended for each other and my mum is as well. There's no point in delaying anything."

"But what about the money to pay for the ring?"

"Don't you worry about that, Honey. Anyway, you've got to choose one yet. We'll go to town on the first bus next week before the show starts and you can have a look in Palmerston's Jewellers. We can be back in plenty of time. Are you okay with that, Honey?"

Martha quickly computed the timing leading up to the start of the race and the bus timetable.

"Of course, Teddy. I'll take my running gear with me, if that's alright with you."

"Course it is." He kissed Martha gently and a warm glow reached deep into her heart.

Chapter 26

The day of the season's final country show fell race had arrived at last and the twins were already on the events field in anticipation of an exciting day. Beaming from head to toe, Martha flashed her engagement ring at Sarah, who grabbed her hand and examined it closely. "It's beautiful, Martha, and it fits perfectly. When are you and Teddy going to make the big announcement about your engagement?"

Martha turned to Teddy and smiled, then looked at her sister and revealed, "We're not, are we, Teddy?"

"No. Your mum and dad know, and my mother knows, but we've told them we don't want a song and dance about it. Your mum has invited my mother to a small celebration at your home next week. The Reverend Boniface will be there to give us his blessing as well. Oh, and your Nan and the Reverend's wife will be there too."

"That was fast organising, if you don't mind me saying so, Teddy."

"It was sorted out during the week, Sarah. I thought you knew," said Martha.

"Of course I knew, Martha; you can't keep any secrets from me. Is it okay for Patrick to come as well?"

"Hmm, let me see." Martha giggled. "Of course he can, Sur. Teddy has already invited him. Anyway, I'm going to the entry tent to see whether I can race or not. Leave me to it and I'll see you later." Martha turned and kissed Teddy on the cheek, smiled at him and then left to go to the entry tent in the intense mid-afternoon heat.

"I'll have a look in the poultry tent then and see you back here in a few minutes. What are you going to do, Sarah?"

"I'll come with you, Teddy. Like she said, we'll leave Honey to it."

There were two hours before the start of the race and Martha wasn't optimistic about being allowed to compete. She was resigned to running on the side lines again. As she neared the tent, Orla Rowley called to her, "Martha dear, Patrick and I have both talked to his Lordship on your behalf but I'm afraid he isn't willing to give up the tradition of an all-male fell race." She lowered her voice and whispered in Martha's ear, "Personally, and between only you and I, I think he's an old fossil. Don't say a word though, I value my employment with him."

Martha wasn't surprised by Orla's statement. "Thanks for asking, Orla. I half expected it anyway. Do you know where Patrick is by the way? I thought he might be here by now."

"He has been here all morning with Shaun, setting up the show tents and the events ring under his Lordship's direction. I think he's gone back to the farmhouse to get ready for the tug-of-war and the race."

"Tug-of-war? I don't think he's done that before."

"He's substituting for one of the young farmers who can't be here today. I don't think they need him really, Shaun is strong enough for two!"

Charles Smythe appeared from the nearby horticulture tent and walked towards Martha and Orla. As soon as he arrived, Orla linked arms with him and, turning to Martha, she smiled and said, "Maybe next year, Martha." Charles tipped his hat at Martha and walked away with Orla at his side.

Martha called out, "Yes, that's what my Father says: 'Maybe next year'." She sighed and wandered slowly back to Teddy with her duffle bag containing her running gear slung over her left shoulder, her right shoulder drooping.

"Well, that's it, Teddy, there's no chance according to Orla Rowley." Martha sighed. "We can still enjoy the show though. Father's putting Shep in the ring with our ducks, he's going to

Chapter 26

have him round them up. I've seen him practising with Shep on the allotment, he's pretty obedient is our Shep."

Out-of-the-blue Martha enquired, "Hey, Teddy, what do you think about Charles Smythe and Orla Rowley? They're courting! If you lined fifty men up and asked who you think would be most suitable for Orla, he'd be the last choice."

"Well, to quote Delwyn Williams, Honey, who would put a beanpole like you with someone like me?"

Martha pushed Teddy and they both fell over. "Oh, Teddy Moore, you can be so funny, you're about as funny as an itchy rash sometimes. What you do mean is who'd have put an elegant young lady like me with a swot like you?"

Teddy replied, "We must be two opposites that attract each other then, Honey," and he kissed her.

The sweethearts walked around the show looking at the various competition tents. Martha fingering her engagement ring from time to time and smiling to herself.

Ruth had entered a plate of scones and a Victoria sandwich in the baking competition.

"Come on, Teddy, let's see if Mother has won anything in the baking competition and then we'll see how Sarah has done with her crochet entry." Martha stopped in her tracks. "Just a minute, Teddy. Father, Mother, and Sarah are all in the show and I'm not. That can't be right; I'm the most competitive! Even Nan's entered some knitting."

"I don't want to upset you, Honey, but I've entered a bantam cock in the poultry competition as well."

Martha looked at Teddy not knowing whether to laugh or cry; she laughed. "Well, we had better see how it's gone on then after we see how Mother's cakes have done."

As Lord Letherby was about to hand out the prizes for the sheepdog trials, Lady Letherby noticed a forlorn looking, droopy-shouldered Martha walking behind Teddy towards the tug-of-war competition, duffle bag in hand. She felt terribly sorry for her and turning to her husband pulled at the sleeve of his tweed jacket and stated forcefully, "Montague, I would like a word with you."

"Can it not wait, Prudence?"

"It most certainly cannot. Those farmers can wait a few moments but this will not."

Lord Letherby knew from past experience that when his wife had something significant to say she would not wait. "Yes, dear, what is it?"

"You have been in Ireland for most of the summer and into the autumn. I have kept you informed of everything that has occurred at Letherby Hall, on the Estate and in the village. You have missed a village wedding, and the most beautiful summer in our time here on the Estate and I believe it is time you took more notice of village affairs."

"What do you mean by that, Prudence?"

"For instance, do you know that we have two young men who have made the academic grade necessary to take places at Cambridge? For the first time in the village's history! And in contrast, there is a young woman, who works full time at Bradshaw's mill and dedicates all the leisure time she has to training in order to be able, one day, to run in a country show fell race. I have seen her and believe you me she can run like the wind."

"Yes, Prudence I know who you mean, our housekeeper Orla and farm labourer Patrick have both mentioned her to me, saying she is more than capable of competing in a fell race."

Well, you have said she cannot run in our fell race today and I would like to know why, Montague? She most certainly can do it."

"She's a female and fell running is for men, dear Prudence."

"Do not patronise me, Montague. What has being female to do with not being allowed to compete against males if one is capable? Do tell me."

Lord Letherby was stuck for words.

"Woman can compete on horses, play football and do what has been described as 'men's work'. During the Great War and the Second War we held this country together while our men were away in France and further abroad and we nursed them on

CHAPTER 26

the battlefield in dangerous situations. If we had been allowed, we would have fought too. Do not tell me that a fit and healthy young woman cannot compete with young men in a foot race. It is preposterous! And do not refer to Patrick as a farm labourer when you know exactly who he is. Give him his rightful title."

A few minutes later Patrick approached Martha, "Marta, go and get your racing kit on."

"I'm in no mood to go round the course like the last race, Patrick. I'd rather just watch it from here."

"No Marta, you're racing."

"What?" Martha shrieked.

Two dozen curious heads turned towards her.

"You're racing. Say no more. Go and get changed and warm up, you have half an hour before the start. Sarah, will you guard the tent entrance while Marta changes into her racing kit?"

Martha turned to a smiling Teddy, he hugged her and said, "Go on, Honey, do your best, I love you." She kissed him.

Martha grabbed her sister's hand. "Quick Sur, as soon as I'm changed, find Father and Mother, oh, and Nan and tell them I'm actually racing, will you?"

"Of course I will, Honey."

Martha changed into her racing kit, strapping her breasts down, pulling on her pink short sleeved top, thigh length shorts and making sure her racing shoes were fastened sufficiently. She prayed quickly, "Thank you, Lord."

After doing some stretching exercises she set off in a slow jog at first then gradually speeding up as she headed out of the showground and onto the fell course. She stopped and placing her hands on the trunk of an oak tree she stretched her calf muscles and tendons. Martha jogged again for five minutes and then sped up until she was at flat race pace. After striding up three sections of short grassy slopes, she jogged toward the showground.

As she ran back, Arthur Beardsworth came striding up to her. "What are you doing, Martha?"

"I'm warming up and I'm going to race."

"Good luck then."

Martha was momentarily astonished. "Same to you, Arthur," she replied.

Back at the showground she ran to the entry tent. Her father called, "Oh there you are, Martha. Here's your number. Lord Letherby himself has entered you just in case the race officials wouldn't allow it, which they wouldn't have without his say so. You will need to thank him after the race – or more precisely – thank Lady Letherby."

Martha was puzzled but apart from saying thank you for her number didn't question her father. Five minutes before the race was due to begin the athletes congregated around the start area. Some were jogging on the spot, others stretching, and David Sanderson and Jonny Jones were striding down the first sixty yards of the course and jogging back. Martha stood quite still mentally visualising the course and recalling the race plan she had settled on earlier in the week. She was ready to race. A voice boomed out over the public address system, "Will all runners take their mark behind the start line, please. His Lordship, Lord Letherby will start the race in two minutes."

Lord Letherby stood slightly to the right and in front of the start line. He held his left arm up and in his deep aristocratic voice boomed out, "Take your marks. Go!" simultaneously dropping his hand.

The front line runners sped away; nine vying for the lead. Like the two previous shows, Jonny and David were prominent on the initial downhill stretch with Sam Kendal, Arthur Beardsworth, Roger Thompson and Billy Wilson four abreast. Patrick was back in tenth place and seemed to be struggling. Martha held back, contrary to her earlier race plan, simply because she felt the start was too fast, and stayed in fifteenth position within the thirty-two runners.

The sun beat down unrelentingly just as it had done all afternoon when the runners reached a rippling, rough and stony single-file track. Martha had moved up three places without speeding up, mainly due to those who had set off too fast, drifting back towards her. She was one position behind Patrick who had

CHAPTER 26

lost a place.

"Are you okay, Patrick?"

"Yes, they're going too fast, I've eased a bit."

After half a mile of racing, the first climb had been reached and the leaders had started to string out. Billy Wilson had taken the lead over Sam Kendal, last year's three-race champion, and they had started to pull away slightly from Arthur. David and Roger were thirty yards behind, walking with hands on knees, side by side on the steep, grassy, clump-headed ascent. Jonny was starting to suffer and slowed dramatically after his fast start. Patrick had gained three places and started to make rapid inroads on Jonny who was losing places. Martha picked her way through the uneven ascent, light-footed, jogging more than walking. Toward the top of the climb she pulled alongside Jonny. He gasped, "Don't say anything, Martha, just get going."

Martha reached the top of the climb and, sure-footed, she started to speed down the long descent to the beck before the final long, steep, merciless climb up to Wickelton Pike – not her usual ascent but the near vertical ascent she had avoided in training – apart from one time with Patrick. She could see Patrick gaining on Roger and David who had both closed down on Arthur. Billy Wilson had relinquished the lead to Sam Kendal.

"Who's leading, Ted? Can you see Martha?" Ruth asked apprehensively.

"I can see some figures running down the steep descent, Ruth. I can't make out who they are for certain. I think there's nothing between Sam Kendal and Billy Wilson who seem to be leading. At least, I think it's those two. There's another three and one who seems to be gaining on them. Ay up, I think our Martha has just come into view. Yes, it's her alright, long ponytail it must be her. She's doing well, Ruth!"

"Let me have a look, Ted." Ted passed his wife the field glasses and she trained them on the runners. "I can see one in front with four chasing. It's Martha leading, Ted and four just behind her."

"The leaders must have gone out of view, love, Martha's about eighth, that's if those two were leading."

"They are the leaders, Mr Hunney, and Murphy's about fifth or sixth, he seems to be closing on those two in front of him," Shaun informed them.

"Oh, let me have a look out of your binoculars, Shaun," begged Sarah and he quickly passed them to her.

"You won't see him now until they run out of the beck on to that monstrous climb. That's why I'm not doing it, Sarah. I went out with Patrick last week to have a look at the course, and took one look at that climb from the beck and said to Murphy, there's no chance of me going up there. I bet even mountain goats would get into a cold sweat at the thought of it."

Sarah laughed at him. "Well, Patrick will get up it and our Honey will too, she won't be frightened of it."

"If you look just over to the left of the descent you'll see the leaders appear shortly on that monster."

"Yes, there's two of them, they've just come into view now. They're not running or even jogging now, they're walking hunched over."

"That shows how steep it is, Sarah. Have you ever been up there?"

"No, it's out of bounds, no one's supposed to go on that hill, well evidently, apart from you and Patrick that is."

"And your Marta, she's been up with Murphy. That's the beauty of working for his Lordship. Murphy called him up in Ireland, and his Lordship said yes to him. I don't think Murphy mentioned Marta though. He definitely wouldn't allow her to go."

"He's letting her race though."

Shaun looked at Sarah, winked and grinned. "Oh well, he had to, to be sure, he had her Ladyship on his back, he had no choice!"

Ruth looked anxiously through the field glasses to the final hill and shrieked, "You're not telling me our Martha has to go up there, Ted? She'll never get up there – it's full of rocks, and look at those two in front. They're actually climbing over boulders. Martha's not a rock climber, Ted; I hope she doesn't hurt herself."

"Ruth dear, Martha knows full well what she has let herself in for. She's more than capable of getting up there, in fact, Shaun's

CHAPTER 26

just told Sarah, Martha's been up with Patrick before and she got back home then, didn't she?"

Ruth sighed. "I hope you're right, Ted."

Martha reached the beck having caught and passed Roger, who had twisted an ankle, slowing him to a limp. She took one look at the ascent ahead then gasped, and groaned, "Here goes. I must be mad doing this, whatever was I thinking." She started to jog upwards after dousing herself thoroughly in the beck and soaking the handkerchief she was carrying. To her surprise, she began to close on David and Arthur, who had both started to struggle on the climb, but three runners had also caught and passed her.

Patrick was a clear third now but not making any impression on the two leaders who were interchanging positions and pulling further ahead. Martha passed David, who gasped, "Not enough training, Martha. You keep going, I'm done for."

Arthur started pulling away from Martha again and was making inroads on Patrick who, once more, seemed to be struggling. Martha reached the rocky outcrop and climbed up, dragging herself over an overhang. Her hands slipped off a slimy moss-strewn rock and she fell backwards but managed to grab hold of an outshot tree root, haul herself up again and scramble up a narrow gully. She had reached a stony section which she walked up and then after a grassy slope half way up the ascent she started jogging a few steps and then walking a few. She gained on Arthur yet again and pulled away from those who had closed the gap on her from the beck upwards.

Jonny, who seemed to have given in on the first climb, had started passing runners again and was gaining on Martha. The last hundred yards of the climb were the steepest, bringing Arthur to a stop. Martha pulled alongside him and he waved her forward saying nothing. The two leaders were about three quarters of the way up the last section but had slowed dramatically. Patrick had made inroads on their lead again and was only twenty yards behind them.

"What's happening, Ted, can you see Martha?"

Ted passed Ruth the binoculars. "Here look for yourself, love."

She trained her vision on the climb and shouted excitedly, "Martha's got over the boulders, Ted and she's going up that really steep part now. She's going slowly but so are the others. I think she's passed some more runners. Who said a woman can't compete in a man's sport? Martha's three-quarters of the way up the field. She's in front of most of those rough tough farmers, as well as the miners and builders."

Ted laughed. "Martha doesn't have an easy job, Ruth. I know it's not all manual work but she's lifting those heavy boxes of material and gets plenty of arm exercise folding those heavy blankets – she's a tough one herself."

Sarah shouted, "Father, Mother, Martha's running really well and Patrick has gone into third position; he's catching Sam Kendal and Billy Wilson."

At the top of the climb the terrain changed, three hundred yards of lumpy tussocks to be negotiated lay ahead leading to a half mile descent on a fast, stony, and grassy surface. The last half mile of the race was on a slight incline. Martha struggled over the tussocks, turning her left ankle slightly; she hobbled for fifty yards and then managed to start running again. Arthur and Jonny passed her, neither saying a word. Martha was glad; she was mentally preparing for her final push to the finish. No sooner had she finished the rough tussock section, than she literally hurled herself down the long descent. Her long lean legs ate the ground up with each enormous stride, her feet placed firmly and precisely but fleetingly on the difficult surface. She pulled away from the three who had closed on her across the tussocks, and made inroads on Arthur, but Jonny was still pulling away and after a kamikaze descent, was closing on the three in front.

Ted was standing near the finish where a sizable crowd had gathered. "We won't see them until they come up round that bend about four hundred yards down there past the woods, Ruth. Keep a sharp eye on that oak tree standing on its own. That's where we'll see the first runner appear any time now."

Not a minute after Ted had spoken Sam Kendal came into view. Ten yards behind him, Billy Wilson and Jonny were locked in a

CHAPTER 26

battle, with Patrick a further twenty yards adrift of them. The crowd was were shouting and cheering the runners to the finish.

Sarah shrieked, "Come on, Patrick," as soon as she saw him.

With two hundred yards to race, Jonny made his bid to win. He burst past Billy – there was no response from last year's runner-up, only a grimace of pain on his face as his legs buckled on the incline to the finish. Jonny pulled level with Sam and then passed by. Five yards rapidly turned into a fifteen yards advantage. Two hundred yards from the tape, Patrick launched a massive sprint, overhauling Billy and then a waning Sam. He fixed his eyes on the finish and lengthening his stride, legs and arms pumping like pistons, Patrick raced past Jonny and pushed all out towards the finish.

With fifty yards to go Jonny raised a final sprint to overhaul Patrick. The crowd bellowed for their respective heroes. Sarah was hoarse with frenzied shrieking and Shaun, with his high pitched tone, yelled until his larynx seized up.

Bradshaw's employers screamed for Jonny as he pulled two yards in front of Patrick, but one last devastating burst by the Irishman saw him breast the tape and then fall to the ground exhausted. Jonny fell on his back at his side and laying his arm across Patrick's chest he gasped, "Well done, Murphy."

Patrick, chest visibly heaving up and down and his heart thumping groaned, "Thanks, great race, Jonny."

Suddenly a massive shout from the crowd went up as Martha appeared, ponytail lashing from side to side, legs and arms pumping, as she tried to hold off Arthur Beardsworth. Teddy ran down the side of the finishing area and bellowed to his sweetheart, "All the way, Honey. Brilliant, well done! Keep going right to the finish."

Martha managed a short smile, then grimaced and raised her pace as Arthur passed her, but thirty yards from the finish she spurted past Arthur as he slowed to a jog, his legs giving way, muscles saturated with lactic acid.

Ted and Ruth, beaming smiles on their faces, shouted Martha home, and Sarah, jumping up and down cried, "Come on, Honey, well done."

Martha ran through the finish to a crescendo of cheers from the crowd. She walked thirty yards from the finish and sat down with a thump. Teddy had managed to push through the crowd to reach her. "I knew you could do it, Honey."

Martha raised her head and smiled at him, then lowered it and sobbed. She managed to speak in a whisper, "Thanks, Teddy, for supporting me. I couldn't have done it without you. I don't know what I'm going to do while you're away at university."

Teddy sat down beside his sweetheart and placed his arm around her waist. "You keep running, Honey; we'll keep in touch, and we can speak over the telephone and write to each other. You need to get in the shade or you're going to boil over. Come on, see if you can get up and we'll walk to the shade of that tree over there." Teddy lifted himself off the parched grass and held out his hand. "Here, give me your hand."

Martha did as Teddy asked and they walked slowly to the shade of the beech tree. Martha sat down in the shade of the outstretched leafy branches and Teddy jogged to the refreshment tent to get her some water. Ted and Ruth walked over to their daughter, both with beaming smiles on their faces. Ted was first to speak. "Well done, Martha, you should be proud of yourself."

"I'm proud of the Good Lord, Father; he's the one who got me to run. That's what I believe and that's what Reverend Boniface believes. Have you seen the Reverend here, Father?"

"I do believe he's here and should be presenting prizes later. So you'll most likely see him."

Ruth came out with the understatement of the day. "How do you feel, Martha? You do look rather flushed, and that's not like you."

"I'm shattered, Mother," was her daughter's short answer.

Teddy came back with a pot of cool water and a glass of lemonade. "Here you are, Martha, these will cool you down."

"Thanks, Teddy, I need to get on my feet and have a walk around, my legs are cramping up. Where's Nan, Father, is she still here?"

CHAPTER 26

"Oh, yes, she saw you finish, love and was completely overtaken with emotion. Don't worry, your Nan's in a safe pair of hands, with a young burly soldier."

Martha shrieked in delight, and jumped up and down totally forgetting her cramped legs. "Where is he? Where's Oliver?"

Ted pointed to the horticultural tent. "Over in yon tent. He's with Scarlett and your Nan, and don't worry, they all saw you finish."

"Come on, Teddy, let's go see Oliver and Nan." Martha hobbling as her legs stiffened up struggled over to the horticultural tent. As soon as Martha saw her brother she raised a jog to reach him and threw her arms round his neck. "How are you, Oliver? I'm so glad you are home."

"Not as much as I am, Martha," Scarlett interjected.

She let go of her brother. "Of course not, Scarlett, you must be over the moon. Isn't he looking fit and tanned?"

Scarlett grabbed Oliver and smiled. "Yes he is and he's home for a whole two weeks aren't you, lover boy?"

Nan's eyebrows raised at Scarlett's forwardness and she turned to her granddaughter, saying, "You did well today, Martha love; it's about time as well. Those men trying to keep you out all time, it's not fair. Even that old skinflint Josiah Leveridge won't have the gall to stop you racing next year. You showed them – and how, Martha! I could hardly believe my eyes when I saw you racing Arthur Beardsworth in. And you beat him as well!"

"I paced my race well, Nan, that's how I beat him. He's been pleasant to me today has Arthur, I'm glad to say."

As Martha left the tent with Teddy, she overheard Donald Bradshaw, who was standing at Lord and Lady Letherby's side comment, "That's Martha Hunney, one of my employees and an excellent worker I might add, and the young fellow who finished second also works for me. We keep them fit at Bradshaw's textile mill, your Lordship."

"Yes, that young woman has raced magnificently I must admit, and in this hot weather too. Extraordinary." Lord Letherby, with a haughty look and an air of arrogance, paused for a moment and then continued, "The young fellow who won is one of my employees, Patrick Murphy. He's Irish, and heir to this Estate, don't you know."

Lady Letherby whispered quietly in her husband's ear, "You admit it then at last. Are you going to tell him or is he going to find out through village gossip?"

"Prudence dear, Patrick already knows, and so does his stepfather. The young man has known for quite a while and we have both decided to keep the matter to ourselves. Of course, you already knew dear, but Bradshaw hasn't a clue about what I have said to him; he thinks it's a joke and doesn't believe it. The man's a fool, granted he's a rich fool, but he has no breeding."

Lady Letherby held her forefinger under nose and held her head back. "He's a war hero and a fine employer; the trouble with you Montague is that you are a snob, an inveterate first class snob at that."

Lord Letherby, eyebrows raised, responded in a deep guffaw. "I know, my dearest, and proud of it."

Martha was standing with her parents and Teddy, as the race presentation was taking place. Sarah was standing nearby with Patrick and Shaun. Lord Letherby announced the winner, "In first place, after a blistering finish, Patrick Murphy." There was loud applause and as Patrick walked forward to collect his prize, his fellow competitors congratulated him, some patted him on the back and others cheered. Lord Letherby announced second and third places and then handed over to Reverend Boniface.

"Today has seen a landmark sporting achievement in this area, and it gives me great pleasure in announcing the first female to complete the fell race, placed in an incredible fifth position, is Martha Hunney."

As Martha walked forward, tears in her eyes and a smile on her face, there was rapturous applause and noisy cheering. A gruff voice bellowed from the crowd, "Well done, young lass." Martha turned to see where the voice had come from and saw Josiah Leveridge with a look between a grimace and smile on his lived-in face. Martha smiled back.

CHAPTER 26

It was Lord Letherby who spoke next. "Well done, Miss Hunney, you have proved to be the equal of these men by participating in this tough race today."

Martha semi curtsied. "Thank you, your Lordship."

Lady Letherby smiled widely and offered her hand to Martha as she walked by. "Well done, Martha. You have done the fair sex proud this day. This ground-breaking moment will have an impact on how males view women in sport in the future; I'll make sure of that."

Taking Lady Letherby's hand, Martha smiled. "Thank you, Lady Letherby."

"Martha, you are quite welcome to attend the Women's Institute, if you would like – your mother is a valuable member and perhaps you could be too."

Martha smiled again and repeated, "Thank you, Lady Letherby."

When she reached Reverend Boniface, he said, "The race organising committee did not envisage a female winner, Martha, so there is no official prize money. However, at their discretion, they have realised a sum of ten pounds as a prize for the first female."

Martha interrupted, "Please don't take offence, Reverend Boniface, but I go to work for my wages and I have no intention of racing for money or accepting a monetary prize, so please don't be offended but I can't take the prize. I apologise to the organising committee but that's my stance."

"That's very noble of you, Martha. You have taken the same stance as Patrick Murphy who also declined his monetary prize. I believe the committee have decided to give to a charitable cause and so I think the female prize money will possibly be donated in a similar fashion. Thank you, Martha."

When the presentation was over and the country show was in its last throes, Martha sought out Reverend Boniface and had a private word. "I did pray like you said and God answered my prayers. Thank you for the advice you gave me."

"I am glad to hear that you do pray, Martha; keep it up, always."

"I will, and thank you again. I'll see you at chapel tomorrow."

Mort had opened his café late in the day to catch the departing show visitors' trade. The twins had been home to change and met Teddy and Patrick at the cafe.

"Father's won a few quid on the race, Mort – he bet on both of us, Patrick to win and me to finish in the first ten."

"I won a few quid myself. Well done both of you."

Patrick, touching his neck with the tips of fingers, commented, "This is a day to remember if ever there was one, and I haven't half caught the sun. My neck's burning."

"Well you should have worn a hat, Patrick. Martha's neck was covered by her hair. I thought you'd have had more sense."

"Oh come on, Sur, he won, didn't he? If you had any sense, you'd be comforting him. Have you any cream in your handbag."

"Marta, I don't want to smell like a woman."

Martha raised her eyebrows. "Patrick, for your information, we don't smell, we give off a pleasant scent and anyway it won't mean you're a sissy, will it, Teddy?"

"Don't involve me, Honey. I wouldn't be wearing women's perfume either."

"Let your neck burn then, Patrick," Martha said impishly. "Or you could let Sarah kiss it better."

"Marta, I think the sun has got to you, drink your drink and pipe down."

Sarah and Teddy laughed. Martha with her glass of lemonade raised in the air and an impish smile on her happy bronzed face said, "Here's to today, and to the future, whatever it may bring."

Printed in Great Britain
by Amazon